THE DIVA SPICES IT UP

THE DIVA SPICES IT UP

KRISTA DAVIS

WHEELER PUBLISHING
A part of Gale, a Cengage Company

LIBRARY OF CONGRESS CIP DATA ON FILE.
CATALOGUING IN PUBLICATION FOR THIS BOOK
IS AVAILABLE FROM THE LIBRARY OF CONGRESS.

ISBN-13: 978-1-4328-8482-6 (softcover alk. paper)

Published in 2021 by arrangement with Kensington Books, an imprint of Kensington Publishing Corp.

Printed in Mexico
Print Number: 01   Print Year: 2021

To my dad.

To my dad.

ACKNOWLEDGMENTS

The incident with the red soda can actually happened to me. If the man hadn't been about my age and very cute, I probably wouldn't have been watching him. Like Sophie, I stopped in the middle of the street. I was with a friend who didn't notice anything! We were in Washington, DC, at the time, and I was very tempted to follow him down into the metro where he had disappeared. Sanity prevailed and I went on to lunch with my friend. But I never forgot about that guy. I suspect it's a rarity to actually catch someone in the middle of a dead drop.

I hope you'll enjoy the recipes. Now that I know how easy it is to make a Pumpkin Spice Latte at home, I have a feeling I'll be drinking more of them.

Diane Alice Tucker calls herself a country cook. I loved watching her whip up dishes with ease and the confidence that only

7

comes with experience. Diane was kind enough to share her recipe for meatloaf with me. You'll find it in this book under the name Wesley's Favorite Meatloaf. Thank you so much, Diane!

I have to thank my editor, Wendy McCurdy, and assistant editor, Norma Perez-Hernandez, for their patience and kindness, and their sharp eagle eyes! This wasn't the easiest manuscript to edit, so thanks also go to the nameless copy editor for navigating the maze of codes.

As always, my lovely agent, Jessica Faust, continues to be a source of inspiration and strength. Many thanks, Jessica!

CAST OF CHARACTERS

Tilly Stratford
  Wesley Winthrop, her husband
  Briley, her daughter
Mia Hendrickson
  Dr. Pierce Hendrickson, her husband
  Schuyler, her daughter
Abby Bergeron, previous ghostwriter
  Benton Bergeron, her ex-husband
Charlene Smith
  Fred Conway, her boyfriend
Eunice Crenshaw
Francine Vanderhoosen, Sophie's neighbor
Nina Reid Norwood, Sophie's friend and
  neighbor
Mars Winston, Sophie's ex-husband
Natasha

CAST OF CHARACTERS

CHAPTER 1

Dear Sophie,
My mother-in-law takes great pride in her cooking. But it's so hot that I can't eat it. Seriously, my tongue goes numb. I watch the others eat with gusto. Do you think she's adding something to my plate so I won't come to dinner at her house?

Mrs. Numb Tongue in Hazardville,
Connecticut

Dear Mrs. Numb Tongue,
Next time, surreptitiously swap plates with your husband. I think you'll have your answer soon enough.

Sophie

Daisy, my hound mix, sniffed along the bank of the Potomac River following her nose. She wore a halter and a long leash so she could wander in the park. I let her

11

investigate scents that I couldn't smell and trailed along after her.

A breeze blew off the Potomac. The summer humidity was beginning to abate, and the air already held the promise of brisk days ahead. Sun glinted off the water as it rippled with the wind.

Daisy had stayed with my ex-husband, Mars, for the last four weeks. I had promised her a long walk and a visit to the river as soon as I wrapped up a marathon of events. As a self-employed event planner, I realized that I had scheduled myself non-stop, without so much as a hint of a breather, but when you work for yourself, sometimes you just have to keep going while the opportunity is there.

Mars had thoughtfully brought Daisy to my house earlier in the day. When I arrived home in the afternoon, sweet Daisy had been waiting for me. I had quickly swapped my suit for stretchy jeans and taken her for that long-promised stroll while I wound down.

A shout from the pier alarmed both of us. On this beautiful Sunday afternoon in Old Town Alexandria, Virginia, quite a few people were out walking or fishing. Daisy tugged me in the direction of the pier, and I went willingly, thinking someone might need help.

"I've caught something huge!" The man was a stranger to me, into retirement age and well fed. "Must be a catfish. It's fighting like the dickens! Here, can you hold on to my fishing rod? Good and tight now. That's my lucky one."

I took it from his hands and immediately felt the pressure of the fish. The rod bent precariously. I hoped it wouldn't snap in two. "This is really heavy. Can the fishing line take this much pressure?"

"I sure hope so. He's a big one. Keep reeling in. I'll try to snag it with my fishing net. . . ."

He had stopped talking, and I understood why. I didn't know of any blue fish that came with a handle on top.

He lay down on the pier, and as the object came within reach, he nabbed it with a bony hand.

I kneeled on the rough wood and helped him pull a blue suitcase out of the water.

The man looked at me with rheumy eyes. "I have no idea how to cook this."

I giggled. "Do you think it's packed full or just waterlogged?"

"We're about to find out." He clicked the latches and opened the top. "Mmm. This is a pretty skirt. But it's not my size."

He was very cute. I found myself smiling even though I was wondering why and how a woman's suitcase had come to be in the Potomac River. "I think we'd better report this to the police."

He stared at me with obvious confusion. "I don't think they'll be interested."

"Don't you find it odd that someone's suitcase is in the river?"

The fellow scratched his head. "Well, now that you mention it, I can't think of a good reason for it to be there among the fishes."

I called the Old Town Alexandria police department on my cell phone and told them about the suitcase.

"Ma'am," said the 911 operator, "is this an emergency?"

I winced. "No."

"No one is drowning?"

"No. But why would someone lose a suitcase in the river?"

The operator laughed aloud. "Why would there be garbage, motorcycles, or furniture? People are slobs. One lady dumped her husband's golf clubs in the river to get back at him for seeing another woman."

Clearly, this was not a priority for them. "Thank you for your time." I hung up. "I guess it's yours if you want it."

The old fellow was peering into the water.

"I can't see anything. Do you think the owner is down there, too?"

I hoped not.

He stood up and held out his hand. "Sam Bamberger."

"Sophie Winston. Can I help you carry it to your car?"

"Naw. I'm old, but I can still carry a lady's suitcase. Even if it is drenched."

I said goodbye to the funny man and headed home, looking forward to a quiet evening.

The next morning, I fed Mochie, my Ocicat, who was supposed to have spots but instead had a fur pattern more like that of his American shorthair ancestors. In various shades from white to cream and dark brown, he had necklaces and bracelets. And on his sides, his coat colors created circles like bullseyes. In lieu of my usual routine, I suited up Daisy in her halter and headed to my favorite coffee specialty shop for a treat.

The barista at the take-out window waved her hand at me, refusing my money.

I squinted at her in confusion. "I'm not sure this is my order. There's an extra drink and two chocolate croissants here."

"The gentleman paid for it."

Gentleman? I groaned inwardly. I hadn't

showered and wore no makeup. I had pulled on elastic waist stretchy jeans and an over-sized top, feeling secure in the knowledge that the entire world was busy. It was ten o'clock on Monday morning. Why wasn't everyone at work?

Trying to hang on to Daisy's leash without spilling my mocha latte and her Puppy Paw-Tea, I twisted around to see who the barista was talking about.

My ex-husband, Mars, short for Marshall, came to the rescue. "It's my two favorite girls!"

Daisy made a fuss, wagging her tail and turning in circles at the sight of him. I was more subdued. Even though we had di-vorced, Mars and I got along well. Neither one of us could bear to give up Daisy, so we had arranged a schedule and she went back and forth, living with both of us. I didn't have to worry about my appearance. He had seen me without makeup and in far worse clothes before. I relaxed. "Thanks for pick-ing up the tab."

Mars took Daisy's leash and led us to an outdoor table. Daisy didn't know whether to be more excited about Mars or her Puppy Paw-Tea, a dog-safe scoop of ice cream with a bone-shaped cookie on top.

"Are we celebrating something?" asked Mars.

A chilling breeze blew, making me glad I had worn the cozy fleece pullover. I sipped my hot drink. "Four back-to-back medical conventions are over. I worked non-stop for a month. I'm looking forward to a break."

Mars held out his coffee in a toast and touched it to the latte I held. "A break. How fortuitous."

Fortuitous? Ugh. What was he up to?

Mars smiled at me. "Soph, I need a big favor."

I never should have looked into his eyes. They crinkled at the outer edges and always softened any resolve I had to stay out of his business. A political consultant, Mars had been blessed with looks that could compete with his telegenic clients.

"I'm taking a break," I said very clearly, imagining that he probably needed me to arrange a party for five hundred people in two days.

He ignored my protest. "The wife of one of my clients is writing a cookbook."

That wasn't what I had expected. "Cool."

"Except she's not really writing it, she's using a ghostwriter."

"That's interesting. Why doesn't she do it herself?"

"She says all the celebrities use ghostwriters for their cookbooks."

"Celebrity?" I inquired.

"She's the wife of a congressman. Tilly Stratford. Her husband, Wesley Winthrop, is my client."

I'd heard the former TV star had moved to Old Town Alexandria. "No kidding!" Just to be sure we were talking about the same person, I asked, "The one who played the daughter in *American Daughter*?"

"The very same."

I chomped into one of the chocolate croissants. The chocolate was still warm and soft inside. The favor Mars needed was becoming clearer. He probably wanted me to arrange a huge party for the debut of the cookbook. I might be an event planner, but most of the time I dealt with conventions and large events.

"But the ghostwriter quit on Friday." He sipped his drink and then said casually, "I was thinking maybe you'd be interested."

"In ghostwriting a cookbook? I don't know the first thing about that."

"Nothing to it," he said with way too much confidence for someone whose cooking expertise was limited to grilling meats and mixing cocktails. "And it pays very well."

18

"Is she difficult?" I asked out of curiosity.

"Who?"

"Tilly."

"Not at all. She's very sweet. You'll like her. She's . . . a little intimidated by the congressional scene. She's out of her element. But you'll love her."

"Then why did the ghostwriter quit?"

"We don't know. She told Tilly she was sorry but she had to quit, and that was it. She walked out, leaving poor Tilly high and dry. No one has been able to reach her since Friday."

I tilted my head and gave him my best doubtful look. "Mars, that doesn't make sense. People don't take a job and quit in the middle of it."

"Are you kidding me? People do that all the time. One of my clients advertised a job and hired six people. Guess how many showed up on the first day of training."

It was clearly a trick question. "Three?"

"Zero." He made a zero with his thumb and forefinger. "Not the best example, but my point is that people don't always come through with what they promise. I'm told that there has to be a personal connection between the ghostwriter and the chef. I feel a little guilty because I was the one who hooked her up with Abby Bergeron. She

19

came highly recommended. Maybe they just didn't mesh."

Daisy finished her Puppy Paw-Tea and then watched us, probably hoping we had another one hidden somewhere.

Mars persisted. "Tilly is a sweetheart, Sophie. She's so disappointed. It would mean a lot to her if you could help out."

I slurped the remains of my mocha latte in a most unladylike manner.

Mars wrote something on a napkin and slid it across the table to me.

I took a look and felt my eyes widen. "Is that a dollar sign?"

"I told you it paid well. They're in a hurry to get it done and are willing to pay extra. The thing is" — he looked at me with his best imitation of Daisy's puppy eyes — "I know *you* wouldn't let them down."

He didn't need to shower me with empty flattery. I was torn. The money would be nice, but I had been looking forward to some downtime. "Mars, thanks for thinking of me, but I'd really like to have a little time off. Besides, a cookbook is a huge project. We'd be working on it for a year, and I would need to get back to my real job soon."

"Ah! But the bulk of it is done." He leaned toward me. "Tilly is very disappointed. This cookbook is a big deal for her, and" — Mars

20

locked his eyes on mine — "I know I can depend on you. I don't want some other highly recommended person coming in and making a mess of it or walking away."

"I'll think about it." I scowled at him. "In spite of your assurances that it's easy, I don't know what's involved in ghostwriting a cookbook."

"There's nothing to it. You write down recipes. How hard could that be?"

I stood up and collected Daisy's leash. "I'll let you know."

As I walked away, Mars called out to me, "You were my favorite wife!"

I was his only wife. He had lived with our friend Natasha, but she never did manage to get him to walk down the aisle with her.

Fall was my favorite time of year in Old Town. It was way too early for pumpkins, but they already decorated the front stoops of some historic homes. Others had lush wreaths on their doors, featuring dried flowers and giant sunflowers. The leaves on the trees that lined the streets were still green. It was that transitional time between summer and fall. School had started, and weekend beach trips had ended. Warm summery days were still the norm but they were interrupted by chilly days that reminded us fall weather was already on the way.

Traffic had picked up, and people had begun to leave their offices in search of lunch. At an intersection with King Street, Daisy and I waited for the light to change and the line of cars to stop.

A man paused near us. About my age with a neat appearance, he reminded me of my old beau, Alex. His brown hair was neatly trimmed. He wore a blue Oxford cloth button-down shirt with a striped yellow tie. Quintessential Old Town attire for gentlemen. He smiled at me, which made me totally self-conscious. He even reached down to pat Daisy.

But the second the light changed he was off in a hurry, walking across the street in great, confident strides ahead of the crowd. When he reached the sidewalk on the other side, he lifted the end of his tie and placed it in his mouth. In one swift movement, he raised the lid on a public garbage bin, bent over, reached inside, and pulled out a red soft drink can.

I was so stunned that I stopped walking in the middle of the street.

He dropped the top of the garbage can in place, let his tie fall back to his chest, and strode away.

I looked around. No one else seemed to be watching him. Hadn't anyone else noticed what he just did?

A car honked at us, and we dashed across the street. I couldn't help myself — I turned right and followed him.

Chapter 2

Dear Natasha,
I love your TV show. You inspire me! I'm throwing a party and I'm planning to serve your jalapeño poppers. What do you recommend as a drink to go with them?

Hot Mama in Volcano, Hawaii

Dear Hot Mama,
As much as I love those jalapeño poppers, I'm afraid they're passé. Look for recipes involving smoked salts or peppered fish and meats. Or go all-out with fermented garlic! That's what's on trend right now.

Natasha

Unfortunately, Natasha intercepted me. "Sophie! Sophie! Where have you been? I went by your house half a dozen times last week, but you weren't home. You really should let me know if you're going out of town."

I watched the man round the corner at Cameron Street and debated whether to run to catch up to him. It was ridiculous, of course. Even if I saw him go into a house or building, it would be meaningless. And then I did something completely out of character.

"Excuse me, Natasha." I took off after the man with Daisy romping alongside me. I was out of breath by the time I reached the intersection where he had turned. He was gone. I stood there for a moment, scanning the sidewalks. They were nearly empty. I'd have seen him if he hadn't turned somewhere or entered a building.

I sucked in some deep breaths. Maybe I had lost my perspective. I thought there was something sinister about the suitcase in the river, and now I was chasing a man who had caught my attention. I was being ridiculous.

When I turned back, Natasha still stood where I had left her. She wore an angry expression and had crossed her arms in irritation.

I trudged back. "Sorry."

"What was that about?"

"I thought I saw someone I knew," I lied. If I told her about the soda can she would think I had lost my mind.

"I was saying that you should keep me informed if you leave."

"I have a phone," I said wryly.

"But this is important. It's the best thing that ever happened to me. I wanted to tell you in person."

I bit back the temptation to be snarky. "What is your wonderful news?"

Natasha looked me over. "What are you wearing? Oh, Sophie! I don't know what to say. Have you fallen on hard times?"

I laughed. "Natasha, are you going to tell me your good news?"

"I thought we might get a cup of coffee, but if you're dressed like that . . ."

I paid no attention to what she was saying. I had known Natasha since we were in grade school. The two of us had competed at everything except the beauty pageants that Natasha had treasured. She still maintained the kind of figure that clothes were meant to hang on. No elastic waistbands for her. She wore a black sweater with the sleeves pushed up and a black-and-white plaid skirt. The kind of skirt with a gathered waist that I longed to wear. But unlike Natasha, I was short and not slender. I would look twice as wide as I already was. She finished the outfit with black leather boots.

While part of me hated to admit it, she looked chic.

And now she gazed at me, raised her eyebrows, and nodded. "You will, won't you?"

Oy. Natasha was prone to outlandish ideas. I didn't dare say yes without knowing to what I was agreeing.

She tilted her head. "I would offer you something to wear, but I don't think you would fit in my size."

"Thank you. It's really not necessary. I'm heading home." I started to walk in the direction of our houses, and she went with me. "Now, what was it you wanted me to do?"

"Come to my party? I'm worried about you, Sophie. Didn't you hear a word that I said? I found my sister!"

CHAPTER 3

Dear Sophie,
My boyfriend's mother uses black pepper in one of the cakes she likes to bake. I try to be open-minded, but that strikes me as odd. Who would bake sweets with black pepper in them?
                    Girlfriend in Pepper Pike, Ohio

Dear Girlfriend,
Pepper is used in cookies from South Africa to Norway. It's not uncommon to find it in spice cakes, either. You might like it!

                                    Sophie

Now I was the one who was worried. "But you don't have a sister."

"Okay, so she's a half sister, but you know how I've always loved your little sister, Hannah. Now I'll have a Hannah of my own!"

I was quite certain that her mother was

no longer of childbearing age. And the biggest blow in Natasha's life was her father's disappearance when she was only seven years old. Where could a half sister have come from? "Your mom adopted a child?"

"No! I told you. I sent off one of those DNA saliva tests, thinking I might be able to find my dad. And this woman popped up as my half sister. That means my dad is alive! I always knew it. It was like a visceral thing that he was out there somewhere in the world. And get this. She lives right here in Old Town! What are the odds of that? We might have been shopping side by side or eating in the same restaurant at the same time and we never knew it!"

I was stunned. If I hadn't heard so many stories about killers being tracked down through the DNA of relatives for acts committed decades before, I might not have believed her at all. "Have you met her yet?"

"No. That's why I'm having the dinner party. I want all my friends to meet her."

"You didn't run right out to meet her immediately?"

Natasha stared at me. Not a muscle in her face moved. Had she gotten Botoxed?

"It took me a while to work through the situation. Please don't mention this to your

29

parents. I don't want my mother to know yet."

My parents and her mom still lived in the town where we had grown up. It wasn't as though they were close friends, but a new half sister was the kind of thing a person might mention in a casual conversation at the supermarket. "No problem. But I think your mom would love to meet her."

"I'm not so sure. It might be very painful for her."

Natasha would know. The fact that she even considered her mother's reaction suggested to me that it had been painful for Natasha. And why wouldn't it be? It meant her father had left his family without so much as a fare thee well and went off to start another family.

"We talked on the phone. You won't believe what she asked me."

I could hardly believe Natasha had found a half sister. I didn't think anything could top that! "What?"

"She wanted to know where Dad was."

"He left them, too?"

"I don't know all the details. I hope she'll tell us when she meets us. You're good at prying into other people's business. You'll get it out of her."

I ignored her slight. She was probably

30

right. Among my many faults, I was definitely nosy. "What's her name? Maybe I know her."

"Charlene Smith."

"Doesn't ring any bells with me. I look forward to meeting her. When is the party?"

"Tomorrow evening."

"What can I bring?"

Natasha's expression turned to horror. "Oh, Sophie! Please don't bring a dish. Everything has to be perfect. This is my night to shine."

Natasha had a local TV show about all things domestic and a rabid fan base. I couldn't help wondering if she was being set up somehow. "Did she know who you are?"

"If she did, she didn't mention it."

We had reached my house. "I look forward to meeting her, Natasha. I truly do. And I'm super happy for you."

Natasha smiled at me. "Wear your best outfit, even if it's last year's fashion."

I turned on my heel to stalk away and with total horror realized suddenly that the half sister might be just like Natasha. After all, Natasha's mom was an interesting woman who worked in a diner, believed in spirits and potions, and was an incurable flirt. What if the annoyingly pompous side of Natasha came from her dad? Not two of them!

I unlocked the front door of my home and stepped inside with Daisy. Mochie came running and meowed complaints about being home alone. I unlatched Daisy and swept Mochie up into my arms. "You wouldn't have liked it. We didn't see a single mouse."

He purred as I carried him into the kitchen and spooned some salmon delight into his bowl.

I looked forward to a leisurely hot shower and headed upstairs.

Sometimes fate just toys with a person. On that particular day, while I was in the shower, a green tile fell off the wall and crashed into the bathtub.

Daisy and Mochie came running to see what had happened.

Three more tiles fell in quick succession. I could see the row of tiles beneath them beginning to bulge. This was fate's way of telling me I had put off the bathroom renovation long enough. I felt fairly certain that the black and green tile and the green sink perched on weird aluminum legs that splayed like a colt standing up for the first time must have been the height of fashion once. For years I had longed for a modern bathroom, but I had taken out a whopping loan when I paid Mars for his half of the house in our divorce, and it didn't leave much for pricey renovations.

Green and black tile bathrooms excepted, I loved the old place with its creaking floorboards, tall windows, and huge double lot. Houses were pricey in Old Town Alexandria, and I was lucky that Mars's aunt had left us this house. She had been a terrific cook and loved nothing more than to entertain. So much so that she had renovated the house by extending the dining room and living room to accommodate large gatherings.

I wrapped a towel around myself and gazed at the space where the tiles had been. I could probably pry off a few more tiles, then glue them back in place and caulk around them. It was the kind of fix that might work, but only for a while.

The figure Mars had written on the napkin hammered at me. Maybe it wouldn't be so bad helping Tilly with her cookbook. I tried to imagine the bathroom in white, with a vanity and drawers for storage. There would be a place for the blow dryer and, be still my heart, maybe even a closet for towels!

If the tiles hadn't fallen off, I would have averted my eyes and continued to live with the ghastly old bathroom. But the truth was that the tiles had sounded an alarm. I knew the kind of damage that would occur if water leached behind the wall. Then I would be paying even more to repair the damage.

I had noticed that things in life often happened with an odd synchronicity. I wasn't particularly superstitious, but the timing was certainly interesting. Maybe it was a sign.

I pulled on a fresh pair of elastic waist jeans, noting that their tightness was also a sign. I needed to cut back on my caloric intake, which definitely did not mesh with ghostwriting a cookbook. But there were slender chefs, I reasoned. Maybe I could learn to take one or two bites and not more.

Fat chance that would ever happen!

I slipped on a soft periwinkle blue top made of cotton, added a little makeup, and blew my hair dry. Daisy and Mochie watched me from the bed, not bothering to disguise their boredom.

I gave some thought to flipping a coin about the cookbook. That wasn't my style, though. I preferred to weigh the pros and cons and make a thoughtful decision. And to do that, I should probably meet Tilly Stratford.

Daisy and Mochie followed me downstairs, where I phoned Mars to set up a

34

meeting.

I could hear him speaking to someone in the background. "How about right now? I'm at their house."

That was sooner than I had expected. But why not? I agreed, and Mars gave me their address on South Royal Street.

Daisy and Mochie had settled in for naps, so I quietly grabbed my purse and left the house. I took my time, enjoying the wonderful weather. The Stratford and Winthrop home was a typical Federal-style house with tall windows and a red brick facade.

Urns filled with conical evergreens flanked the front door. Gray shutters accented the windows and matched the color of the door. I turned and followed a short brick sidewalk to the house. The plaque on the wall designated the house as historical, which many people would have guessed from the aged appearance of the building.

Most door knockers were brass, so it caught my attention that the bald eagle on the door was brushed silver. I clanked it three times.

Tilly swung the door open. Blond strands of hair had escaped from a messy bun at the nape of her neck and blew around her face. Her eyebrows had been carefully penciled in light brown, and she had pale skin that looked as if it would burn easily, leading me to believe that she was a natural blonde. She looked at me in fear for the briefest moment before she smiled and held out her arms to hug me. "Sophie! I love you already!"

She gave me a hug, which was interrupted by two teenaged girls. They were both out of breath when they darted toward us from the sidewalk, but only one of them was giddy.

"Mom! You won't believe what happened!"

Tilly introduced me to them. "This wild one is my daughter, Briley."

Briley looked uncannily like her mother. Blond hair a few shades lighter than her mom's danced around her face. Briley wore tight skinny jeans, an oversized baby blue sweater, and dangling drusy earrings that matched her sweater. I recognized the earrings as trendy designer jewelry.

"And this is her friend and our next-door neighbor, Schuyler." Copper-colored hair fell over her shoulders in waves. I assumed they had coordinated their outfits in advance, because Schuyler wore the same type of tight jeans and oversized sweater with matching drusy earrings. The only difference was that her sweater was a pine green.

Tilly reached out to her and placed an arm around Schuyler's thin shoulders. "How are you holding up?"

"I'm okay," she said softly.

She didn't look okay. I wondered what was going on.

"What's so exciting?" Tilly asked her daughter.

Briley could barely contain herself. "Troy Anderson! I think he might ask me to the homecoming dance!"

The girls looked at each other, and Schuyler broke into an unenthusiastic smile. Briley raced inside and up the staircase with Schuyler following at a slower pace.

Tilly ushered me into the foyer and closed the door. "Do you remember how wonderful life was when we were that age? They're having so much fun. We were worried about Briley changing schools when we moved here. Luckily, Schuyler lives next door, and the two of them hit it off right away."

"What's wrong with Schuyler?"

"It's the saddest thing. Her mother, Mia, has simply disappeared. Her husband is an obstetrician. He was called out to deliver a baby on Friday night, and I took the girls and some of their friends to a football game. When we came home, Mia wasn't there. Naturally, I insisted that Schuyler stay with us until her parents came home. She's here all the time, anyway. Eventually her dad returned, but her mother still hasn't shown up or even called! The poor child is distraught."

The story reminded me a little bit too much of Natasha's father disappearing. "I'm so sorry. Poor Schuyler."

Tilly paused in the foyer and gazed at me. "I have to confess that I was scared to death to meet you. Mars told me you were his former wife, and someone else told me he had been married to Natasha, whom I've seen on TV."

Mars hadn't married Natasha, but I let it pass without correcting her.

"I was afraid you might be like her. I'm sure she's a very nice woman, but I don't think she eats, or she wouldn't be so thin. I just couldn't work with someone like that. I mean, these are *recipes* we're talking about. We *have* to taste them! I hope you won't be offended, but you're more my kind of gal."

I knew the feeling. I fought extra pounds all the time. And it was far too easy to feel self-conscious about not being slender. Tilly obviously liked to eat. We would get along fine.

Tilly chattered as she led me to the living room, where I caught a glimpse of Mars.

A man rose to his feet and came to meet me, his hand outstretched to shake mine. He had what I thought they were calling a "dad" body. Definitely not muscular but not overly flabby, either. What stood out to me was his face. Mars had a knack for working with attractive politicians. Wesley had a full head of well-trimmed silver-white hair, which enhanced his tan. I assumed Wesley and Tilly were around fifty years old, but Wesley's face was that of a younger man, leading me to believe that he'd had some tweaking done. Long dimples ran along both sides of his face. He had what Mars called *the look.* Wesley would have been equally at home on a farmhouse porch drinking lemonade as he would in the Capitol, which would make him appeal to a wide group of people. He was blessed with the ability to make other people comfortable, a trait I had seen in many of Mars's political clients. He smiled at me as if I were the most delightful person in the world. "Wesley Winthrop. Thank you so much for coming to Tilly's rescue, Sophie. This recipe project means a great deal to her."

"I hope I can be of assistance."

Another man, who seemed vaguely familiar, called out, "Hi, Sophie." I smiled at him and said hi, all the while wondering who he was.

Tilly steered me away from him. "Isn't this the most wonderful house? The minute I saw Old Town, I told Wesley that I had to have an authentically historical house. I just adore them."

We entered her kitchen, which had clearly been remodeled but was so charmingly colonial that Natasha would have broken out in hives. She simply did not appreciate blending the old with the new.

But I did, and I was amazed by how cleverly someone had incorporated what had probably been the original kitchen with a modern one. A brick-lined fireplace, almost big enough for me to walk into, anchored one end of the expansive room at the back of the house. Soot covered the back wall of the fireplace. An iron arm with a hook on the end appeared to have been used to hold pots over the fire. I'd heard they also served to hang heavy cloths to dispel the draft from the chimney.

"Is this kitchen from the 1800s?" I asked.

Tilly beamed. "Isn't it wonderful? Of course, the house must have been very different at the time. The previous owners incorporated the modern wall next to it." She gestured toward a television, which had been mounted in built-in wall units that had been carefully crafted to resemble roughly hewn timber. Tilly paused in the center of the room at an island painted the color of moss. It held a six-burner gas cooktop mounted on granite. Behind the island, a floor-to-ceiling wall of maple cabinets swung around the back of the room and the interior wall. A small breakfast table was located near French doors that led to a walled garden. The room was stunning and cozy.

"Your kitchen is beautiful," I murmured.

"This room sold us on the house. Wesley can spend all the time he likes in the formal living room, but this is where we live. You are so kind to come on board and help me finish this project. Could I offer you some coffee?"

I readily accepted a mug. It smelled like fall, with notes of cinnamon and nutmeg.

"What prompted you to write a cook-book?" I asked.

Tilly sighed. "Have you met many congressional wives?"

I had, but she kept talking and I didn't stop her.

"They're brilliant. Clearly the lady congresswomen are, too. But the wives are like a Who's Who of overachieving women.

41

They're doctors, judges, and engineers. I think one of them told me she was an astronaut! Honey, have you seen some of these women? They run miles every day and lift weights. I break into hives when I pass a gym on the sidewalk. One of Wesley's staffers suggested the cookbook to sort of give me an expertise."

"But you're a cool TV actress! Nothing's more impressive than that. You're already a star!"

"Aren't you sweet. I'm afraid that's very much in the past. You'd be surprised how many of them are too young to remember me. Or maybe they were too busy studying for PhDs and curing diseases to watch TV. Really, they intimidate me!"

I had heard some mean comments about Tilly's current appearance. She had put on weight since her days on TV, but a lot of people gained weight as they aged. After all, she was a teenager when she was a TV star. She still radiated the same kind of enthusiasm that had made her popular. She was gorgeous, with intelligent eyes, jolly cheekbones, and a friendly smile. I bet some of those accomplished women were intimidated by her.

Tilly placed a stack of papers on a pine coffee table. It was bound by a red gingham ribbon. We sat down, and she scooted it toward me.

A shout arose elsewhere in the house. There was a solid stream of angry words, although I couldn't tell what was being said.

Tilly's eyes grew large with alarm. She rose and ran down the hallway. I was on her heels.

Everyone in the living room appeared to be in a state of distress, except for Mars. He clearly wasn't happy, but he seemed calmer than the others.

Wesley's face was a frightening shade of magenta. Tilly went to him. "What happened?"

"Somebody" — he looked from Mars to the other people in the room — "released a private e-mail from me without authorization, and now it's been leaked to Twitter and is all over the web."

"What was it? What did it say?" asked Tilly.

"I'm toast. It reveals information about our position on North Korea."

I gazed at their faces. If one of them was responsible, he was very good at hiding his emotions.

I was proud of Mars when he said calmly, "We can fix this. You'll survive it."

"What if the person who released it has more?" Wesley slumped into a chair. "I better not ever meet whoever did this. I'll strangle him with my own two hands."

Tilly whispered, "Maybe I should make some chamomile tea."

In an angry tone, Wesley said, "Tea is not going to make this any better, Tilly."

Mars flicked his fingers discreetly. He wanted us to leave.

I whispered to Tilly, "Maybe they need some privacy."

Reluctantly, she followed me to the kitchen. Tilly didn't have to say anything. Her expression made clear that she was worried.

"Mars will handle it. It's what he does, Tilly."

"How could that happen?" she asked.

"I don't know. But I do know that all e-mails go to someone. Maybe it was released by the recipient or someone in his office."

"Then it might not have been one of the people working for Wesley. That's a relief!"

We sat down again, and I tried to focus on the recipes bound in red gingham. The cover page was pristine. "There's quite a stack here."

"I suppose Mars told you what happened."

I wanted to know more, and Mars's explanation had been sketchy at best. "Only the bare bones."

She tilted her head and squinted. "Honestly, I don't know what to think of it. Wesley says I take everything too personally. He might be right, but I find it odd that a person would contract to do a job and then quit working without any notice. She hasn't even phoned about her paycheck."

"She didn't tell you she was leaving?"

"Not a word until Friday. It was so abrupt. Now, I'll admit that she was acting a little bit peculiar the last time I saw her here. But if you were going to stop working, wouldn't you have given some advance notice? She knew I have a deadline. If she didn't have the courage to tell me sooner, at least she could have explained in a text. Even my ultramodern daughter says that's the least she could have done."

I untied the ribbon and turned pages. The ghostwriter had scribbled extensive comments in the margins and made notations about the amounts of ingredients.

"We had accomplished so much," Tilly prattled. "It's odd that Abby would have left when she did. It was so sudden. We hadn't argued or anything. Why wouldn't she have the courtesy to face me and give me two weeks' notice? Wesley thinks she got

45

a job that pays more. Call me old-fashioned, but in my book a person has an obligation to see a job through. You don't just flit from one to the next."

I didn't think I had met Abby. Old Town Alexandria was a relatively small place, but each season and new administration in nearby Washington, DC, brought new faces, so it wasn't surprising that I didn't know her.

"Abby was as nice as she could be. I guess that's why it hurts a little that she just up and left. I thought we were getting along pretty well."

"Was she very young? Maybe she wasn't confident enough to finish the job or didn't know she was supposed to give notice."

"In her forties, I'd guess. And recently divorced. She thought Wesley was fabulous and told me how lucky I was to have found such a great guy."

I wasn't psychic. And I wasn't a genius. But a little chill ran through me. What she was describing didn't bode well for Abby. Had she left because of Wesley? I tried not to sound critical or rude. "I guess you tried to phone her?"

"Of course. Her cell phone rolls over to voice mail. Isn't that always the case? People see who's calling and they don't answer."

Tilly laughed. "Except for me. Honestly, half the time I can't answer fast enough. My phone is usually stuck in my purse somewhere, and by the time I find it, the caller has given up."

"Do you know where she lives?"

"Oh sure. She has the cutest little place. You'd know it in a second. She made the most adorable wreath for her front door. It's all lemons with touches of eucalyptus and magnolia leaves."

I knew that house. Daisy and I walked by it regularly. The unique lemon wreath had caught my eye.

Tilly studied her hands for a moment. In a soft voice, she said, "I went over there. Wesley said I shouldn't go. That I should let her be. But I went, anyway." She looked up at me. "I just couldn't understand what had happened. I thought maybe I had offended her. You know? It's so easy to do that accidentally. I try to be nice to everyone. Well, I'm sure you do, too. You understand. I haven't told Wesley that I went to her house. I'm not sure *why* I haven't told him. Nothing happened. Either she wasn't home, or she wasn't answering the door."

Tilly shrugged. "So here we are. What you need to know about me is that while I love to cook, I don't measure ingredients and I

47

don't use the exact same ingredients every single time."

Ack! That would make it much more difficult to establish the recipe.

Tilly went on. "Abby would come over here and watch me make the recipes for the cookbook and write them down. All the scribbles on those pages are her notes." Furrows formed between Tilly's eyes.

"Is something wrong?"

"I hadn't given it any thought before, but Abby usually took these pages home with her. I wonder how long she knew she wouldn't be returning."

"Maybe she'll have a change of heart and give you a call."

"At least she thoughtfully left them here for me so I wouldn't have to start over from scratch. She knew she wasn't coming back!"

"Why did she take them home? Did she try re-creating each recipe?" This was beginning to sound like a lot of work!

"Yes. That's what you see there in the margins. We only have a few more recipes to go, so would that work for you?"

I flipped the pages to a recipe for corn bread. Abby had crossed out the original amounts of sugar and baking powder and written new amounts in the margin of the page. I pointed as I spoke. "Are you comfortable that the notations in the margins are the correct amounts for the recipes, or would I have to cook or bake every recipe again to test it?"

Tilly turned positively green. "That would be like starting all over again! We don't have time for that. We would have to cook and bake nonstop." She picked up the corn bread recipe and studied it. "I don't think we need to start over on everything. Good grief! That would take a year, and the publisher is waiting for it. Besides, most of these changes are fairly minor."

I had to agree. But it was her cookbook and would bear her name, so she needed to be satisfied.

Tilly moaned. "Here's what we'll do. How about if I select a few recipes and you select a few recipes and we make them with the amounts noted in the margins? Then we'll know how close they are and whether we need to recreate all the recipes."

I smiled at her. I liked reasonable people. "That's an excellent idea."

"You know, they tell me that some of the big chefs don't write their own cookbooks. There's simply no time for it. The ghostwriters watch them cook and write down the recipes, just like Abby did for me."

"Really?" I had no idea that was how it

49

worked.

"And it's hard to find a good ghostwriter. Apparently, you need to adopt my voice so it sounds like me."

"I don't think that will be too difficult. And you can always change anything that doesn't sound quite right to your ear."

"Did Mars tell you we're in a hurry?"

"He mentioned that. How much of a hurry?"

"I'd like to finish the last few recipes and turn it in three weeks from now."

I took a deep breath. It wasn't too late to walk away. We spoke briefly about the payment. Mars had been correct about that.

"We realize that this is an imposition," said Tilly. "It's hard to find someone who can drop everything and take on a three-week job. I'm sorry that it came to this. We would have been right on schedule if Abby hadn't abandoned the project." She shook her head in dismay. "Why did Abby have to leave me?"

CHAPTER 4

Dear Sophie,
I'm bringing a casserole with a crispy bread crumb topping to my church potluck dinner. I can keep it warm in an insulated carrier, but how do I keep the top from getting soggy?

Choir Director in Crum,
West Virginia

Dear Choir Director,
Ovens are rarely available at potlucks, but if you're lucky and one is available, you can pop it under the broiler briefly to crisp it up again. Either way, cover it with paper towels during transit to absorb the condensation.

Sophie

Later that afternoon, armed with a steaming mug of tea, I sat down at my kitchen table with the pages of the recipe book and got to work. The first thing I noticed was that the pages appeared to be out of order. They weren't numbered, which I thought odd, but even stranger, they weren't organized in any logical way that I could discern. Strawberry Shortcake and Grandma Peggy's Sunday Go-To-Meeting Cake were followed by Chicken Sausage Lasagna, Heavenly Toffee Blondies, and Melt-in-Your-Mouth Kale Greens.

I would have to ask Tilly about that. Maybe they were supposed to be arranged as complete meals. I had seen cookbooks set up like that before.

I stopped at Creamy Macaroni and Cheese. That would probably be a good test recipe. And I had all the ingredients on hand. I set a pot of salted water on the stove to boil and placed flour, Colby cheese, Irish cheddar cheese, milk, and powdered mustard on the kitchen island. Abby had written *1 teaspoon paprika and 1 tablespoon yellow mustard* in the margin. She'd also jotted *BCS417.* What did that mean?

While I shredded the cheeses and the pasta boiled, I thought about the guy I had followed the previous day. What on earth would possess a person to open a municipal garbage can? Even more baffling, why would anyone withdraw trash from it?

It had to be something he had done before. The maneuver of placing the tie between his lips was completely automatic for him. And he had moved so swiftly. I would have had trouble figuring out how to open the top of the trash can.

But the biggest question in my mind was, *Why?* It made no sense unless someone had left something there for him. It must have been the soda can. The whole thing was strange. It amazed me that he had pulled off this bizarre act in broad daylight in front of at least a dozen people, yet I appeared to be the only one who had noticed it.

Forcing my thoughts back to cooking, I drained the macaroni and set it aside while the cheese melted into the milk I had warmed in a large saucepan. I liked the way Tilly cooked the onions first and added flour to them. The recipe was very simple except for the *BCS417* notation that I didn't understand.

If that was some kind of recipe shorthand, I wasn't familiar with it. Was there a shorthand for recipes other than standard measurement abbreviations? I opened my laptop and searched. It was pretty much what I thought. A person might write *cinn* instead of *cinnamon,* or *bs* for *baking soda.* But overall, the only shortened versions were common standard abbreviations, like T for *tablespoon* and t for *teaspoon.* I saw nothing at all about numbers. Maybe she meant 1/4 or 1/2 of a tablespoon? But that kind of measurement would be written as teaspoons.

I preheated the oven, poured the macaroni into the delightfully aromatic cheese sauce, and stirred to mix it. After pouring it all into a casserole dish, I mixed panko with grated Parmesan and sprinkled it over the top.

As I closed the oven door, my kitchen door opened. I knew who it was without looking. My best friend and across-the-street neighbor, Nina Reid Norwood, had an uncanny ability to know when something was cooking in my kitchen.

"It has to bake for twenty minutes," I warned.

"It smells wonderful!" Nina opened a drawer and took out a spoon, which she used to scoop up the dregs of cheese sauce in the pot. "Mmm. There's just nothing better than cheese."

She gazed at the stack of recipes on the table. "You're writing a cookbook?" she asked excitedly.

"Not exactly. I'm ghostwriting one for Tilly Stratford."

Nina nearly dropped her spoon when she squealed. "You've met her?"

"She's very nice. You'll like her."

"I'm sure you need an assistant. Right? Don't all ghostwriters have assistants? And tasters?"

I doubted that was the case, but I laughed and said, "Your help would be most appreciated. Actually, it pays pretty well because she's in a hurry to get it done. I'm hoping I can finally rip out the old bathroom. Hey, Nina, do you know someone named Abby Bergeron?"

"Don't think so. What did she do?"

"She quit working as the ghostwriter for Tilly rather abruptly."

Nina licked the spoon and asked, "Did they have a fight? Maybe Abby wanted her name on the cover along with Tilly's?"

"If they had a spat, Tilly isn't admitting it."

Nina scraped the pot, trying to get every last drop. "Maybe you should have a chat with this Abby and find out what's really going on."

"I think that might be a good idea. I found an odd notation on this recipe, too. I have no idea what it means." I pointed it out to her.

"*R P C one four two*," she read. "I don't

have a clue. Maybe it doesn't have anything to do with the recipe. Maybe she was on the phone and didn't have anything to write on. It sounds like an apartment number."

"It does look like one, doesn't it? Maybe she was supposed to meet someone." I pawed through the recipes in search of something else to try. "Oh yum! How do Bourbon Apple Fritters with Caramel Sauce sound?"

"That's the kind of thing Tilly cooks? Why am I not her best friend? Now I really have to meet her."

The recipe sounded simple enough. I had some apples in the fridge and usually had a bottle of bourbon around. And then I drew a sharp breath. "Nina, I don't think it's an apartment number."

She looked over my shoulder. *"C C T one thousand eighty-five,"* she read aloud.

Trying to keep the recipes in order, I flipped through the pages. "Here's another one. *M G B four one four three.* And another. *C P S three eight one one.*"

"Sophie, I don't mean to put you down, but are you sure this isn't some kind of cooking lingo?"

"I am the first person to admit there's a lot I don't know in this world, but I've never seen anything like this on a recipe. I would

56

guess that it might mean something as to the order of the recipes, but there doesn't seem to be a logical pattern that I can discern."

"Plus, it would be easier to just number the pages, or write out the name of the section, like appetizers and desserts," she observed.

"Nina! A and D!" I shuffled back through the pages. "Maybe you're onto something. That would make sense." I scanned the pages for a D reference. "So much for that. There isn't a D. I'll have to call Tilly and ask her."

I took the bubbling macaroni and cheese out of the oven and placed it on a trivet to cool a bit. Nina eyed it, and I knew it would only be a matter of minutes until she dipped a spoon into it for a taste.

I phoned Tilly, who answered the phone a bit breathless.

"It's Sophie. Is everything okay?"

For a long moment, Tilly didn't speak. I was certain that only seconds had passed, but it was long enough for me to wonder what was going on.

Nina waved at me. She held a large serving spoon and doled the mac and cheese into a pretty blue casserole dish. "We could bring some to Tilly," she said in a loud voice.

I made a face at Nina. She would do anything to get to meet Old Town's newest famous resident.

"Everything's fine. I just walked in. What are you going to bring me?"

"Your macaroni and cheese."

She gasped. "You already cooked it? That's fabulous. I haven't started anything for our dinner yet, so that would be perfect."

"We'll drop over in a few minutes. There's something I wanted to ask you about the recipes."

When I hung up, Nina was frowning at the casserole. "Aluminum foil?" she asked.

"Let's cover it with a few layers of paper towels first since it's so hot. I don't want the crunchy crust to get soggy."

We packed a generous portion into an insulated carrier and pulled on our jackets. I dressed Daisy in her halter, folded two recipe pages, stuck them in my pocket, and we set off for Tilly's house.

Evening was setting on Old Town, and the lights in windows were starting to illuminate. There was something magical about Old Town when the lights came on. It was as though the historic houses came to life and we lived in a quaint village of another time.

As we approached Tilly's block, Daisy

58

carefully sniffed the unfamiliar territory. I didn't know how Tilly felt about dogs, but it wasn't like we were planning to stay long. We walked up the short sidewalk to the front stoop.

"So this is Tilly's house? I drive by all the time but had no idea a TV star was living here." Nina gazed up at the three stories while I clanked the door knocker.

Tilly opened the door, her hair flying out of place even more than it had earlier. Her face was flushed, with cheeks so red I wondered if she was sick. "Mac and cheese delivery," I said lightly.

"This is perfect timing. The girls are ravenous." Tilly smiled at Daisy and patted her.

I introduced Nina to her and pulled the recipe pages from my pocket. "I was wondering if you know what this means." I pointed to the letter and number combination.

"I haven't a clue," said Tilly. "Don't you know?"

"Not all the recipes have a notation like this. They're not any standard cooking instruction as far as I can tell."

Tilly stared at the pages. "I'm clueless. Can we just leave them out?"

I certainly didn't think it advisable to leave

59

anything *in* if we didn't know what it meant. "I don't see why not."

A man's voice inside Tilly's house said something that I didn't hear clearly.

Tilly handed the pages back to me with a smile. "Thank you so much for bringing this by. I know we'll enjoy it. Nice meeting you, Nina." She backed up and quickly closed the door.

CHAPTER 5

Dear Sophie,
I have a limited budget for herbs and spices. Which ones do you recommend for a starter kitchen?
                    Spice Girl in London, Kentucky

Dear Spice Girl,
Thyme, sage, rosemary, oregano, and cinnamon would be a great way to begin. Of course, don't forget salt and black pepper. You can pick up others as you need them.
                                        Sophie

"Is it just me, or was that weird?" asked Nina.

"She seemed in a hurry to get rid of us, didn't she?"

"What does her husband do?"

"Wesley Winthrop is one of the new congressmen. From Texas, I think."

"Oh, that's right. Do you suppose she's scared of him?"

"I hope not. How would you feel about taking a walk?"

"To enjoy the night air?" asked Nina.

"To pay the previous ghostwriter a visit."

"Okay. But if you're going to get rid of the weird letters and numbers, then why are we going?"

"Abby must have written them on the recipes for a reason. Maybe it's her personal code for something. Maybe it means to exclude a recipe or . . . Oh!" I pulled the two recipes out of my pocket and looked at them. "Could it be a date? Maybe she marked them to indicate that she had tested them? Maybe she assigns a ranking?" I studied the two pages. "Or maybe not."

"Are we going to ask her about Mr. Tilly?"

"You mean Wesley? Let's see what happens to come up in conversation."

We turned left. I spied the elegant lemon wreath right away.

"That's very clever. I might have to copy that wreath," said Nina.

"Since when do you make wreaths?"

"Perhaps I misspoke. By *copy* I meant *buy.*"

I looked up at the dark house. No lights were visible through the front windows.

"Doesn't look like anyone is home."

Nina banged the door knocker, which was in the shape of a woodpecker. "This woman has got a great sense of humor."

We waited, listening for the sound of footsteps.

"She's not home," I repeated.

Nina tried again, rapping on the door with her knuckles.

The front door to the house on our immediate left opened. The television inside the house blared. The porch light illuminated an elderly woman with a cane. "If you're looking for Abby, she hasn't been home for a few days."

The woman's voice sounded familiar. I walked toward her to see who she was.

"Is that you, Sophie?" she asked.

"Eunice Crenshaw?" I ran up her front steps and held out my arms for an embrace. "I haven't seen you in ages."

Eunice, whom I guessed to be in her late eighties, was dressed in a purple velour sweat suit. She wore her gleaming silver hair in a short bob and didn't bother with makeup. "Aw, I don't have any interest in going to all those parties anymore. Don't know anybody. They're all strangers to me."

It made me sad to hear that. Eunice had been born to money. Her father, an ex-

tremely successful builder, had left everything to his only child. For years she had
been a fixture on the social scene in Old
Town, generous to a fault when it came to
charitable donations. But now she had
reached an age at which she faded into the
background.

My neighbor, Francie Vanderhoosen, was
only a bit younger than Eunice. "There's
always Francie. I bet she would love to hear
from you."

"She hasn't passed yet, has she? I should
give her a call. So many of my friends have
been buried that I can't remember who's
still around and kickin'. If you're looking
for Abby, I haven't seen her since Thursday."

"Thank you. Maybe she left town. I hope
we didn't disturb you."

"Not at all. I've been worried about Abby,
so I'm glad to see somebody checking up
on her. Her cat, Oscar, is an indoor fellow,
but Friday night he came and hung around
in back of my house. Must have jumped the
fence. I took him in, of course, but I'm
concerned about Abby. Oscar is her baby.
She'd never let him run around by himself.
I thought she'd surely show up looking for
him. I called the police for a welfare check.
When the officer came, nobody answered
the door, but the sliding door in the back of

the house was unlocked. He went in and looked around, but nothing was amiss."

I didn't like the sound of that. She abruptly stopped going to work. Her indoor cat was outside of her house, and her back door was unlocked? I tried to rationalize. Maybe Abby had been searching for Oscar and didn't know Eunice had him. Or maybe he escaped when a cat sitter came to take care of him. I didn't know many people who would leave their back doors unlocked while they were away, though. Surely that meant she was nearby and planned to return soon.

"Sophie!" called Nina. "I can see a light on in the back of the house."

A few minutes earlier, I might have scolded Nina for snooping, but now I feared something was amiss.

Eunice patted my shoulder. "You better check on Abby. If she's home, tell her that I have Oscar."

I nodded and joined Nina, who had opened the gate to a small alley between Abby's and Eunice's houses.

Daisy sniffed the air and pulled on her leash, something she rarely did. She all but propelled me through the passage along the side of the house. A light shone through a window far in the back.

Nina flicked on the flashlight in her phone

so we could see our way to the rear of the house. The small, fenced backyard was quiet and calm.

"Abby?" I called.

No one answered.

Daisy pulled me toward the sliding glass door. I flicked on the light in my phone and shone it on the back of the house.

Nina and I approached the door slowly, calling Abby's name.

Still, no one responded.

Between our phone lights and the dim light inside, we were able to see a tidy living room. A cat carrier sat in the middle of the floor.

Nina shrieked.

CHAPTER 6

Dear Natasha,

You were so right about gray being the trending color. I'm painting my living room and I'd love to know what color you see trending next.

Pinkie in Blue Ash, Ohio

Dear Pinkie,

You are wise to think ahead so your living room won't be outdated. I'm predicting a return to bold 1960s orange, which will coordinate beautifully with all our grays.

Natasha

"What? Do you see Abby?"

"Turn around."

She had aimed her light toward bushes near the gate to the alley. A blue cat collar decorated with rhinestones hung on a branch of a holly tree. "There's no way a cat could shed its collar that high off the ground."

Cats were fairly crafty. I wouldn't put it past one to have somehow managed to leave its collar hanging from a branch five feet in the air. On the other hand, maybe Nina had a point. Had Abby taken off her cat's collar and flung it? If she doted on her cat like Eunice had said, then surely she wouldn't have done that.

"Sophie," said Nina softly. "The door is unlocked. . . ." She pulled the sliding glass door open about four inches.

I grabbed Nina's arm. I was thoroughly confused about the right thing to do. Part of me wanted to yank the door open and go running through Abby's house flicking on lights. But part of me knew that wasn't right. If, heaven forbid, her house was a crime scene, we would be contaminating it. And worse, if Abby came home and found two strangers in her house, she would have every right to call the police and report us. For all we knew, Abby had been coming and going as usual.

"That cat collar hanging on the tree isn't normal."

"We can't just go inside," I protested.

"You have to be kidding me," said Nina. "What if she's upstairs dying in a closet?"

"Honestly, Nina, I think we'd better not go in."

"I hope using the light on my phone hasn't drained the battery." Nina turned off the light and dialed 911.

"What are you doing?"

"I'm calling for a wellness check," said Nina.

"Eunice already did that."

"Hmm." She gave me a wicked look. "What if it were you? What if Mochie were wandering around the neighborhood without his collar and I didn't see you for a week? What if you didn't show up for one of your events? Wouldn't you want someone check on you?"

"I would. I would most certainly want that."

"Why is that cat collar in the tree? It won't hurt to do a second wellness check."

While we waited, I filled Nina in on what Eunice had said.

Wong arrived in ten minutes. She was African American but continued to use the surname of her ex-husband, a marriage that she claimed had been a huge mistake. Wong loved to eat, and her uniform strained against the buttons. I was delighted to see her because she was smart. She was brilliantly logical, and she didn't put up with

69

nonsense from anyone.

Nina explained the situation to her, ending with, "And Sophie won't let me go in to look around."

"You should listen to Sophie," grumbled Wong. "Did you touch the door handle?"

"Yes. There isn't another way to open the door."

"When's the last time you heard from her?" asked Wong.

Nina sighed so loud that Wong flicked her flashlight in Nina's direction.

"We don't actually know her." Nina launched into an explanation of the ghost-writing situation.

"Her neighbor Eunice hasn't seen Abby recently, and Abby's indoor cat showed up at Eunice's house," I added.

"I'll go inside and check on her. You two stay out here, but don't touch anything. Did you hear me, Nina?"

I tried to hide my smile. Wong knew Nina would be nosy.

"Yeah, yeah, yeah. I thought we could go inside with you." said Nina.

"Sometimes you can for a welfare check. Usually it's family members who are worried, and they would know if something was out of place or unusual for the person. Most of the time the person is fine, but once in a while we find that someone fell down stairs and broke a leg or something. But I have to clear the house first. It's my job to make sure no one is hiding and that it's not a crime scene. You two stay out here."

Wong knocked and shouted, "Ms. Bergeron? Police, Ms. Bergeron!" She slid on a glove, opened the door, and slowly walked into Abby's house while Nina and I waited on the back patio. Wong continued to call out Abby's name.

Nina started to talk, but I shushed her. "Listen! If she's weak or tied up she might not be able to scream."

I didn't hear a thing. So much for that theory.

We watched Wong's flashlight as she walked through the first floor. There must not have been any sign of Abby in the kitchen or dining room.

Nina sidled through the open door and into the living room. She flashed around the light on her phone.

"Nina!" I hissed. "Get back here."

"Sophie, the cat bowls are gone," she pointed out.

I squinted. "The cat carrier is sitting out in the living room. Maybe she was planning to take him someplace."

Wong returned in short order. "Everything

71

was neat as a pin. The beds were made, and there weren't any clothes lying around. The shower is dry as a bone. Ladies, I believe Abby Bergeron has left town."

"And let her cat run outside?" I asked.

"Maybe he escaped, and she had to catch a flight," said Wong. "I've seen people leave their pets at home without food or water. It happens."

Nina gasped.

I was horrified by the thought. But I didn't think that was the case here. If that had been Abby's plan, the cat carrier wouldn't have been in the middle of her living room. And the cat's collar wouldn't be hanging in a bush.

"So can we come in now?" asked Nina.

"You don't even know her. You wouldn't know what was out of place. I don't see the point. Besides, I still have to clear the basement."

She opened a door and disappeared.

Nina sneaked back inside.

I hissed at her again. "Get out of there!"

Wong came running up the stairs, each footstep pounding. She breathed heavily. "Nina Reid Norwood, leave the premises now. It's officially a crime scene. Go, go, go!" She pointed to the door. "And don't touch anything on your way out."

"Abby is in the basement?" I asked.

Wong nodded. "Somebody is. I popped open the freezer and found toes."

"Toes? Like . . ." I swallowed hard "Chopped off?"

"Eww, no. They appear to be attached to a foot. I didn't move anything. It's in one of those chest freezers. I expect the entire body is inside."

"It must be Abby," breathed Nina.

I nodded. "I would think so."

Wong sighed and shook her head. "What is wrong with people?" She looked at us, and her mouth pulled into a straight line. "Now that this has changed from a wellness check to a crime scene, I'm afraid you two have to depart. I've called it in. The place will be swarming with cops in a couple of minutes."

"Poor Abby," I whispered.

It was totally dark behind Abby's house. Especially now that our phone batteries had run down and our phone flashlights had died. We were relying on the moon and ambient city light to make our way out to the street. Someone walked around the corner, which caused Nina and me to scream.

A strong flashlight beam caught us. Thankfully, we recognized the male voice that said,

"Not you two."

Daisy whined, and her wagging tail smacked my legs as she greeted Wolf Fleishman of the Criminal Investigations Division of the Alexandria Police. Wolf patted Daisy, whom he knew well because we had dated.

I gave him a break about his sarcastic comment. After all, Nina and I *had* been involved in solving several murders.

The silver in Wolf's brown hair gleamed as the light from Wong's flashlight briefly hit it. It appeared that he had lost some weight. Like me, Wolf was fond of good food. One year, determined to lose weight, we had grown a vegetable garden together in my backyard.

Nina raised her free palm in protest. "We didn't even know her! But I wish we had. She seemed like a fun person."

"Who is she?" Wolf shot the beam from his flashlight around Abby's backyard.

"Abby Bergeron," I said. "She was ghostwriting a book for Tilly Stratford, but she unexpectedly quit on Friday. Her neighbor says Abby's indoor cat turned up at her place on Friday night, so that's probably around the time she was murdered."

"How do you know she was murdered?" Wolf's back was to me and he was tilting his head to get a better look at the cat collar

74

hanging on the tree branch.

"I've never heard of anyone dying a natural death in a freezer surrounded by food."

Despite the darkness, when he turned to look at me, I caught his surprised expression, which was saying a lot. I had often been frustrated by Wolf's ability to hide his emotions. "Where's the freezer?"

"In the basement."

Wolf grunted. "Okay. I know where to find you. Get out of my crime scene."

Daisy led the way through the passage to the sidewalk. A second police vehicle pulled up as we walked toward Eunice's house.

"I'd like to tell Eunice what's going on if that's okay with you," I said to Nina.

"Sure." Nina shook her head. "It's so sad. We didn't even know Abby, but I still feel a loss. She was probably about our age. It could have been one of us!"

Eunice was standing in her doorway, holding onto a cane and watching the police who were arriving. "What's going on? Did you find Abby?" She stepped aside and motioned for us to come in.

A large long-haired black and orange tortoiseshell cat with green eyes meowed at us as we walked in.

"That's Abby's cat, Oscar." She shook her finger at the cat. "Hush now and behave," she said to him.

I was about to introduce Eunice to Nina when they hugged. "I haven't seen you at the shelter lately," said Nina.

Eunice nodded and tapped her cane on the hardwood floor. "As you can tell, I'm not getting around as much as I used to. That's the one place I miss. I find I don't care about seeing people, but those sweet babies need and deserve help."

A completely white cat walked up to Daisy without a qualm, and they touched noses.

Nina, Daisy, and I followed Eunice into a large living room, where I counted seven more kitties. Daisy stayed close to me but didn't seem distressed by the presence of so many cats.

Eunice slowly sat down in a recliner. From the looks of it, I suspected that she slept there, too. The elegant living room with a marble surround on the fireplace had turned into an all-purpose room for Eunice.

A table next to her chair contained lotions, a clock with extra large numbers, tissues, a Bible, a laptop computer, and a couple of bags of cat treats. I could see into the kitchen, where little had been put away in cabinets. The counters and floor were covered with boxes and bags of food. Cans of cat food cluttered the counters, too. I assumed that the bags of dry cat food on the floor were too heavy for her to lift.

As gently as I could, I asked, "Eunice, do you have anyone who comes to help you?"

"No!" she barked. "I don't need any help. I'm not a doddering old fool yet. My cleaning lady, Lula, comes over once a month and we have a grand old time catching up on gossip."

From the looks of things, Lula wasn't doing much in the way of cleaning. I could understand wanting to keep things close at hand, but Eunice would be tripping over the mess on the floor fairly soon if someone didn't straighten things up for her.

"What's going on over there at Abby's place?" Eunice asked. "I can't imagine it's good news, or all those police cars wouldn't be pulling up."

My eyes met Nina's. "I'm sorry, Eunice. It appears that Abby has died. We don't know for sure that it's Abby, but it's not very likely that it would be someone else."

Eunice pulled a tissue out of the box and wiped the tears that spilled from her eyes. "It's just not right when a young person goes too soon. I knew something was wrong over there. What happened to her?"

"We don't know yet, Eunice," said Nina. "But we think she may have been killed about the time her cat showed up at your house."

"Killed?" Eunice's eyes widened. "Mercy! Right next door? I thought you meant she had fallen or taken ill. Someone murdered my sweet Abby?"

"I'm afraid so," I said gently.

"So that's why Oscar came to me. How'd he get out? Abby was so careful and adamant about him being a house cat."

"The sliding glass door in the back was unlocked," I explained. "Maybe he made a dash for it when someone opened the door to check on Abby?"

"Or perhaps her killer was a cat lover," Eunice observed. "How odd. Cat people are usually very kind."

Her comment caught me by surprise. Had Abby's killer opened the door for the cat? Suddenly the collar hanging on the bush seemed more sinister than bizarre. Why would someone remove Oscar's collar? I wondered how many murderers took the time to close doors. A killer would probably be in a state of panic and rush to leave. Maybe it was commonplace that doors were left open after a murder. In fact, that might be a clue to her killer. Most strangers wouldn't know where the keys were and would have to leave a door unlocked. That indicated the murderer wasn't someone who was close to her.

"How well did you know Abby?" I asked.

"Pretty well. She came over here a lot. Used to bring me leftovers when she was trying out recipes. I ate like a queen!"

"Was she married?" asked Nina. "Did she have children?"

"She had an ex-husband but no children. I think that was the one thing she regretted. She loved kids and would have been a great mom. Her ex is a good-looking fellow. I saw him come by once in a while."

"Did you hear anything unusual around the time Oscar showed up?" asked Nina.

Eunice buried her head in her hands for a few moments. "Honey, I wish I had." She pointed at her ear. "My hearing isn't what it used to be. Visitors complain that I have the TV on too loud. I tell them it's on the right volume for me and if they don't like it, they can leave. But I guess it's right loud for people with normal hearing. I didn't hear a thing. I'd have called the cops if I had." She winced and dabbed at her eyes. Speaking softly, she added, "I have hearing aids, but I don't wear them because I loathe the stupid things. Now I wish I had worn them."

On a whim, I asked, "Did Abby say anything about Tilly Stratford's husband, Wesley?"

CHAPTER 7

Dear Sophie,
There's a restaurant where I live that serves the most delicious macaroni and cheese. It's so creamy! I have tried everything. Adding heavy cream, cream cheese, and soft cheeses, but I can't get the combination quite right. Any suggestions?

Mac and Cheese Lover in
Caerphilly, Wales

Dear Mac and Cheese Lover,
Have you tried using cream cheese and Colby cheese in your recipe? Colby contains more moisture and is creamier when melted. A relative of cheddar, it's a natural for mac and cheese.

Sophie

"Now that's an interesting question," said Eunice. "I watch a lot of those crime shows, and I know they'll suspect Abby's former husband first. But if he has an alibi, they'll sniff around the other men in her life."

"Are you saying Tilly's husband was involved with Abby?" asked Nina.

Eunice pointed her forefingers and waggled them. "If you ask me, Abby liked him a little bit too much."

"They were having an affair?" I asked, trying to get to the bottom of her innuendos.

"She never said as much, but she raved about how wonderful he was and how he always made it a point to drop by the kitchen and sample the dishes she and Tilly were cooking. You girls understand what it means when another woman thinks too highly of a married man. It's always trouble."

"Sophie's going to take over ghostwriting Tilly's cookbook," said Nina.

"Did Abby tell you about it?" I asked.

"Abby talked about it all the time. She liked Tilly, and she loved the two girls —"

"Two girls?" I interrupted.

"Only one was Tilly's. The other was her friend." She paused to think.

"Schuyler?" I asked.

"That's it. Must be a family name. Abby thought they were wonderful."

If she liked them all so much, then I had

to wonder why she quit.

Eunice continued. "She was always telling me stories about them. They're at that age when every little thing is such a big deal. When you get to my age, you've learned not to let the little things bother you. You have to let things go."

"What did Abby say about the cookbook?" I prompted, hoping she'd said something helpful. Or maybe Abby had even shared the odd code.

"Mostly she was worried that Tilly's recipes were too bland. She wanted to spice them up a little. Not so that they burned your tongue or anything. I'm very sensitive to spicy-hot foods. Never could eat 'em. But she felt that Tilly cooked a little too plain."

It wasn't the kind of information I had sought, but it was extremely helpful to know. She was adding spices to the recipes? Maybe that's what the odd notations meant. Could they be her personal shorthand for spice ideas? D for dill? B for basil? That wouldn't explain the numbers, but maybe they represented amounts? They hadn't looked like measurements. After all, if they meant half teaspoons or quarter teaspoons, wouldn't a lot of them be fractions? And wouldn't there be a lot of ones?

I took out the two recipes I had brought

with me. "She made notations on some of the pages that I can't quite figure out. Three letters followed by numbers. Does that mean anything to you?"

"Sophie, it has been quite a while since I cooked. I imagine everything has changed. Do you still use measuring cups?" Eunice winked at me.

I rose and showed her the pages.

Eunice was quiet for a long moment. "Sophie, they look like codes."

"Yes, but for what? What do they mean?"

"You'd have to figure that out. Sometimes people have a particular book, and the numbers represent pages and a line where a letter or a word is located. If you have the identical book, you can unravel the code and read the message."

"Thanks, Eunice."

She scowled at me. "Like this one. *B C F four one seven.* The B might mean chapter two. The C could mean the third paragraph. I'm not sure about the F. The four could indicate the fourth line. Are you following me? Once you know the book and understand the pattern, it's easy to decipher."

I didn't want to offend her, but I hardly thought Abby was writing secret messages on the recipes. The only people who would see them would be Tilly and maybe the editor.

Nina asked, "Did you ever see Wesley Winthrop at Abby's house?"

"I've seen him on TV, so I know what he looks like, but I can't say I've ever seen him in the flesh. I suppose Wolf will be over here soon asking me the same questions."

I suspected she was right about that. Leaving Nina to chat with Eunice, I tried to unobtrusively tidy up Eunice's kitchen. I washed a few dishes and put them away.

"Leave that stuff out where I can see it," Eunice shouted. "I don't have enough years left to waste my time looking for things."

I took out everything that I had stashed in cabinets and placed it all neatly on a table. I gathered empty cookie bags and old newspapers and placed them in trash bags. I wondered if Lula the housekeeper was the same age as Eunice.

I flicked the light switch by the back door so I could see where I was going and stepped outside. Holding the trash in one hand, I grabbed the railing and walked down three steps to a brick patio, where I could hear the police going about their business next door. They were being very quiet, but I overheard one of them say, "No computer, no phone, no tablet, watch, or iPad."

If someone had said that about Eunice, it wouldn't have surprised me. But Abby was probably closer to my age. It was odd that she wouldn't have a cell phone or a tablet. I supposed some people still didn't. I carried the garbage bag to the trash can. Out of curiosity, I opened the gate in the fence and stepped into the alley that ran behind the houses. It was dark and silent. A couple of houses had electric lanterns mounted near their gates. I'd have to come back during the daytime for a better look, but preliminarily I'd have said it would be an easy way to drive or walk up to a house without being noticed.

I couldn't see much in the dark, but it appeared to be a lovely patio. A deck box for cushion storage sat behind two comfortable armchairs. Someone had placed yellow cushions on them and opened a yellow-and-white-striped umbrella over a round dining table. I bet Eunice didn't get out here much to enjoy her backyard. The stairs and uneven bricks probably made her dread a trip to the garage or an afternoon outside.

I returned to Eunice and Nina.

Eunice dabbed at her eyes with a tissue. "Abby was always tidying up around here.

She pretended she wasn't, but I knew what she was doing. Like Sophie did just now."

"Eunice, do you know if Abby had a cell phone or a computer?" I asked.

"Oh sure. She loved that kind of stuff. She's the one who showed me how to play bridge online." Eunice tapped on the laptop near her chair. "I thought I'd have to give it up since I don't get around much anymore. But playing online is almost as good! The only thing I miss is the gossip." Eunice heaved a great sigh. "Abby was a blessing to me. She was a friend." She grasped Nina's fingers. "How did she die?"

I wasn't sure we should tell her. Would she ever sleep again knowing what happened to her friend right next door?

Nina looked at me with large eyes. She was probably thinking the same thing.

"I'm not sure," I said. "Wolf might know after the medical examiner takes a look." That was actually the truth. We didn't need to mention that her dear friend had been folded up and mashed into a freezer. All Wong had seen were her toes. That hadn't told us anything about how she had died.

Eunice held a hand out to me. "I want to hire you to solve Abby's murder. That's the least I can do for Abby when she was so very kind to me. Name your price."

I took her gnarled hand into mine. "I don't charge anything, Eunice. But don't forget that Wolf is very competent and has a lot more resources than I do. I bet he'll figure it out in no time."

"You and Nina will look into it as a favor to me, won't you?" asked Eunice. "I would do it myself, but I'm not as spry as I used to be."

"Of course we will." I gave her hand a gentle squeeze.

"I can do any research you need online!" she offered.

She was adorable. "You'd better be careful what you offer, or we'll be back here with work for you," I teased.

Nina and I gave Eunice hugs and saw ourselves to the door. I made sure it locked behind us.

"I guess I should call Tilly before she hears about Abby through a rumor," I said.

"Do you think Tilly's husband had something to do with Abby's death?"

"I hope not. Do you think she overheard something nefarious? Maybe she threatened to go public with information that could ruin Wesley's career?" I squinted into the night as cops walked in and out of Abby's home. "Who lives on the other side of Abby?" I asked.

We turned together as if our move had been orchestrated. Even Daisy was happy to swing in the other direction. We crossed the street, and for a long moment we stared at the house next to Abby's.

"I have no idea who lives there," I said.

"Me either." Nina's mouth twitched. "We can ask around." She scribbled the house number on a scrap of paper.

"Maybe we should drop by with questions for Eunice every day. That would give us an excuse to bring her food and check up on her," I suggested.

"She's pretty sharp. I think she would catch on. Wasn't she friends with Francie?"

"She was." My elderly neighbor, Francie, was a long-time Old Town resident. "I wish we could find someone to help her. Maybe Francie is clever enough to persuade Eunice to hire someone who could cook and clean and keep her company."

We walked home in the dark. Even though streetlights and porch lights provided enough illumination, both of us were jumpy and overreacted when a cat darted in front of us. Only Daisy strolled along as usual.

An automatic light had turned on in my kitchen. We could see Mochie waiting for us in the bay window. As we approached, he leaped off his viewing perch and raced to the kitchen door, where he waited, thrilled to see us.

After greeting Mochie, I phoned Tilly to tell her about Abby, but her phone rolled over to voice mail. It didn't seem right to leave a message about Abby's death, so I simply asked her to call me.

Nina popped the remaining mac and cheese in the oven to warm it up. She heated a pot of apple cider and disappeared to the dining room, where I kept alcohol.

We wouldn't eat six chicken breasts, but I baked them all, anyway, planning to use the rest for future meals. I tossed a salad of baby spinach leaves, slices of red onion, a handful of crunchy walnuts, and halved grape tomatoes. Still thinking of Abby, I whisked together a quick dressing of apple cider vinegar, extra virgin olive oil, minced garlic, a pinch of dried mustard, and a couple of tablespoons of brown sugar.

Nina returned and splashed a healthy amount of bourbon into the apple cider.

When the chicken breasts registered 165 degrees on my cooking thermometer, I placed them on plates and poured some of the buttery juices from the pan over them. A sprinkle of salt and fresh parsley, and they were ready to eat.

Nina brought the macaroni and cheese to

the table, which bore a tablecloth of burnt orange, gold, and maroon. I fed Mochie chicken in aspic and cut up a chicken breast for Daisy to eat with her dinner.

Nina and I sat down at the table, but I couldn't help feeling guilty. What was Eunice eating tonight? I knew she had some food in her cupboard. Was she eating peanut butter on toast? Crackers with cheese?

Nina gazed at me. "You're thinking about Eunice, aren't you?"

"We should bring her dinner."

"I'm in."

I packed the hot food in an insulated carrier on wheels. Nina wasn't about to leave her drinks behind. She poured them into thermoses and fastened them to the carrier with bungee cords.

I suited up Daisy in her harness, left Mochie snoozing in the bay window, and locked up. It took us less than six minutes to walk back to Eunice's house. As we turned onto her street, it appeared that the number of police and emergency vehicles had doubled.

Daisy stayed close to me, probably worried about the busy people moving around ahead of us.

When we reached Eunice's house, we stopped and watched them for a moment.

Neighbors and onlookers had gathered to see what was going on.

We walked up the three stairs to Eunice's door. I banged the elegant lion's head door knocker, which had to be antique.

To my surprise, Wolf answered the door.

"We brought dinner for Eunice," I blurted.

He stepped aside so we could enter. "That was thoughtful of you."

Nina sang out, "Eunice! We're back!" She smiled at Wolf. "We brought enough to share if you're hungry."

"I need to get back to work. But I might find time for just a bite."

In a low voice so I wouldn't cause Eunice more distress, I asked, "Can you tell how Abby died?"

He shook his head. "We'll have to wait for the autopsy."

"Is she out of the freezer yet?"

CHAPTER 8

Dear Sophie,
I work a nine-to-five job, then I pick up my children from three different schools. We have athletic events some nights, and I'm okay with eating pizza or takeout on those nights. What can I cook that's fast but still a real meal?
Overworked Mom in Sleepy Hollow,
Illinois

Dear Overworked Mom,
When you cook, do it in a big way so that you'll have leftovers for other dinners. Chicken breasts and chicken tenders can bake in 15 to 20 minutes. Make a big casserole of mac and cheese on a Sunday, and you'll be eating well all week.
Sophie

Wolf took a deep breath and muttered, "Not

yet. I would guess it was easier putting her in there than it will be to get her out."

"Hi, Eunice! We brought you dinner." I took the food from Nina and hustled to the kitchen.

Eunice rose from her chair and shuffled after me. "It smells wonderful."

"The mac and cheese is one of Tilly's recipes."

"Oh gosh. I remember Abby having a fit about that mac and cheese. It was not to her liking at all."

Eunice's words struck a chord with me. Was it the ghostwriter's job to improve the recipes? We all had different tastes. What I might find bland and boring could be the exact way someone's mother cooked a dish and the way that the person thought it should taste. Was that my job? Was I supposed to tweak the recipes? Maybe not. For all I knew, other moms had cooked a dish in the same manner and some readers would think they had finally stumbled upon the authentic recipe that they remembered from their childhoods. I'd had that happen to me.

"Uh-oh. I made it according to Abby's notes."

Eunice held her hand against her chest. "Abby," she said with a sigh. "If only I could have helped her in some way. Maybe I could have saved her."

"Eunice, you can't blame yourself. Whatever happened to Abby had nothing to do with you," I said firmly.

Eunice wiped a tear off her cheek. "I keep telling myself that. But it doesn't make it any easier to know that I was right next door and I did nothing. I could have at least called 911 or shouted out the front door to passersby on the street."

"Eunice, have you considered one of those medical emergency buttons?" I asked.

She blew air through her lips in disdain. "I don't need anything like that. That's for old people."

What could I say? I wondered exactly how old she was.

I found some beautiful Lamberton china in her cabinet. Soft rose and blue flowers were connected by a delicate scroll around the rim. "Do you have everyday china somewhere?"

"Use that old stuff."

"But it's so pretty."

"All the more reason to use it, Sophie. It's not like anyone is lining up to inherit it. I might as well enjoy it."

She had a point. I doled out the chicken breasts, macaroni and cheese, and added a serving of the salad on each plate.

Nina bounded into the kitchen. "Wolf is working, so he's not interested in spiked apple cider. How about you, Eunice?"

"I've never been known to pass up a good drink. Bring it on, Nina!"

"Would you like to eat at the dining table, or are you more comfortable in your chair?" I asked.

Eunice blushed. "I don't think the dining table is fit for company."

"The chair it is!" I felt terrible for having embarrassed her.

When we were settled in Eunice's living room, it grew quiet. Through the window that was open a crack, we could hear murmuring outside, a reminder of Abby's terrible death. I watched Eunice. She didn't seem to hear it at all.

"Was Abby from around here?" asked Wolf.

I had to give Eunice credit. She was a strong woman. His question didn't seem to bother her a bit.

"I got the impression she had moved around quite a bit. She wasn't a born-and-bred Southerner, that's for sure. I know she lived in Savannah and somewhere in Texas for a while. But she said a few things that led me to think she might have hailed from

Wisconsin. I know she loved children and had been a kindergarten teacher before going to culinary school. By the way, Sophie, I believe she'd be very happy with this mac and cheese. It's delicious. My favorite part is that it's so creamy."

"That's the Colby cheese in it. It melts better than cheddar."

"Wolf, do you know who lives on the other side of Abby's house?" I asked.

Eunice answered. "Bob Hughes and Jerry Schwartz. They were away for the weekend and horrified to learn what had happened."

I looked over at Wolf, who took a big bite of mac and cheese. He nodded in confirmation.

I couldn't help thinking that the killer had gotten very lucky. A lady on one side who was hard of hearing and no one home on the other side.

Nina tried to keep the conversation away from the subject of Abby's death, but it hung over us like a dark cloud.

Wolf ate quickly, thanked me for dinner, and excused himself to get back to work. "Eunice," he said, "I know Abby was working for Tilly Stratford. Did she mention any other jobs she had?"

"She was beginning to look around for another freelance gig. She said she always worried about her next job, but every time one ended, another one came along."

I saw Wolf to the door. "Did anyone find her phone or computer?"

Wolf raised his eyebrows. "How did you know about that?"

I wasn't about to confess that I had overheard it. "Just a hunch."

"All that's left is a printer."

"What about her purse?"

"Sophie, I don't have the time to give you a complete inventory of exactly what we found in Abby's house."

Aargh. It was just like Wolf to clam up. Okay, I could snoop around her garage to see if a car was there. But I couldn't go into the house. "I'll only ask about the purse."

"You know how it is. Women are always changing purses to match their clothes. All I can say is we haven't found one with her wallet in it. Okay?"

It wasn't very helpful, but it would have to do. Wolf said good night and left me thinking that whoever had murdered Abby had taken her computer, telephone, and purse. That had to mean something. Could she have a file on her system that someone would have wanted? Had her killer taken her electronics to prevent anyone from finding out what Abby knew? Suddenly, I couldn't wait to get home. Could the codes on the recipes be related to information on her computer? It seemed unlikely, but stranger things had happened.

I cleaned up Eunice's kitchen and stashed the leftovers in her fridge before we left and walked home.

That night, I built a small fire in my kitchen fireplace and sat at the banquette in the kitchen with all the recipes in front of me. Methodically, I went through each page. When I found a recipe that contained Abby's mysterious code, I wrote the code on a small yellow sticky note and adhered it to the outer edge of the page. There were twelve in all.

HPS5106	BAC149
MGB4143	RPC142
BCS417	CPS3811
WFM2912	GPP251
BAF7168	GMP434
CCT1085	CMC3610

I studied them, but they made no sense to me. I couldn't see a logical theme or rhythm to them. I considered what Eunice had told us about a book being the key to a code. I flipped through the pages in search of anything that resembled a book title. At midnight, I gave up, doused the fire, and went up to bed with Daisy and Mochie.

My phone rang at four in the morning. I hoped it was a wrong number, because I was not ready to rise and face some kind of emergency. And why else would anyone call at that hour?

"Hello?" I croaked.

"Soph!" It was Mars's voice. "Is it true that Abby Bergeron is dead?"

Oh no. I would never get back to sleep now. "Yes."

"Why didn't you tell me?"

The truth was that it didn't even occur to me to notify Mars. "It was late when I came home."

"You were there?" The phone line went dead.

"Mars? Mars?" Ugh. He was on his way over. And he had a key. We had swapped keys for ease of picking up Daisy. If I didn't get up, he'd sit on the edge of my bed and bombard me with questions.

I dragged myself out of bed, pulled on a fluffy white bathrobe, and stumbled down the stairs. Mochie sprang ahead of me, and Daisy was as alert as if she'd slept the whole night.

I flicked on the outdoor light just in time to see Mars run across the slumbering street and up to my kitchen door. I opened it for him.

I yawned. "Why is this such an emergency?"

He held out a plastic container full of croissants and breakfast breads. "A peace offering."

"You came prepared to bribe me?"

"They're from the Laughing Hound. Day old but still good."

After breaking up with Natasha, Mars had moved in with our friend Bernie, who ran The Laughing Hound, a popular local restaurant. The two of them lived in a mansion catty-corner from my house.

"No wonder you haven't moved out of there."

Mars shrugged. "It's convenient and comfortable. Bernie brings home a lot of leftovers, so I never have to cook. Altogether convenient. Not to mention that Natasha still hasn't paid me for my share of our house."

I wasn't getting involved in their financial dealings. "Coffee or tea?"

"Better make it coffee. I need to be fully awake when I talk to Wesley."

"How did you hear about Abby?" I asked.

"Wesley called me ten minutes before I phoned you. He was distraught. I figured if anyone knew what was going on, it would be you."

"Thank you so much," I said wryly. "How did he hear about it?" I poured coffee for Mars and steeped hot English breakfast tea for myself. I brought the mugs to the table with milk, sugar, spoons, and napkins, and I placed the breakfast breads on a platter.

"One of his staffers, I think. Bernie said the news made it to the Laughing Hound last night, so I assume it's spreading like wildfire."

"You woke Bernie, too?"

"He turned over and went right back to sleep."

I should have been so lucky.

Mars stared at the mugs listlessly. A faint smile crossed his lips. "Sophie's brew. I've put a spell on you!" he read. "Where did you find these?"

"A gift from Nina."

"Figures. Very funny."

Mars stirred his coffee, and the smile faded. "I liked Abby. What happened to her? Heart attack? A bad fall?"

"I doubt it. No one, not even Wolf, knows much yet. She was in her freezer."

Mars's spoon clanked to the table. "Are you kidding me? Someone stuffed her into a freezer?"

"I'm afraid so." I took a long drag on my hot tea.

"How would you do that? Aren't the shelves in the way?"

"Not in chest freezers. They're basically a big box. There might be a couple of baskets to divide the space, but they can be lifted out very easily."

Mars cupped his coffee in his hands as though he had gone cold. "It never occurred to me that she might have been murdered. I thought for sure that she had some medical emergency or a disease that I didn't know about." He looked me in the eyes. "Who would want to kill Abby?"

"You're the one who knew her. I wasn't aware of her existence until you told me about her." I watched his expression. "She had an ex-husband."

"So I've heard."

"They'll probably suspect him first."

Mars stared into his mug. "Um, Soph, there's something you should know. It's not a big deal actually, but I went out with Abby a couple of times."

CHAPTER 9

Dear Natasha,
My mom has a cooking blog. She's very proud of it, and she's a great cook. But when she serves a casserole and takes a photo, it looks like garbage! How can I tell her it's turning people off?
Worried Son in Difficult, Tennessee

Dear Worried Son,
What is your mother doing making casseroles? Is she stuck in the 1960s? Bring her up-to-date by explaining that no one eats casseroles anymore!
Natasha

It was far too early in the morning for that kind of revelation. I shouldn't have been surprised, though. Mars was a smart, good-looking guy with a sense of humor. I'd heard that single women our age were chasing him in Old Town. Still, it came as a shock to me.

"Don't look at me that way. We went out twice."

"And . . . ?"

"And nothing. She's still in an I-just-got-divorced fog. She was nice enough, but there wasn't a spark."

It wasn't funny, but I had to swallow an urge to giggle. "A spark?"

"No chemistry. Does that sound better?"

I knew what he meant. And this really wasn't the time to tease him about it, anyway. "Are you trying to tell me that Wolf will be coming to talk to you as soon as he's done with the ex-husband?"

"I'd say that would be very likely."

There was no point in asking if he had an alibi. No one knew yet when Abby had died. And I didn't have to ask if he had murdered Abby. I knew Mars better than anyone. He didn't have it in him to kill someone. Even if it had been an accident, he would have been a stand-up guy and called an ambulance. That was Mars. Still, the cops would have to consider him a possible suspect. "Was she dating anyone else?"

"If she was, she didn't tell me about it," he said. "Maybe Tilly knows."

"They spent a lot of time together in the kitchen. They probably talked about many things. Wouldn't hurt to ask."

I wasn't sure how I could broach the subject of his client without sounding accusatory, so I just blurted it out. "Any chance Wesley was involved with her?"

Mars's face lost all its color. "No!" He thought for a moment. "No," he stated firmly. "What would give you that idea?"

I turned the tables on him. "Why would Wesley call you about Abby in the middle of the night?"

"Because she was working with Tilly. The newshounds will be all over this. It has to be handled very carefully. I'll write a press release about how sad they are and what a wonderful person she was."

I didn't press him, but our eyes met across the kitchen table.

Mars massaged his forehead. "Wesley isn't that stupid."

I bit my lip to keep from laughing. As if that would prevent a politician from straying. The newspapers were full of stories about infidelity in the political arena.

"Please tell me that you haven't heard rumors to that effect." Mars winced.

"Pretty embarrassing to date your client's paramour, huh?"

Mars's eyes widened in horror. "Can you even imagine the headlines?"

106

"Relax, Mars. I don't know anything," I said. "Do you remember Eunice Crenshaw?"

He frowned. "The wealthy socialite?"

"That's the one. She's Abby's next-door neighbor. According to Eunice, Abby was quite fond of Wesley."

"That doesn't mean they were having an affair."

"I'm in total agreement about that. I just thought I'd point it out to you. It's always better to be forewarned. Right?"

Mars did not seem happy. He rubbed the side of his face in discomfort. "You really don't know how Abby died? Wolf didn't tell you?"

"Not the first clue. To be honest, I don't think the cops know yet. They're waiting to see what the autopsy turns up."

"Mind if I call Wesley?"

"Not a bit." I wondered if I should give him some privacy, but I decided he knew his way around. He'd lived in this house. If he wanted to speak privately, he could get up and go into the sunroom. I plucked a croissant off the platter and tore a piece off. Mars was right. They were almost as fresh as the day they were baked.

Mars didn't leave the table. He punched a number into his phone. "Wes, Sophie confirms that Abby has died." He was silent for a moment. "The cause of death wasn't immediately apparent. Uh-huh. I have some contacts, so we'll probably know what happened before it hits the news. I'll draft a statement and be over" — Mars glanced at his watch — "by five. That should give us enough time." He hung up and took a croissant from the platter. "At least your clients don't wake you in the middle of the night to confirm rumors."

"I don't know how you do it. Wesley seems like a nice guy, though." Still, I was a little surprised that he found Abby's death to be of such concern that he was up phoning people about it in the middle of the night. That made me suspicious of Wesley. I didn't care what Mars thought on the subject. People didn't call a guy in the wee hours of the morning about a woman's death unless there was a very close connection.

"The news will identify Abby as working for TV star Tilly and her husband the congressman. It will make me sound like a complete jerk to say this, but the truth is that Tilly's fame and her husband's powerful job are what make Abby's death sensational. If she was just Abby Bergeron who had a boring job and no interesting connections to the rich and powerful, she'd probably get a passing mention or two."

"Did you smooth over the e-mail that was released?"

Mars groaned. "What a mess. I'm not sure we'll ever know who the culprit was. For now, I've hired a security consultant to put up a new firewall on the computers at Wesley's office. That will make it more difficult to penetrate them."

"Assuming it wasn't simply someone *in* his office," I pointed out.

"True. But if another e-mail is released, then we'll know where to look for the offender."

"Are you going to have him send some fake e-mails as a test?"

"What a great idea!" Mars finished his coffee and croissant, patted Daisy, and took off. He had work to do.

Meanwhile, I was wide awake, and it wasn't even five in the morning yet.

I took Daisy for an early walk. It was absolutely chilly. Naturally, I couldn't help wandering in the direction of Abby's house. I stopped and observed it from across the street. The lights were off. It looked dead and dreary. At that very moment, the gate that led to the back patio opened and a man stepped through. I didn't recognize him but I wondered what he was doing there before daylight.

Daisy tugged at her leash. I thought it wise not to follow him in the dark. I coaxed Daisy to turn around. Two blocks later, she pulled at the leash again. This time I let her steer me. I had no particular destination in mind. All I could think of was the man I had seen. What had he wanted at Abby's house?

I felt more secure when we were back in our house. I went straight to the den and looked up Abigail Bergeron on my computer. There were a lot of women by that name. It didn't help that I had never seen her, though it appeared to me that most of them were probably too young to be our Abby Bergeron.

I rose and locked the kitchen door before pouring myself another mug of tea and looking through the recipes for something to cook.

It was more than a little bit eerie to know I was reading through the work of a woman who was no longer alive. I had read lots of things written by people who had passed on, but Abby's handwriting in the margins screamed out to me. I wasn't usually melodramatic about this kind of thing, but I couldn't shake the feeling that this project had been meant to fall into my hands.

Nonsense! I was letting Abby's gruesome death get to me. I tried to focus on the recipes, making note of the ingredients I needed. I had everything for Grandma Peggy's Pumpkin Bundt Cake, and it sounded good.

I took eggs and butter out of the fridge and placed them on the counter to come to room temperature. Meanwhile I took a shower, trying to aim the stream of water so it wouldn't hit the spot in the wall that no longer had tiles.

Half an hour later, I watched my bright red KitchenAid mixer cream the butter and sugar. Following the recipe carefully, I mixed the flour with nutmeg, cinnamon, and a tiny bit of cloves. My kitchen was beginning to smell like fall. I poured the thick batter into a Bundt pan and popped it into the oven to bake.

Grandma Peggy's Pumpkin Bundt Cake was one of the recipes that bore the odd code. I knew I should give up on the strange markings. Now that Abby was dead, we would probably never know what she meant.

Nevertheless, I studied the codes again.

They meant nothing to me. Just numbers preceded by letters. Each had three letters at the beginning, followed by three or four numbers.

I chided myself for being obsessed with the notations. If I ever figured them out, they would probably mean something ridiculously unimportant, like whether Abby approved of a recipe.

The sun was rising by the time I poured a glaze over the pumpkin cake. The scent of the cake had filled my kitchen, and I was itching to try a piece.

I decided I would wait and reward myself with a slice for breakfast, after I made fall wreaths for my doors.

Daisy accompanied me to the storage room on the third floor of my house, which was actually a finished attic. Someone, probably Mars's aunt Faye, had converted it into one lovely bedroom and one mini-bedroom, which despite its size often came in handy and had been very popular with my niece when she was young.

I opened the door to the storage room, and Mochie leaped inside to sniff the array of storage boxes. I located straw wreath bases and a box of dried and silk flowers. Remembering the lemon wreath on Abby's door, I wondered if it was too early for miniature pumpkins on a wreath. Huge dried hydrangea blossoms in creamy pink and green and others that had turned light brown looked like good choices for the season. I affixed them to the bases and tied them with a coral — almost pumpkin-colored — ribbon with a velvety texture.

I coaxed Mochie out of his playroom and carried them downstairs. I hung each of them by the ribbon. The ends draped onto the flowers in the wreaths.

That done, I cut a large rectangle out of an old plastic tablecloth that I had used outdoors. With the aid of waterproof repair tape, I affixed it to the shower wall where the tiles were missing. I wasn't sure it would hold up, but it was better than nothing. I sprayed water on it and was pleased that it didn't peel off.

I swapped my now-damp clothes for jeans, a long-sleeved T-shirt, and a fuzzy vest and headed for the grocery store.

It was early enough for traffic to be light. There weren't many people shopping yet, either. I started with Brussels sprouts, bell peppers, and potatoes. I placed some Fuji apples and bananas in my cart. Chicken breasts were on sale and always a favorite of mine, so I added a couple of packages along with a whole chicken and bacon. Suddenly a chill swept over me, and it wasn't from the cold meat section. I felt as if someone was watching me.

I turned and saw the man who had pulled

the soda can out of the garbage. He smiled at me, placed a steak in the basket he was carrying, and walked away.

I shivered and kept an eye out for him. Strolling along and trying to focus, I grabbed Parmesan cheese, panko bread crumbs, cornmeal, ketchup, frozen corn, heavy cream, and more pumpkin puree. I thought I had most of the spices I would need. But I added some staples. Eggs, bread, milk, and a box of Daisy's favorite dog treats.

I drove home and unpacked my groceries. When I stepped outside to get my mail, Nina emerged from her house and ran across the street. "I love your wreaths! But wait until you see what I'm doing."

"Something new?" I asked.

She smiled. "They should be here today!"

"Sounds like fun. How would you feel about a slice of Grandma Peggy's Pumpkin Bundt Cake?"

"Perfect. I haven't had any breakfast. I had to get up before the crack of dawn to drive my husband to the airport. He's off to Los Angeles again." Nina's husband was a forensic pathologist who spent more time traveling than he did at home. She didn't seem to mind, though.

For the second time that morning, I sat

114

down at my kitchen table with a friend, a cup of tea, and a delicious nosh.

"Mmm." Nina swallowed a bite. "Grandma Peggy knew how to bake. This is perfect for fall."

I had to agree with her. "The pumpkin makes it so wonderfully moist. I'm going to bring some over to Tilly to be sure the recipe is correct. Want to come with me?"

"Would I turn down the opportunity to rub elbows with a TV star?"

"Never."

"Any news yet on poor Abby?" asked Nina.

"Only that word made it to Wesley in the middle of the night."

Nina's gaze met mine. "I know she worked for them, but who would have called in the middle of the night to tell Wesley that Abby was dead? Wouldn't a normal person wait until maybe seven in the morning to call?"

"Thank you! That's precisely what I thought. Mars seemed to think it was perfectly normal. Exactly who knew and why was it so vital that he had to inform Wesley immediately?"

"A sinister aura begins to surround Wesley Winthrop." Nina plucked crumbs off the cake plate. "Do you think he murdered Abby? Or is afraid their affair will be made public?"

"Could be neither. Politicians are a strange breed. They need to watch their backs all the time. There's one additional little hiccup. Mars went out with Abby."

"Our Mars?"

"The very same."

"You know he didn't kill her," said Nina.

"Of course not. But that doesn't mean he won't be a suspect."

I cut the remaining cake in thirds and placed one portion in a turquoise-and-white cake carrier with a handle on top. I stored the other two pieces.

Daisy was roaming underfoot as if she knew we were going somewhere. But Mochie was bored and ambled into the sunroom, probably to watch birds.

Nina carried the cake as we walked over to Tilly's house. This time Tilly opened the door wide and invited us inside.

"I'm so glad you're here. I'm just sick over Abby's death. And now I feel terrible about not pursuing the reason she quit working for me." Tilly led us into the kitchen, which smelled like cinnamon.

Nina sniffed the air. "What are you cooking? It smells like Sophie's kitchen."

"I was just experimenting with the pumpkin spice latte recipe. Would you do me a favor and try one? I'm not sure I have the recipe exactly right."

We readily agreed.

I handed her the cake I had brought. "What did you think about the mac and cheese? Was it worthy of your cookbook?"

Tilly pulled three mugs out of a cabinet. "It was better than my usual mac and cheese!"

Nina watched, and I jotted notes while Tilly assembled the drinks and topped them with whipped cream and a sprinkle of nutmeg. Tilly suggested we sit outside and led the way out the French doors to a charming fenced patio.

Tilly had a good eye for form and color. She had thrown a blue-and-yellow tablecloth over a round table. An arrangement of fresh yellow and orange sunflowers sat in the middle. Freshly tilled soil in flower beds along the brick fence in the rear featured masses of yellow and purple mums. We settled into comfortable chairs with thick cushions. The high brick fence blocked the breeze, and the fall sun warmed us. Daisy lifted her nose in the air and sniffed something I couldn't detect.

"Grandma Peggy's Pumpkin Bundt Cake was Abby's favorite recipe in my collection."

I could hear the grief in Tilly's tone. Her

bubbly nature was hidden, and her eyes were rimmed in red.

"What happened?" she whispered. "Why would anyone harm Abby? She was such a sweet, normal sort of person. I don't mean this in a cruel way, but Abby was so nice that she bordered on dull. She wasn't into drugs or drinking or anything dangerous, you know? Who would want to kill a woman who writes cookbooks? What could possibly be a more benign profession?"

"I'm sorry, Tilly," I said. "She was very kind to an elderly friend of ours. Abby touched a lot of lives. It's a terrible tragedy."

"You spent time with her," said Nina. "Abby must have told you about herself. She never mentioned anything worrisome? Problems she had? Neighbors or men she dated who were stalking her?"

I shot Nina a look. Surely she didn't mean to imply that Mars was following Abby. She may have dated other men, though.

"Like me," said Tilly, "she wasn't from Old Town. We talked about how we didn't have any relatives close by. That's always difficult. She and her husband moved here because he worked for the government, some technical job, I don't recall exactly. She had thought about leaving since nothing was keeping her here anymore, but she seemed fairly happy up until the last day she worked here."

Now she had piqued my attention. "Did something unusual happen that day?"

CHAPTER 10

Dear Sophie,
I love fall spices. They smell great, and they taste even better. But there's something about pumpkin pie spice that bugs me. I can't put my finger on it. Is it possible to make my own?

Sour Puss in Spice, West Virginia

Dear Sour Puss,
To make pumpkin pie spice, mix cinnamon, nutmeg, ginger, and cloves. Go heavy on the cinnamon, then add lesser amounts of the other spices. Maybe you can identify the one you don't care for and omit it.

Sophie

"That's the odd thing. I've been over and over it in my mind, but I can't think of anything that would have upset her. It was a lively day because the girls were off from school. A teacher's workday, I think. They were in and out sneaking tastes of the pumpkin cupcakes I was baking. I remember joking about them having a salon day, because they were pulling their hair up into those messy buns that are so popular. If you ask me, it's easy to look messy, but they were watching videos and trying all kinds of crazy things. Schuyler's mom, Mia, came over for a while."

Tilly stopped speaking for a moment. "You know, she still hasn't come home. I'm so sad for Schuyler. I think Mia was disappointed that the girls weren't hanging out at her house on Friday. But she's one of those hovering helicopter moms. I think that's why they spend so much time over here. I try to give them room to do their own thing. My days were so structured when I was a teen that I missed out on a lot of silly fun. Moms like Mia don't understand that."

"And what was Abby doing?" I asked.

"Wesley brought some of his staff over. Mars was here, too. I made them my roasted Parmesan chicken, maple syrup Brussels sprouts, and garlic mashed potatoes for lunch. Abby was very busy watching me and writing down the recipes as I cooked. And she kept flipping through the recipes and making notes. I think she was arranging them in order. Maybe it was too much of a madhouse for her that day with people coming and going? Most days it was just the two of us. Wesley was working, and Briley was at school. I really didn't give it much thought at the time. It all seemed so normal to me. It was just another day at our house."

"That was the last time you saw her?" I asked.

"Right. As she walked out the door, she said she wouldn't be able to finish the cookbook but she wished me all the best. I was stunned. She walked away as fast as she could. I never heard from her again. I called her number because I was totally perplexed, but her phone rolled over to voice mail."

"What made you think she was upset that day?" I stroked Daisy for being such a patient dog while we talked.

"She seemed quiet. More withdrawn than usual. Like she was doing her job, but she was thinking about something else. Now that I consider it, she seemed anxious. Honestly, it wasn't a big deal, or I would have asked her if something was wrong."

Tilly sniffled. "I'm old enough to know that I can't blame myself, but now I wonder why I didn't ask Abby what was troubling her. Maybe I could have helped. If someone was giving her a hard time, she could have stayed in our guest room and we could have protected her." Tilly placed her hands over her eyes. When she removed them, she shook her head. "There are so many solutions to problems. I'm devastated that we didn't prevent her death."

Was that an unusual reaction, I wondered. Maybe not. We all wanted to save people if we could. "Did you have any reason to think she was in danger?"

"Heavens, no! If I had, you wouldn't be sitting here right now. Abby would be sitting in that chair drinking latte with me and I probably wouldn't have met you." Tilly sipped her latte and licked a smidge of cream off the rim before eyeing us. "Mars says that you two solve murders."

Before I could say anything, Nina piped up, "We're definitely looking into Abby's death."

"I hope you'll be careful. Her killer must have been a madman. Who stuffs a person into a freezer?" Tilly shivered at the thought.

She had a point. It was certainly unusual, but perhaps clever from the perspective of the killer. It could have taken six months or longer before anyone opened the freezer and looked inside. I shuddered to imagine that a relative could have found her body while cleaning out her house. That would give me nightmares.

"It must have been planned, don't you think?" asked Tilly. Suddenly she gasped and sat up straight. "The phone call! Abby received a phone call that day. Now what was it that she asked? It was somewhat odd. 'The squirrel has landed?' I remember teasing her about that because it sounded like a line from a movie. Who asks if *the squirrel has landed*? That has to be code for something."

"Did she tell you who the squirrel was?" I asked.

"She laughed it off, like it was unimportant."

"Be sure to tell the police about that," I said. "Tilly, was Abby dating anyone?"

The expression on Tilly's face was priceless. I guessed she knew about Mars dating Abby but wasn't sure whether she should say so. "Besides Mars," I added.

Tilly fanned herself with her hand. "I'm so relieved that I wasn't the one who had to tell you about Mars and Abby. That would have been awkward! She didn't mention anyone else to me. Just her ex-husband and Mars. She was married for a long time."

"Did she say why they divorced?" asked Nina.

"She never came right out and told me the reason, but one day she said to me that we are all products of our pasts and nothing can change that."

"You thought she was talking about her husband?" I asked.

Tilly shrugged. "It could have been about him or her. I didn't pursue it. She appeared happiest when Wesley and the girls were around, but something was off on that Friday. Sometimes we sense these things but can't put a finger on the problem."

The door knocker sounded at that moment. Tilly excused herself to answer the door.

Nina leaned over to me. "I love the latte. But do you get the feeling that someone in this household might know more than she's saying? After all, she's an actress."

"I think it's odd that Mia didn't come home. Tilly doesn't seem too worried about that. I wonder if Mia has done this before."

The French door opened, and Tilly walked out followed by Wolf. Daisy jumped to her feet and ran to him.

"Good morning, ladies. I see you beat me here," he said as he greeted Daisy.

"For your information, I baked a cake as part of my job for Tilly and brought some by for her to try."

"Maybe you would like a slice?" Tilly moved as fast as Daisy had.

But one of them had wanted to see him and the other appeared to want to get away from him.

"Back in a jiffy," Tilly said brightly.

Wolf sat down with us. "Has she told you anything I should know?"

Through the French door, I could see Tilly pick up her phone and make a call. I averted my eyes when she looked out at us.

"Only a throwaway line about a squirrel. Totally unimportant," grumbled Nina. "But don't forget that she's an actress and can lie convincingly."

Wolf tried to hide a smile. "Thank you for that reminder, Nina." He glanced at our latte mugs on the table. "I hope you won't mind if I speak with Tilly alone?"

"We can take a hint. Come on, Nina." I rose and called Daisy.

When I walked into the kitchen, I caught Tilly's fearful expression. "You're not leaving?"

"Wolf needs to speak to you privately. Don't worry, he's a nice guy."

Behind me, Nina added, "Sophie dated him. She should know."

Thank you, Nina.

"That's reassuring. Sophie is probably

very selective about the men she dates. Wesley told me this morning that I shouldn't speak to the police without our lawyer present. I called him while you were outside with Wolf. He should be here any minute."

"Oh? Who's your lawyer?" asked Nina.

I braced myself. *Please, just don't let it be —*

"Alex German. Do you know him?" asked Tilly.

Of course. In a town swimming with lawyers, it had to be the only lawyer in the world whom I had dated.

Nina burst out laughing.

"What?" Tilly froze. "Is he the worst lawyer in town?"

I took a deep breath. I might as well confess before Nina blabbed. "I dated him, too. It's going to be like a conference of my old beaus here in a few minutes. I believe it's time for me to take my leave. Thank you for the latte. It was fabulous. I wouldn't change a thing."

I didn't wait a second longer. I waved at Tilly and hurried Daisy through the house and out the front door.

Nina was still laughing when she caught up to me. "I didn't know you could move that fast."

"So not funny," I said drolly. "Let's cut

over this way," I suggested, turning right blocks sooner than I normally would have.

"You're going to run into Alex one of these days," Nina pointed out.

"It doesn't have to be today." There wasn't actually a good reason to avoid him. Alex was a genuinely nice guy. I was the one who had broken off the relationship, which, if I thought about it logically, meant I shouldn't be avoiding him. But I wasn't ready for that awkward meeting. And I certainly didn't want to have it with Wolf sitting there watching. The mere thought of that gave me chill bumps.

"The glamorous social life of the single woman," Nina quipped. "At least we got some exercise out of it."

Nina peeled off at her house after making me promise to phone her the second anything exciting happened. I went home and did something Daisy did every day but I rarely had the opportunity to indulge in: I took a nap. In spite of all the coffee I had consumed, I drifted off and woke in the early afternoon.

The first thing I thought about was the cookbook and how I should have been working on it instead of snoozing. But that brought me back to Abby. By now Wolf had probably talked to her ex-husband. I wondered if he was a suspect yet.

Mochie yawned and stretched, and then the little stinker curled up again and went back to sleep. The luxuries of being a cat.

I took my notes from the morning and a recipe from Abby's stack and retreated to my tiny home office. Following Abby's format, I wrote out the recipe and added as though I were Tilly:

After I tried a pumpkin latte, I couldn't get enough of them. I whip up this version when my girlfriends come over for a mid-morning gabfest. Cold fall days are the perfect time to serve it with a slice of Grandma Peggy's Pumpkin Bundt Cake and enjoy the company of friends.

I printed it out and carried it into the kitchen to add to the stack. That done, I put the kettle on for tea.

The two recipes I made from Tilly's collection had been delicious. I grabbed a note-pad and jotted a reminder to ask her if the cake had turned out to her liking. If it had, then the next steps would be to add the remaining recipes, organize them all, and come up with more notes as though Tilly had written them herself so the cookbook would feel authentically hers. That didn't seem so difficult. There was probably a story behind most of the recipes, and that was what would make the cookbook special to her fans.

The only thing that disturbed me were those silly codes. I would have to come to terms with the fact that Abby was gone and I would never know what they meant. But I had become obsessed with them.

I browsed through the recipes for a dish to take to Eunice. Tilly's Shortcut Chicken and Dumplings sounded interesting. Plus, it made a good amount, so Eunice could reheat leftovers another night. Tilly's recipe used leftover rotisserie chicken, which I didn't have on hand. I did have a whole chicken, though. I popped it into my Instant Pot to cook and wasted the next hour browsing bathroom ideas on Pinterest.

When the chicken had cooled a bit, I chopped up the meat and added thyme, sage, and minced garlic. Tilly used a lot of butter in her dumplings. She was a true Southern cook. I made them her way and dropped them into the liquid, then slid the pot into the oven and let it all bake for twenty minutes.

When I removed the lid, a fabulous aroma wafted out. I ladled most of the dish into an oven-to-table microwave-safe bowl to make things easy for Eunice. I packed it into a bag along with a third of the cake I had baked. Daisy eagerly waited at the door for me to help her into her halter.

I locked up, and we walked toward Eunice's house. It was early for dinner, but she could stash it in the fridge and warm it up when she was ready to eat. On King Street, I saw the man who had pulled a soda can out of the trash. He was on the opposite side of the street. There was no reason for him to remember me, of course, yet I felt certain he noticed me. I was sorely tempted to follow him to find out what he was up to, but he was probably just going about his business.

I knocked on Eunice's door but didn't hear the *thump-thump* of her cane as she made her way to open it. To my total surprise, my neighbor Francie opened the door. Daisy, who was usually very polite, barged inside to greet her pal Duke, Francie's golden retriever.

Francie had spent a lot of years birding and gardening in the sun, which had left her with a road map of lines in her face. I thought she was slightly younger than Eunice, but Eunice's unlined skin helped her appear more youthful.

"I'm so glad Eunice called you."

"Called me?" Francie frowned. "I saw her house on the news because of the murder next door and thought I'd better check on her."

"I'm glad you did. I brought her some chicken and dumplings to try. And a little pumpkin cake for dessert. There's enough for two."

Francie smiled at me and whispered, "I had no idea she was having trouble getting around. This house has a lot of stairs. If I wanted to take her somewhere, I think both of us would fall just trying to get her out of the house."

"Maybe it's time for her to move to an apartment?"

"Lord have mercy! Don't mention that to her. She nearly threw me out of the house for suggesting it. I'm going to call a contractor and see what we can do. She's bound and determined to stay here."

"That's very thoughtful of you. Let me know if I can help." I stepped inside.

"Is it Wolf?" called Eunice.

"Nope. It's just Sophie. I brought dinner for you and Francie."

Eunice leaned forward in her lounger. "How lovely! I need to move a chair to the front window. I'm missing all the action. Francie said she saw Wolf outside. I thought he might drop by to give us an update on Abby."

I hurried into the kitchen and removed the contents from my bag. "If Francie will dish out the food, I'd be happy to track down Wolf for you."

Francie wasted no time. "Go, go, go! Before he takes off!"

I left Daisy with Duke and rushed back through the living room and out the front door. Wolf's car was parked across the street. On a hunch, I opened the gate to the passage along the side of the house and walked to Abby's patio.

Wolf stood in the middle of the patio, staring at the spot where the cat collar had hung in the bushes.

"Wondering why someone tossed the cat collar up there?" I asked.

"You noticed that, too? Cats get stuck on all kinds of things, but those branches don't look strong enough to hold a cat."

"That's what Nina and I thought."

"I'm glad to see you. I was planning to stop by."

"Is everything okay?"

"That would depend on your definition of *okay.*" Wolf faced me and looked me in the eyes. "Turns out the woman in the freezer isn't Abby."

CHAPTER 11

Dear Sophie,
My family loves chicken and dumplings.
But everyone complains about my recipe
because the dumplings aren't biscuit-y
like my grandmother's version. She's
gone now, and all I have is a list of the
ingredients. She kept the instructions in
her head. What am I doing wrong?
Frustrated Cook in Chicken Creek,
Alaska

Dear Frustrated Cook,
Instead of the conventional method of
steaming the dumplings on the stove
top, try baking them in your oven.
Maybe that's Grandma's missing trick.
Sophie

I blinked at Wolf. "What? How is that possible? Who is it?"
"I don't know the answer to either of

those questions. I've been asking myself the same thing since we found out. We were operating under the assumption that Abby was a nice woman who met a terrible fate for reasons unknown. I've been talking to people who knew her and trying to figure out who had a beef with her. But this changes everything. It throws all our theories in the air again."

"Do you think Abby murdered the woman in the freezer?" I asked.

Wolf took a deep breath. "I don't know what to think. I've got one unidentified dead woman, one missing woman, and one cat collar way up higher than it should be. What are you doing here, anyway?"

"The two sleuths next door sent me to find you. They're eager for an update. But I don't think they were expecting this."

Wolf nodded. "No one was. Who is the second sleuth?"

"Francie Vanderhoosen."

Wolf smiled. "Come on, let's fill them in. It will be on the evening news, but they'll feel special hearing about it early."

If I had known there would be four of us, I would have brought more food. When we walked into the house, Francie and Eunice were eating, with both dogs shamelessly watching and hoping for a bite.

"I found Wolf, and he has big news."

Both of them stared at Wolf expectantly but continued eating their dinners.

"The body in the freezer isn't Abby Bergeron," said Wolf.

Eunice and Francie stopped eating. There was a long moment of silence before they peppered him with questions.

"How do you know?"

"Does that mean Abby is alive?"

I longed to add my own questions, but I figured he'd get around to answering them if we gave him a chance.

Wolf sat down. "We brought Abby's ex-husband in to identify the body."

"I could have done that for you," Eunice said. "I know what she looks like."

"That might have been preferable. It was a very difficult moment for him. He clearly dreaded it. And then when it turned out it wasn't Abby after all, you can imagine his joy. But that was tempered with guilt because you don't really want to be happy about anyone being dead. Even if she is a stranger."

Eunice slapped a hand against her chest. "The divorce was hard on Abby. She never said a mean word about him. From what she said, he seemed like a decent fellow."

"Then who was in the freezer?" asked

136

Francie.

Wolf held up his open palms. "We don't know yet for sure. Abby's husband, Benton, didn't recognize her."

"No purse or identification?" asked Eunice.

"Her pockets were empty, and the only other things in the freezer were frozen foods. No purse, no phone."

"Will they be releasing a photo?" asked Eunice. "Maybe someone in town will know who she is."

"It will be a drawing," said Wolf. "A photograph would be too graphic. It should be on the local news tonight."

Eunice's eyes narrowed. "That's the strangest thing. Do you think someone kidnapped Abby and killed this other woman?"

It was interesting to me that Eunice jumped to the idea that Abby had been kidnapped, when my first thought was that Abby had killed the unidentified woman and made a run for it. There were a lot of possibilities. But I hadn't known Abby, and Eunice knew her well.

Wolf shrugged. "I have to be honest with you. Anything is possible. All we know is that a woman was in Abby's freezer and no one knows where Abby is. Eunice, did Abby give you any indication that she planned to go away? Did she say anything about a trip she wanted to take? A sick relative she planned to visit?"

Eunice answered quickly. "She most certainly did not. Listen here, Wolf, something untoward has happened to Abby. There is no way she would have let her cat run around loose in Old Town. No way! Abby is a decent and responsible woman."

"Could the woman in the freezer have been Abby's cat sitter?" I asked. "Maybe she had to go away in a hurry and Oliver got out when the cat sitter was murdered."

Wolf gazed at me in shock. "I have considered a lot of scenarios, but that's one I hadn't thought of."

"Eunice, maybe Duke and I should stay with you for a while," said Francie. "Something very strange is going on in the house next door."

"Nonsense! Whatever horrible thing happened there has already taken place and I didn't even know about it. I am quite safe here, Francie," Eunice said emphatically.

Francie shot me a knowing look. "We'll talk after these two leave, Eunice."

I took that as a cue that it was time to go. Motioning to Wolf, I said, "Ladies, have a good evening. And call me if you need anything."

Wolf rose. "I'm sure you'll be fine. And let me know if either of you recognize our victim from the sketch they'll show on the news."

I called Daisy, who reluctantly left Duke and accompanied me to the door. When we were outside, I asked Wolf, "How did the woman in the freezer die?"

"I don't have the autopsy reports yet. They're waiting for her to thaw. There wasn't anything immediately obvious like a bloody stab wound. But she was kind of, um, folded up, so it was hard to see if she had injuries."

"I guess you're searching for Abby?"

"Naturally."

"What do you think happened to her? Could she be the killer, or did she run away to save herself?"

"We sprayed luminol and found some blood spatter. At this point, all we know is that it doesn't match Abby or the woman in the freezer."

"A third person was there?" I reeled at the thought.

"Looks like it."

"So Abby and the third person might have run off after committing murder."

Wolf grunted. "At this point, anything is

possible."

"Wolf, the other day I saw a guy grab a soda can from a municipal trash can. It was the strangest thing. It was like he'd planned it and had done it before. He even stuck his tie in his mouth first."

"I gather he didn't appear to be a hungry vagrant?"

"No. He was well dressed. Typical Old Town style."

Wolf chuckled. "Sounds like a dead drop. If you saw it happen, he's not very good at it. It's a classic spy move to pass on information."

I knew CIA headquarters was only miles from Old Town as the crow flies, but I had never given it much thought. It felt sort of invasive to know spies were among us. Like someone had broken into my sweet, safe city.

My expression must have revealed my discomfort because Wolf said, "It was probably a training run. It's nothing to worry about."

I wasn't so sure about that. "I think it's creepy. It's like something sinister is going on in our streets!"

Wolf turned and looked at Abby's house. "Not as sinister as what went on in there."

He was right, of course. I shuddered to

imagine what the poor woman in the freezer had gone through. "Abby quit her job on Friday. Her cat turned up at Eunice's around then, too. Do you think that's when it all happened?"

Wolf rubbed his chin. "That's a good bet. At this point we don't know much. I hope the autopsy will reveal something helpful."

He hopped into his car and drove off. As Daisy and I walked home, I pondered whether to bring a dish to Natasha's party.

She wanted to impress her new half sister, but I was very familiar with Natasha's insistence on serving trendy food. There would be no elegant chicken breasts or delicious simple salad at her dinner table. I could only hope she had gotten over her hot pepper stage. Even though she had said not to bring anything, I thought it wise and also very polite to bring a dish to her party.

I remembered seeing a tomato tart among Tilly's recipes and planned to look it up when I was distracted by Nina's new autumn decorations. The short sidewalk to her house was lined symmetrically with fall items that graduated in size. It began with large gourds, followed by flowering purple cabbages and yellow and red mums. At the very end, next to her door, were two tall urns. They were packed with orange mums, miniature pumpkins, cascading white flowers, and spiraling branches that reached upward. It was elegant and eye-catching.

Nina stepped out of her house. "What do you think?"

"It puts the rest of us to shame. That's amazing."

"I'm pretty happy with it. I may not have arranged it, but I selected the parts." She followed me across the street to my house.

As I unlocked the door, she said, "You won't believe what happened!"

For a second, I was worried. "Not another death?"

"Not that I know of. Natasha invited me to her dinner party tonight!"

"She likes you more than she lets on."

"I thought she'd never forgive me after the pie throw-down. I'm definitely going. I can't wait to see her sister. Do you suppose they look alike?"

"Hard to tell. I know three sisters who all have similar features. You can see they're related. But I don't think Hannah and I look alike."

I located the recipe and pulled out ingredients for the crust.

"Any word on Abby's murder?"

I filled her in on the gruesome details. While I was still talking, Nina used her

142

phone to pull up the police sketch of the woman found in Abby's freezer.

I was slicing juicy red and yellow tomatoes when Nina brought her phone over to me.

The woman in the freezer was older than I had expected. Squarely middle-aged, she had a broad jaw and prominent eyebrows. There was a mole on the left side of her face.

Nina read aloud. *Police request assistance in identifying this woman thought to be in her fifties. She has chin-length auburn hair. She is wearing black jeans, a black Henley sweater, and a black leather jacket. Please notify Alexandria Police if you recognize her.*

"I've never seen her around, have you?" I asked.

"I always feel like I know everyone, but evidently there are a lot of people in town who run in different circles."

CHAPTER 12

Dear Natasha,
I threw a dinner party for some people I
wanted to impress. One of my guests
brought dessert! I thought that was
highly irregular and somewhat offensive.
Did she think I wasn't capable of pulling off a nice dinner including dessert?

Offended in Sandwich,
Massachusetts

Dear Offended,
You are correct to be offended. A dinner
invitation implies that food will be
provided by the hostess. I hope that you
were kind enough to make that clear to
her so she won't make that mistake
again!

Natasha

At six thirty, I changed into black slacks
and a V-necked lace top with elbow-length

sleeves. I pulled my hair back and pinned it into a bun. I knew towering high heels were still the rage, but I also knew I would immediately twist, if not break, my ankle if I wore them. The brick sidewalks of Old Town were charming but not ideal for stilettoes. I opted for comfortable black flats. I was short, but heels wouldn't make me significantly taller, anyway. A pair of dangling earrings with hearts on them and I was ready to meet Natasha's half sister.

I fed Daisy and Mochie, packed up my tomato tart, and walked across the street and down a few doors to the house that Natasha and Mars had bought together. Even though they had split up, she still lived in the house. From Mars's comments, I gathered that they hadn't come to an agreement yet regarding the house.

A pot of golden mums decorated each step as I walked up the stairs to the front door of the red brick house. At the very top I knocked on the door.

Natasha swung it open. "Oh. It's you." She wedged past me and looked out on the street.

I stepped inside and she followed. I handed the tomato tart to Natasha.

Her eyebrows lifted. "Well, this wasn't necessary! Perhaps I'll put this in the

145

freezer."

I had my doubts about freezing it, but it was her decision. "I hope you'll enjoy it." I had clearly irritated her by bringing it. "I take it your sister isn't here yet?"

Natasha's lips drew thin in disapproval. "I hope Charlene's not one of those fashionably late types who makes everyone wait."

"I'm sure she'll be here soon. Have you told your mom about her?"

Natasha fingered the tight gold necklace on her throat. "Maybe you can help me decide the best course of action after we meet her. I don't want to keep anything from my mom, but it will be such a bitter pill for her to know for certain that it was us my dad didn't want. I always suspected as much, but my mom has always clung to the hope that he lost his way and didn't remember where he came from."

My heart ached for Natasha. For all her bravado, at heart Natasha was still the little girl whose dad had abandoned her and her mom. My own mother thought that was the reason Natasha had such high expectations of herself. She tried so hard to be what she thought was perfect. I guessed that could be the result of feeling rejected by the one man most children knew they could count on, no matter what. Maybe my mom was right.

Natasha felt she wasn't good enough for her dad, and that was why he left. She needed to be perfect to prove something to him and to herself.

"The house looks beautiful," I said. It did, even if she had painted the dining and living room walls charcoal. It was in vogue and provided a good backdrop for her ultramodern furniture. From the inside of the house, there wasn't so much as a hint that it was a historic building.

"Thank you. I'm about to change the paint. I led the way with gray and charcoal. I have a feeling it's time to move to a new color palette. What do you think of 1970s orange?"

I was honest. "I tend to prefer lighter colors for walls, like a salmon maybe."

"Mmm, yes. You've never followed the chic trends, have you?" She led me down the stairs and out to her patio. "I believe you know everyone. I'll just put this tart away."

Vintage-style pear-shaped lights glowed golden on strings that crisscrossed in the air over Natasha's brick patio. A long table had been spread with a beige cloth, and a matching white and beige runner stretched from one end to the other. Votive lights serpentined the length of the table with generous sprigs of rosemary winding between them. White napkins were rolled up and tied with natural twine. She had written our names on place cards that were framed in the same twine.

I spied Mars and Nina speaking with a man who had his back to me. When I walked over to join them, he turned toward me.

He was the guy I had seen removing a soda can from the garbage. The spy.

CHAPTER 13

Dear Sophie,
A group of my friends has begun throwing elaborate dinner parties. I can cook well enough to get by, but last night I was faced with no less than three forks! How do I know which one to use?

Embarrassed in Forks of Salmon,
California

Dear Embarrassed,
Work your way from the outside in. The first course will probably be an appetizer. That will be the smallest fork on the far left. Relax and enjoy the dinner. If you're confused, watch your hostess and follow her example.

Sophie

I hoped I didn't show my shock.
"You're the one who followed me," he said.

I could feel my face flushing. "Who are you?"

"If you don't know me, why did you follow me?" he asked.

"Because I was curious. Your turn. Who are you?"

"Benton Bergeron."

I was pretty sure my mouth dropped open. I snapped it shut and swallowed hard. "Bergeron? Like Abby Bergeron?" I asked.

"Exactly like that." He smiled at me. "Abby is my ex-wife."

Nina giggled. "Mars is Sophie's ex-husband. Am I the only one who can hold onto a spouse around here?"

"That's because your husband is always traveling," quipped Mars.

"I've seen you around town," said Benton. If I hadn't observed that two-second maneuver with a soda in the trash, I might have liked him. He had blue eyes, a square jaw, and remarkably symmetrical features. In a way, he was quite plain because none of his features were extraordinary. No distinctive nose or cleft chin. He didn't have Mars's adorable factor, but he could have played a leading role in a romantic movie. Still, I was leery of him.

"It's nice to finally meet you," I lied. I was a little bit ashamed that my next thought was whether I could get some information about Abby from him. "I wish I'd had a chance to meet Abby."

Benton took a deep breath. "Is that the weirdest thing? I was certain she was dead. I can't tell you how I dreaded going to identify her. And then to find out it wasn't her? Now I don't know what to think. It would be completely out of character for her to kill anyone, yet they found that woman in her freezer."

"Did she have any issues that could have caused her to act irrationally?" asked Mars.

Well put, Mars. Nicely worded without accusing her of anything.

"No. Abby would never have harmed anyone. When pushed to her limit, Abby was the type to walk away."

"So she probably ran away and is in hiding somewhere?" asked Nina.

"All I can imagine is that she went to stay with her sister. But I called her, and she says Abby isn't there."

Oh! That was intriguing. I wondered if it was true. I would lie for my sister if she was running from an ex-husband. "Abby didn't say anything to you about being afraid or needing to get away?"

"You know how it is with ex-spouses. You don't always tell them everything that's going on in your life," said Benton.

Especially if one of them is a spy, I thought.

Benton continued. "Mars might know more about Abby's plans than me. The police have questioned me twice now, but I honestly don't know what happened."

Ouch! He was throwing Mars under the bus already. The only plus for Mars was that Wolf knew him well. Of course, Wolf would never let that interfere with an investigation, but it probably helped to some degree.

Larry Fiedler called me over. A local anesthesiologist, he had lost his wife the year before and was just beginning to get out and socialize again.

As I joined him and Helbert Sullivan, it dawned on me that Natasha had only invited eligible men to her dinner party. Helbert, a tall and scrawny man with deep-set eyes, ran an investment company. His wife had left him, but the local scuttlebutt had it that Helbert had shrewdly insisted on a prenuptial agreement that protected his vast holdings.

"Have you met Natasha's half sister yet?" asked Larry in a whisper.

"No. I know nothing about her. Why are we whispering?" I asked.

"She should have been here by now."

Helbert checked the Breitling watch on his wrist.

"Maybe she chickened out," said Larry. "Natasha has very high standards. I would hate to be related to her. Honestly, she intimidates me! Did you see the array of silverware on the table? Which fork do I use?"

I never would have expected it of him. "Start on the outside and work your way in. But you might have a point about Natasha. If the half sister caught Natasha's TV show, she might have gotten cold feet. It's hard enough to meet a sibling for the first time without that person being a local celebrity."

Natasha tinkled a little crystal bell and called, "Dinner is served."

I happened to be close to the table, and when I turned around, I caught Mars with his place card in his hand. He deftly swapped it with another one.

"What are you doing?" I hissed.

"She had me sitting opposite her at the end of the table, like we're married or still an item. I want to be supportive, but I'm not playing that game."

I hoped Natasha wouldn't make a scene.

"Sophie," she trilled. "Could you give me a hand?"

I walked up the outdoor stairs and joined

her in the kitchen. Natasha had installed a gray and silver kitchen long before it was popular. It was sleek, but cold as ice. "What can I do for you?"

"Nothing. I have everything under control except for Charlene. Where could she be?"

"Did you check your phone?"

"Only a million times."

"Maybe she lost her nerve. It's a pretty big deal to meet your sister for the first time!"

"What if she's just rude and inconsiderate?"

I couldn't help laughing. "Then you'll be like all the rest of us. Everyone has relatives who aren't perfect."

"Oh no, she's like my mom," she moaned. "Wait! She doesn't share genes with my mother. That's a relief. But I had hoped Charlene might be like me. Why can't I have any normal relatives?"

I had no idea what to say. "Natasha, everyone is different. She might not match up to the standards you impose on yourself."

"Obviously not," she snorted angrily. "If she did, she would be here searching for her place card at the table. Well, I guess we'll go on without her. I don't see the point in waiting any longer."

"Now can I give you a hand?"

"Don't be silly. I don't require your services."

When I returned to the table, I realized that Mars might not have been the only person playing Move-the-Place-Card. Everyone else had been seated, which left me with no choice but to sit opposite Benton.

Natasha proudly served her appetizer of crisped pancetta and figs. I had to give her credit. They were actually tasty, if tiny.

"I must apologize to you all," said Natasha primly. "Our guest of honor isn't answering her phone and seems to have disappeared. I hope you will enjoy your dinner in spite of her absence."

"I'm sorry that we won't meet her," said Nina. "If I were you, I would be dying to see what she looks like!"

"I admit that I am quite curious." Natasha sighed. "But I suppose it won't happen this evening."

Natasha's backyard was fenced. Next to the alley that ran behind the house were a detached garage and a workshop for her crafts with a tiny apartment over top of them. In the darkness, I thought I saw something move near the workshop, but as I watched, nothing more happened. It was probably a neighborhood cat.

The next course of cold pea soup arrived in demitasse cups, prompting Larry to whisper to me, "Will she serve anything that's more than a bite or a sip of food?"

I thought he might have regretted that thought after taking a bite of scallop that she had seared beautifully but topped with a peanut sauce that left my tongue numb. I rushed to the kitchen for a pitcher of water and refilled glasses of water and wine before Natasha began to serve the main course.

Benton whispered, "Has anyone else lost feeling in their tongue?"

Happily, the main course turned out to be a crusted prime rib roast with duchesse potatoes.

After one bite, Helbert gasped and drank an entire glass of ice water. "Is it supposed to taste like campfire ashes?" he murmured.

I kicked him under the table and pointed to my plate. "That's the charcoal. Very trendy. Cut off the outer edges," I hissed. The interior was perfect. It was a pity that she insisted on lacing it with charcoal.

It dawned on me as we ate that we were dining with the top two suspects in the murder at Abby's house. Benton and Mars drew that dubious distinction. Nevertheless, both were in good spirits and proved to be delightful company. I was even warming up to Benton.

Just past his right elbow, I could see the spot in Natasha's yard where I thought something had moved. I couldn't make out anything now that it was completely dark.

Benton leaned toward me. "It's probably terrible form to ask out a woman when her ex-husband is in the room."

Oh, dear heaven. I hadn't seen this coming. He was definitely attractive and had been interesting all evening, funny and well mannered. Would it be a bad thing to date a spy?

"Maybe we could have coffee tomorrow?" he asked with a hint of a smile.

Coffee. I could do that. Maybe he was actually as nice as he seemed. "I'd like that." The words slipped out of my mouth far too easily, before I could entertain second thoughts.

When Natasha collected plates, my gaze drifted back to the spot behind Benton. "Excuse me. I feel like there's something in the grass. Maybe a kitten or a lost pup."

Benton accompanied me out on the lawn.

"I thought it was right about here —" We both screamed when an arm flailed in the air.

CHAPTER 14

Dear Natasha,
I have a brother-in-law who always arrives late to dinner parties. I have to include him because the oaf is married to my sister. She's wise to him and drives herself now. When he arrives, do I have to wait on him and bring him each course?
Miffed in Cranberry, Pennsylvania

Dear Miffed,
He's lucky if you offer him food at all! What audacious manners. The correct thing to do is to serve him what the others are eating at that time. If they are on dessert, there is no need to serve him any of the previous courses. If he leaves hungry, perhaps he will learn.
Natasha

In spite of our shock, Benton and I edged

closer. I could hear footsteps pounding on the ground as others ran toward us. A flashlight suddenly lighted the grass and found the person's bruised face. Dried blood was caked in her hair and near her nose.

She was probably in her late thirties with a delicate appearance. She had almond-shaped eyes, high cheekbones, a pointy chin, and jet-black hair. I knew who she was immediately. There was no doubting the resemblance to Natasha.

"Charlene?" I asked gently.

She moaned, and her eyes closed.

"No! Don't leave us," I cried, fearful that she would die.

Natasha pushed past me and screamed. She clasped a hand over her mouth and fell to her knees. "Charlene! It's your sister, Natasha. Charlene!"

"I called 911," Mars announced. "They should be here any second. I told them to use the alley."

Natasha wept. She picked up Charlene's closest hand and clutched it in her own. Natasha's tears fell on their hands.

"Charlene, can you hear us?" I asked.

There was no response. I reached across her for her other hand and felt for a pulse.

"Is she . . ." choked Natasha.

"I feel a faint pulse. She's still with us."

The wail of sirens pierced the night. We heard the ambulance turn into the alley. Its headlights set the alley aglow beyond the fence.

"I'll show them the way," said Mars.

In minutes, emergency medical technicians were checking on Charlene. One of them had to drag Natasha away from her. He asked questions about Charlene, but none of us knew the answers. Her age? Did she have any allergies? What had happened to her? We knew nothing. I wished I had bothered to get up from my dinner earlier and check on the odd movement that had caught my eye.

In fifteen minutes, she was whisked away in the ambulance. All we knew was that she was unconscious but still breathing. For that matter, we weren't even certain that she was Charlene Smith. We had all made that assumption based on her appearance.

I seized Natasha's arm. "Go with her. I'll take care of everything here." I walked to the house with her.

"Do you mean it?"

"Of course!"

"I knew there was a reason that you're my dearest friend. Chocolate curry cake with stout beer frosting is on the kitchen island.

Please serve it on the blue Wedgewood Hibiscus dessert plates. I've already prepared the hot pepper coffee. All you have to do is turn on the machine."

"Don't worry about us, Natasha. Keep us informed about Charlene."

She grabbed a handbag and rushed off to her garage. By that time, no one was outside. Larry and Helbert begged off and departed. I had expected as much. It was hard to stay in a party mood after something that dramatic happened.

The rest of us pitched in to clear the table and extinguish the lights. Back in Natasha's kitchen, Nina wrapped the leftovers and stored them in the refrigerator. I washed dishes while Mars and Benton dried them.

"What on earth could have happened to Charlene?" asked Nina.

Mars put away the clean forks and knives. "It was pretty obvious that someone beat her up."

Nina studied the cake. "Do you think that someone was trying to keep her from coming here?"

"Their father!" I exclaimed. It was a gut reaction, but as soon as I said it, I realized that it made no sense. "Except her hair had dried blood in it. I don't think the attack on her was recent. And from what I gather,

161

neither of them knows where their father is, so it's unlikely he was involved in the attack on Charlene."

"How long does it take for blood to dry?" asked Mars.

Benton polished a plate with a kitchen towel. "One hour for one droplet at room temperature."

Mars, Nina, and I stopped working to stare at him.

"What?" asked Benton. "It's public knowledge. The government did a study. It depends on the ambient temperature."

"Did either of you know that?" asked Nina, looking from me to Mars.

Benton chuckled. "I read a lot of oddball articles on the Internet."

Mars's phone buzzed and he walked away to answer it.

I washed the last plate and wiped the counters clean while we continued to speculate about Charlene's bizarre appearance at the dinner party.

Mars barged into the kitchen. "Excuse me, but something has come up. I need to borrow Sophie."

"What happened?" asked Nina.

"A problem with Wesley and Tilly. Grab your purse, Soph."

"Mars!" I protested.

"We need to hurry," he hissed.

I frowned at Mars. "Are you serious?"

"Come on already!"

"Nina, would you mind locking up?" I asked.

Mars tugged at my hand. In a flash we were out the door in the cold.

"Is this just a lame excuse to leave?" I asked.

"We'll make better time on foot, I think."

"Mars! Will you *please* answer me?"

He looked down at my feet. "I'm glad you didn't wear heels. We can walk faster."

"What happened?" I asked, getting worried now that it was sinking in that Mars hadn't tried to tear me away from Nina and Benton.

"Abby's phone is on the move."

CHAPTER 15

Dear Natasha,
Is it true that it is bad manners not to turn off your cell phone when sitting down to a meal with people? What if you're expecting an important text?
VIP in Hot Coffee, Mississippi

Dear VIP,
Turn off your phone. It is the height of rudeness to take calls or check your phone during a meal. For the etiquette impaired, "during a meal" means from the time you walk into the home or restaurant until you depart from the home or restaurant. I don't care if you haven't ordered yet or if you are waiting to be served or to pay. If the text is that important, maybe you shouldn't be out having lunch, anyway.
Natasha

"She's alive!" I finally walked faster. "How do you know?"

"Sorry, clearly I couldn't say anything in front of Benton."

"I don't see why not."

"Really, Soph? Excuse me, Benton, but your wife the murderess has been located through her telephone. What if he contacts her and tells her the cops are onto her? All she has to do is ditch her phone and *whammo!* They've lost her again."

Of course. I should have realized that. As we walked closer, I saw people watching Wesley and Tilly's house. A TV van was parked across the street

"Hold it!" I seized his arm and brought him to a halt on Tilly's street. "How do *you* know this?"

"Wesley texted me."

I was wondering how Wesley could know, when a reporter ran up to us. "Mars Winston! Is it true that Abby Bergeron was not the woman in the freezer? Is Wesley Winthrop having an affair with Abby Bergeron?"

"What?!" I looked at Mars.

"Just ignore them." He held onto my elbow and ushered me through the cluster of reporters. We were peppered with odd questions as Mars and I hurried toward the house.

I was shivering. My lace top had been fine while we ate dinner, but the night had grown colder and it wasn't warm enough for a hike through Old Town.

Tilly flung the door open and motioned to us to enter quickly. "Isn't this ridiculous? They're claiming that Wesley is a murderer!"

"One of them asked us if he was having an affair with Abby," I said.

"That's so offensive! Where do they get these crazy ideas?"

It might be offensive but it had crossed our minds, too.

Tilly showed us into the cozy family room in the back of the house. A fire blazed, and mugs sat on the rustic coffee table. The TV was on but muted. Wolf paced the room, his phone to his ear.

Wesley perched on the L-shaped leather sofa, his hands knotted into fists. The man I hadn't recognized when I saw him before stood in the shadows watching Wolf.

None of them greeted us. I hoped things would go well, because the tension in the room was enough to make it explode.

"Would you two care for a brandied hot chocolate?" asked Tilly.

"Not for me, thanks," said Mars, who made a beeline for Wesley. "What's the status?"

166

"I'd love one," I whispered to Tilly, so I could hear Wesley's response.

"The police triangulated Abby's phone and were able to zero in a little closer using GPS. It's in Reston, Virginia, and on the move."

"So Abby is definitely alive!" I exclaimed.

"Looks like it. The cops are trying to find her," said Wesley. He gazed at Wolf hopefully. "They'll probably arrest her for murder."

His pupils were large, and his chest heaved with each breath as though he'd been running. This was obviously a big source of stress for him. Not that I could blame him. He would be relieved when Abby was caught and the speculation about his involvement ended.

On the other hand, if he was really having an affair with Abby, he might be nervous because the truth would now come out.

The man I hadn't recognized before edged toward me and said, "Hello, Sophie," as if he knew me. Why did he look familiar? Big bushy eyebrows topped intense brown eyes. He wore a short mustache and a day's worth of beard growth.

I was immensely relieved when Tilly said, "You know Stu Jericho, of course."

Stu smoothly said, "I see Sophie at a lot

167

of the big events in town. Let's see, I think the last one was the art benefit gala."

The room grew silent as we waited to hear an update from Wolf. Tilly handed me a mug of hot chocolate with a marshmallow garnish decorated with green candy melts to look like Frankenstein.

I pointed at it and mouthed, "So cute!"

At long last Wolf said to us, "The phone appears to have come to a stop. They're on foot, searching for Abby."

He continued holding the phone to his ear. Suddenly, he said, "I'll meet you there."

Wesley rose to his feet. "They found her?"

Wolf rubbed his neck like he was tired. "I wouldn't get too excited yet. I'll give you a call when I know more."

While the others talked, I slipped away and walked to the door with Wolf.

"Wesley seems very agitated," I whispered.

"I noticed that."

"Is he involved?" I asked.

Mars shot me a look. "Like I would tell you? Sophie, I don't know much more than you do yet. All I can say is that we're running down all the leads we have, hoping we can start to make sense out of this."

He opened the door and marched into the midst of reporters shouting questions. I closed the door behind him and locked it.

No point in taking a chance that one of them would try to sneak inside.

When I returned to the family room, Tilly was saying, "I've been bugging Wesley about getting outdoor cameras. The kind that are set off by motion sensors. I've been anxious since they found that woman in the freezer. And then people started gawking at our door. The girls can barely come and go. You'd think they would leave them alone!"

"Why don't you have the girls use the alley?" asked Mars. "I doubt that's staked out yet."

Tilly looked at her husband. "I wish we could go away until this blows over."

Jericho, still in the shadows, was quite obviously shaking his head in the negative.

Wesley frowned at his wife. "I'd say we should take a family vacation just to get out of town, but if we do that they'll probably follow us and claim that it's a sign of guilt."

"Or that you're enjoying yourselves when Abby is on the run and an unidentified woman is in the freezer. Also a very bad image," said Mars.

"Can't we stop this?" asked Wesley. "There has to be a way to get this under control."

"Maybe it will calm down when they find Abby," said Mars.

I wondered if that was true. If Wesley had

played a role in whatever happened, then finding Abby could be the beginning of the end for him. For the first time I wondered if Abby could be hiding from Wesley. "Where is Briley now?" I asked.

"Upstairs doing homework. Tomorrow is a school day. While I truly hope they find Abby, I hope we won't be up all night again." Tilly collected empty mugs and carried them to the sink.

"We should go," I said to Mars. "Would you mind if we left through the alley?"

I could swear Wesley looked panicked. The self-assured smooth-talking politician had lost his confidence. He gazed at Mars and asked, "You'll call us if you hear anything?"

"I will." Mars nodded solemnly.

"Even in the middle of the night," Wesley pressed.

Mars placed his hand on Wesley's shoulder. "You don't have anything to worry about. Try to get some sleep."

The clattering of rapid footsteps on the stairs drew our attention. A moment later, Briley burst into the room. "The woman in the freezer is Schuyler's mom!"

CHAPTER 16

Dear Sophie,
I'm headed south for the winter, but I don't want to throw away all the food in my fridge. Can I freeze butter, heavy cream, and cucumbers?
Frozen Grandma in Hazard,
Nebraska

Dear Frozen Grandma,
Butter freezes surprisingly well. Unfortunately, most other dairy products, including cream, are not good choices for the freezer. Alas, neither are cucumbers or other high water-content vegetables. May I suggest pickling the cucumbers?
Sophie

I glanced at the television. There was no breaking news. "How do you know that?"

"Schuyler's dad had to go identify the body. He just broke it to her. She texted

171

me." Briley held up her phone as though that proved what she was saying.

"Mia? I was afraid of that." Tilly sank into a chair. "Oh, Briley! Schuyler must be devastated."

Wesley grasped the back of Tilly's chair. "I'm having trouble computing this. Abby murdered Mia? What was Mia doing at Abby's house in the first place? Were they friends?"

"Honey," said Tilly in a soothing tone, "I'm sure they met over here. But I wasn't aware that they socialized outside of our house."

"Clearly, they must have," he grumbled.

"The good news," said Jericho, "is that they'll probably take Abby into custody tonight and this nightmare will be over."

"Not for Schuyler," murmured Tilly. "Do you want to go over to see her, Briley? You can stay home from school tomorrow to be with Schuyler if you want."

Briley was solemn. "I'd like that. What do I say to her?"

"Honey, let her do the talking. You be a good friend by listening. I'll go with you. Maybe Schuyler's dad needs help with something. Wesley, you should listen to Mars. You haven't slept since they opened that freezer. Maybe you should take a sleep-

172

ing pill tonight."

Wesley said, "No sleeping pills for me, Tilly. I have to keep my wits about me."

"I'll be back soon." Tilly rose and wrapped an arm around Briley's shoulders. Together they walked out toward the alley.

Wesley fidgeted as if he wasn't sure what to do.

"I'm sorry it was Mia," I said. "Is there anything we can do for you?"

"Thank you, Sophie. I think perhaps Jericho is correct. If they bring in Abby, then I'll be okay."

Mars was already outside, eager to leave. "The coast is clear," he hissed. He had opened the door in the brick wall surrounding their garden and held it for me.

I stepped through and into darkness.

We walked along the alley without speaking. It wasn't until we were safely a block away from Wesley and Tilly's house that I said, "Your client is falling apart."

Mars nodded. "I didn't expect it of him. Then again, I never expected anything like this to happen. What did Wolf tell you? I noticed that you slipped away to get the scoop from him."

"Not much. Sounds like they're as confused as everyone else."

"Did he mention Wesley?"

173

"Nope. Are you worried about him? Do you think he's involved in this mess?"

"I don't know. I get that he liked Abby as a person and the situation is distressing. But he's far more upset than I would have expected." Mars glanced at me. "This is hush-hush. Got it? Don't even mention it to Nina."

"Okay."

"The guy named Jericho who was there tonight is bad news. Wesley insists he came highly recommended, and I believe that. Jericho is like a political bloodhound. He can smell trouble a mile away."

"Why is that a secret? What politician wouldn't want a guy with that kind of talent around?" I asked.

"He can't be trusted."

"So how does that play into Mia's death and Abby's disappearance?"

"I'm not sure. But I'm beginning to put some things together."

"Like what?"

Mars walked me to my kitchen door and hugged me like he didn't want to let me go. "It might be better if you don't know." He turned and walked into the night.

Had Abby told Mars something that he hadn't shared with me? I wasn't too concerned about him until that moment. It

174

wasn't typical of Mars. That hug had told me more than his words had. Just like Wesley and Tilly, I found myself hoping everything would be cleared up when they found Abby.

I locked up the house and went to bed but tossed, wondering what Wolf had discovered. Had they found Abby? Was she in hiding because she was afraid or because she had murdered Mia, and stuffed her in the freezer?

And how was Charlene?

At six in the morning, I turned on the local news show, hoping to hear that Abby had been found. I was disappointed when the anchor announced that police were currently investigating a person of interest. What did that mean? Was Abby dead or alive? Was *she* the person of interest?

Reluctantly, I gave up any hope of sleeping and ambled downstairs to make tea. While I waited for the water to boil, I looked through Tilly's recipes for an apple tartlet I had seen.

Inspired, I mixed the dough and placed it in the fridge according to the instructions. I chopped nuts and sliced apples while it chilled. Still in my bathrobe, I preheated the oven and rolled out the dough. I sprinkled it with nuts and lay the apple slices on top in overlapping circles. The recipe made four tartlets. They looked too pretty to eat.

I half expected Nina or Mars to drop by for breakfast, but neither of them appeared. After a quick shower during which I took care not to aim the water at the spot I had covered, I pulled on a teal cotton sweater, light brown pants, and a scarf that contained shades of teal and brown. I slid the apple tarts out of the oven and left them to cool while I took Daisy for a walk around our neighborhood. It was remarkably quiet and peaceful — so much so that it was hard to believe Mia had been murdered and stuffed into a freezer and Charlene had been badly beaten.

On our way back, I stopped by Natasha's house. She answered the door in a flowing icy-green bathrobe. She looked like a 1950s starlet who had just stepped off the screen. Except for her eyes. They were tired.

"How is Charlene?"

"Why is there an entire cake in my fridge?"

"Charlene first."

She cast a glance at Daisy. "I would invite you in if you didn't have the furball with you."

"The furball and I don't need to come in. How is Charlene?"

176

"They don't expect her to survive. She has a broken leg, a broken rib, a bruised kidney, and a bruised liver. Her hands and elbows are raw from trying to drag herself across the ground. The doctor says she was bleeding internally and had so much blood loss that it was a miracle she was still alive and managed to make it to my house."

"No!" I cried. "I'm so sorry, Natasha."

"Isn't it odd to feel such devastation over the impending death of someone I didn't even know? If I hadn't sent off the DNA swab, she would have died and I would have gone on with my life, never having realized that my sister was in a nearby hospital taking her final breaths." Natasha broke into tears. Her shoulders shook as she sobbed.

I hugged her. There wasn't anything else I could do.

When she recovered, she sniffled and wiped her face. "I've called in to work and asked them to run some of my old shows. You know, The Best of Natasha or some such. I plan to stay with Charlene to the tragic end. It's the least I can do for the only sibling I didn't know I had."

It occurred to me that she might have other half siblings who had not submitted their DNA. But it didn't seem like the right time to say that. "Of course. If there's anything I can do, I hope you'll let me know."

Tears welled in her eyes. "You can find the horrible person who did this to her."

She was serious. "I have nothing to go on. Did the doctors say what they think happened?"

"When she dies, it will be a homicide. Someone beat her very badly. She has swelling on the brain. She's so dehydrated that they couldn't believe that she was still alive." Natasha gripped my arm. "She came to me, Sophie! She needed help and she trusted me because we're blood. That . . . that means everything in the world to me. She came looking for me because she knew I would help her."

"You're a great sister, Natasha. I'm certain Charlene would tell you that if she could. Maybe through the fog she realizes that you're by her side at the hospital, looking out for her. I hope you'll keep me posted."

"Find him, please. Find the person who beat up my sister."

I nodded. What else could I do? Daisy and I walked down the stairs and went home. I didn't know anything except Charlene's name. I had no idea where she lived or what she did for a living or whether she was married or had children. I had nowhere to start.

After feeding Daisy and Mochie, I packed the apple tarts and used them as an excuse to pop in on Tilly.

Tilly seemed glad to see me. She ushered me into the family room. I said hi to Stu Jericho, who hovered around. I was glad Mars had mentioned him to me. He looked like trouble.

Wesley waved at me but kept his eyes on the news program on TV. "Enough of this," Wesley barked. Looking at me he asked, "Have you heard from Wolf?"

"No, I haven't."

"For cryin' out loud. You heard him. He promised to keep us informed. The news said they have a person of interest. Do you know who that is?"

He was extremely agitated. As calmly as I could, I said, "I'm sorry. I don't have any information."

Stu Jericho watched me. Shivers ran down my back. I tried not to show my discomfort.

To break away, I walked to the rear of the huge room and placed the apple tarts on the kitchen counter.

Unfortunately, Jericho followed me. "I'm sure Mars has explained the situation to you," he said. "Clearly, Wesley's career can be ruined if aspersions are cast upon him. More than one politician has suffered from false accusations. People only hear the bad and never pay attention when the politician is later cleared of any wrongdoing."

He fixed those brown eyes on me. "I hear you're good friends with Wolf."

I didn't respond. He was clearly getting at something, and I was certain I wanted no part of it.

"Maybe you could act as our liaison with Wolf. Find out what's going on and report back to us?"

Why wasn't he asking Mars? Where *was* Mars, anyway? He had warned me about Jericho. Was that coloring my impression of the man? "I appreciate the importance to Wesley, but Wolf does his job well. I seriously doubt he'll share anything with me that he wouldn't tell Wesley."

I would have sworn that Jericho's eyes were boring into me.

Happily, Tilly charged toward us. "What did you bring? Oh, the tarts! We have to try them."

She chattered as she did what she loved. Tilly was definitely a domestic diva. "You won't believe what happened, Sophie. With all this business about Abby going on, it's sort of getting short shrift around here." Tilly looked over at me. "The station that hosts Natasha's show wants me to take it over!"

CHAPTER 17

Dear Natasha,
I adore your TV show. You have such style. I try to model myself after you. My dear husband's birthday is coming up. His favorite meal is meatloaf and corn bread, but after watching you, I know that's too pedestrian. What would you serve for a birthday dinner celebration?
Loving Wife in Celebration, Florida

Dear Loving Wife,
I am so glad you asked! Chilean sea bass with sweet-and-spicy hot pepper jelly would be such an elegant entrée. Serve it with lima beans and pureed turnips.
Natasha

I was horrified. Natasha would wither and die without her TV show. She might be a pest and have some weird decorating ideas,

but the show was the one thing that anchored her. Maybe they wanted Tilly to fill
in for Natasha while she was with Charlene?

"You mean on a temporary basis?" I asked.

"No. They want me to come in and bring
them down-home flavor."

I tried to sound happy. "That's wonderful. And just in time for your book to come
out, too."

"I know," she whispered. "Things are
looking up for me." She glanced toward her
husband. "I wish I could say the same for
Wesley. He's completely distraught about
the Abby situation. He didn't sleep all night.
And he has barely touched any food. He
just chugs down coffee by the potful."

Was that normal? If he truly had nothing
to do with Abby's disappearance or Mia's
death, would he be so troubled about it?

"Is he usually high-strung?"

Tilly gazed at me in surprise. "Never! Wesley is the calmest man in the world. He's
the one you want to have around in a crisis
because he's so logical and placid. He takes
care of everything. He's a born leader."

Funny how different my impression was
of Wesley. I was itching to ask if she was
certain nothing had been going on between
her husband and Abby, but I didn't dare.

Since I was there, Tilly decided to cook

183

Wesley's favorite meal for the cookbook. While I took notes on her Southern-style meatloaf and corn bread, I eavesdropped on the conversation between Jericho and Wesley.

"You have to ride it out," said Jericho. "This is nothing compared to what I've been through before."

"Call Wolf. I want an update."

"Get a grip, Wesley. You don't want to poke the Wolf. He's the one person we need to handle very carefully." Jericho lowered his voice, and I couldn't understand what he was saying, but I would have sworn that I heard my name.

By noon, I had everything I needed to add the two recipes to the cookbook. Only a couple more and we would be done. I left the three of them to eat meatloaf and corn bread for lunch. I was walking toward the front door when I heard someone jogging down the hallway behind me. Jericho caught up to me.

"Hey, Sophie! I was wondering if you'd like to have dinner sometime?"

No! Either he was very bad at picking up on subtle hints that someone wasn't crazy about him, or he wanted to press me to get information from Wolf. I decided it was the latter. "Look, Stu, you must not know Wolf

184

at all. He's not going to tell me anything unless it will be public knowledge in five minutes."

He rubbed the stubble on his chin. "You think I'm using you. Actually, I just wanted to get to know you better."

I didn't believe a word he said. I grappled with the problem women have had for eons. How to turn down a guy without being rude or hurting his feelings. Not that I particularly cared about his feelings, but no one likes to be hurtful. "That's very kind of you, but I've just started seeing someone," I lied. "If it doesn't work out, I'll let you know."

I smiled at him and hoped I sounded convincing.

"And who is this lucky guy?"

Oh no! I was giving him an easy out. Why did he have to push it? "I'm not quite ready to let people know yet." I winked at him and fled out the door before he could pursue the topic or me!

All I'd had to eat was half a little apple tart. I was famished. I stopped by The Laughing Hound. Located in an old building that was once a huge home, it was broken into several dining areas.

Bernie saw me enter and motioned for me to join him. "You're just in time for lunch. Roasted chicken salad?"

"Sounds great."

He took me through the kitchen, where he asked a waiter to add another chicken salad, then led me out on the back deck, where Wolf sat at a table with a young woman.

Bernie, who had been raised in England and various exotic ports around the world, spoke with a delightful British accent, which made anything he said sound completely brilliant. His mother had dragged him along as she married an assortment of absurdly wealthy men. The last I'd heard she currently lived in Shanghai. Bernie had been the best man at my wedding to Mars. None of us had expected footloose Bernie to settle in Old Town, but to our surprise, he took over management of The Laughing Hound for an absentee owner and turned it into a popular eatery. He had a talent for the business.

Even though he was now a respectable restaurateur, his sandy hair still looked like he'd just rolled out of bed. And he would forever be marked by the kink in his nose where it had been broken once, or possibly twice. The stories about just how it had happened varied and seemed to grow with each retelling.

"Soph, this is Brittany Shelburne," he said.

Brittany wore the restaurant's uniform of black trousers, white shirt, and black vest. When she turned her head, I saw that she wore a sparkling rhinestone ponytail holder.

We gathered at a table under ceiling heaters. We were the only people on the porch.

The waiter brought out hot apple cider and roasted chicken salads for all of us. They were plated beautifully on a mound of mixed greens and red quinoa. Strips of roasted chicken radiated from the top with long pieces of red and yellow peppers between them. A creamy garlic dressing was served on the side.

"Tell Wolf what you told me, Brittany," said Bernie.

"Sure. You know that lady, Abby? I didn't know her name before I saw her picture on the news. She was here Friday having dinner with Bernie's friend."

"Mars?" asked Wolf.

That came as a surprise. I had known that they were dating, and I was certain Mars would have told Wolf. But I didn't realize that Mars had been out with Abby the night she disappeared. I looked at Wolf's expression. He always had a poker face. It was so frustrating not to know when he was surprised or worried. I now wondered if Mars had been the last person to see her alive.

That would mean the police would be taking a harder look at him.

"Did they leave together?" I asked. "Do you recall?"

Brittany thought for a moment. "I'm pretty sure they did. I was their waitperson that night. For what it's worth, they didn't seem to be having fun. You can tell when a date isn't working out. One person does all the talking and the other one looks eager to run out of the restaurant. Also, when it's a lousy date, they *never* order dessert. They want to get away from each other as soon as possible."

Wolf listened intently. Her last comments made him chuckle.

"They said on the news to call the police with any information on Charlene Smith. She's been here, too," said Brittany.

I stabbed a piece of chicken with my fork and listened.

"She comes in with a guy who looks like he's older than her. I always notice them because she's kind of out of his league. You know what I mean? She's strikingly pretty, but he's sort of flabby and plain. Love is a weird thing. You never know who might be attracted to each other. Right?"

"Do you recall his name?" asked Wolf.

"Fred Conway. He usually pays with a

credit card. That's where I saw his name."

"Big tipper?" asked Wolf.

"Not particularly. He pays a normal tip, nothing out of the ordinary."

"When did you last see them?"

"Must have been during restaurant week. They could have been here on one of my days off, but that's the last time I saw them. I remember him liking the crab legs. He asked if we would continue to serve them."

Wolf looked at Bernie, who said, "End of August. I can go through the credit card receipts if that would help."

"I'd appreciate that, Bernie. Thank you very much, Brittany. Sounds like this is our first solid lead to find out more about Charlene."

We chatted about lighter topics while we ate. When we finished, Brittany went back to waiting on tables, Bernie headed to his office to look through receipts, and Wolf said he was going back to his office. I assumed he would be looking up Fred Conway.

I thanked Bernie for lunch and left with Wolf. When we were outside on the sidewalk, I said, "Natasha had spoken to Charlene on the phone. You could track down information on her that way."

"Natasha? They were friends?"

"Ha! You're so far behind. They're half sisters."

"No kidding?"

"You can probably find Natasha sitting by Charlene's bed."

"Thanks, Sophie. I'll pass that along. It's not my case, but everyone is upset about it. I haven't seen anything so brutal in a long time."

"What happened with Abby? I thought I'd be hearing about her arrest on the news this morning. Did you find her?" I asked. "Wesley is dying to know." And so was I.

"Is he? Does the name Dusty Lynton mean anything to you?" asked Wolf.

"Not off the top of my head. I meet a lot of people through the conventions and events I set up. You know, I'm introduced but then I never see them again, so I'm never a hundred percent sure."

"Did you ever hear anyone mention him when you were at Wesley and Tilly's house?"

"I don't think so."

Wolf kept his eyes on me. "He's young, only twenty-two, but he has a rap sheet that you wouldn't believe. A small-time crook. He had Abby's phone in his possession."

CHAPTER 18

Dear Sophie,
I would like to learn how to bake. Do I
need to take a class, or can I learn from
the Internet?

> Sweet Tooth in Upper Pig Pen,
> North Carolina

Dear Sweet Tooth,
You don't have to take a class. Start with
an easy recipe such as a coffee cake or a
dump cake. Look for one that doesn't
have a lot of complicated steps. You can
graduate to more difficult recipes after
you're comfortable with simple cakes.

> Sophie

I took a sharp breath of air. "Do you think
he murdered Mia and stole Abby's phone?"
"I'm not sure. He denies knowing Abby.
He claims he found her phone in a shopping mall."

"But he's a crook," I protested. "Why would you believe him?"

"That's the problem. I'm trying to find the connection between him and Abby."

"Maybe the phone will give you the answers you need. Maybe there are texts between the two of them."

Wolf grimaced. "Our forensic technicians are looking at it now. It would be great if they had been communicating. My fear is that Dusty managed to clear the memory."

"How could he do that if he didn't have the password?"

"There are half a dozen ways, some surprisingly easy. These low-life types use a lot of stolen phones. They cycle through them, tossing each one after a while, which makes it harder to keep tabs on them. And they know it."

"Where was the mall?" I asked.

"In Reston."

"Assuming his story is true," I said, "it would mean that someone, most likely Abby, accidentally left the phone there. Which would probably mean Abby murdered Mia."

"I wouldn't jump to conclusions just yet," warned Wolf. "We haven't corroborated his claims."

"Don't they have a lot of cameras in

malls?" I asked. "That would be an easy way to confirm his story."

"Don't worry. We have people on it. I sure wish we could find Abby, though. She appears to be the key to this entire mess."

Wolf headed back to his office, and I walked home.

It seemed as if everything revolved around Abby. What had Mia been doing at Abby's house, anyway? They had probably become friendly at Tilly's. Maybe they shared some interest like yoga or gardening.

I almost overlooked Schuyler as I ambled toward my house. She sat in the end of a tubular slide in a small children's park, her red hair blowing across her face. She didn't move or make any effort to wipe it away.

Taking a deep breath, I crossed to her and crouched beside her. "I'm so sorry about your mom, Schuyler."

She pushed her hair off her face, pulled it together with her hands, and twisted it, revealing a glimpse of a small red heart on the back of her neck. Was that a tattoo? I couldn't imagine Mia, the overprotective mom, being okay with that. I could envision the argument that ensued when Mia learned about it. Schuyler looked at me with vivid blue eyes. "Thank you."

"Would you like to talk, or do you want to

be alone?"

"Alone." She said it so softly that I could barely hear her.

"Okay."

I stood up wondering if I should just walk away and leave her to deal with her grief, when she said, "I wanted a mom like Tilly."

Remorse. I sat down on the ground beside her.

"I feel so guilty. She devoted her life to me. I was everything to her, but I never appreciated it. She homeschooled me for years. I didn't really know any other kids until I was ten. She never let me out of her sight. She had to come with me, even when I was invited to someone's house to play. It irritated me so much. I was the only kid whose mom was always present."

"You must have been very close to her."

"I hated her! When I was going into eighth grade, my dad told her I had to go to public school. He told me it was the only way he could get her to cut me loose. You know what she did? She came with me!"

"Oh no!"

"It was so embarrassing. One of my teachers finally threw her out and said she wasn't allowed in his class. But my mom didn't understand what *no* meant. She got a job at the school and checked up on me all the time."

"That does sound a little bit obsessive."

"That's why I'm sitting here. I thought it would be wonderful to be free of her control. But when I scooted down the slide and came to the end, I realized that it wasn't freedom, it was just the end. Life as I know it has ceased. I resented her for so long, and now I'll have to muddle through without her. I thought that was what I wanted." In the tiniest whisper, Schuyler said, "I wished her dead and it happened."

"Schuyler, you had no power over her death. You had nothing to do with it at all. She was . . . in the wrong place at the wrong time. That's all. There was nothing supernatural about it. And it's not surprising that you would have felt that way. It sounds like your mom didn't give you much breathing room. Maybe you can talk to your father about this?"

"Maybe eventually. He doesn't know what to do right now. He wanders around the house staring at things like he's never seen them before."

"It sounds like you need each other. You need to be there to help him get through this."

"I feel so guilty. I never appreciated her,

never loved her the way she deserved. And now she's gone."

This was out of my league. I wasn't a shrink. But I tried to give her a reason. "She made it hard to love her. It sounds like you spent a lot of time being angry with her and embarrassed by her. I'm sure she knew that you loved her, but she probably also knew that she was overbearing."

Schuyler looked down at her sneakers. "Why would anyone murder her?"

"I don't know. I don't think anyone knows right now. But I can assure you that the cop on her case is very good. He'll figure out what happened." I stood up and held out my hand. "May I walk you home?"

She took my hand and let me hoist her up to her feet. We began to walk toward her house. "I wish I could make it up to her."

I didn't want her to suffer like Natasha, who was spending her whole life trying to be someone her father would approve of and love. "She knows, Schuyler. I'm certain that she knew every time you held her hand or smiled at her."

Schuyler stopped walking and gazed at me. "Do you really think so?"

"I'm positive. Day-to-day life can be trying. We all get mad at people we love. That doesn't mean we don't love them."

"Hey, Sophie, do you know anyone who has lived in Old Town for a really long time?"

"I do."

"For school we're supposed to interview someone about what Old Town used to be like a long time ago. I have to interview someone old to get the story."

"I see."

"I don't mind talking to people, but a lot of kids have a grandparent they can go to. . . ."

"I have the perfect friends for that. Two little old ladies who would love to chat with you. I can almost guarantee you an A in that class."

As we approached Schuyler's house, Tilly was outside talking to someone on the sidewalk. The moment she saw us, she broke off her conversation and hurried toward us. "Where have you been?" She hugged Schuyler to her. "Your father is worried sick. Come on over to my house, and we'll give him a call."

Schuyler entered the house first. Tilly hung back and said, "Her dad is at the funeral home making arrangements. She either left her phone at home or wasn't answering. He freaked out. It was just like when Mia disappeared! I was about to form

197

a search party."

I followed her into the house. Schuyler had joined Briley at the kitchen table. Briley looked glum.

Wesley and Jericho watched me with interest. "Any word from Wolf?" asked Jericho.

I chose my words carefully. "I saw him briefly this morning. They haven't found Abby yet."

"You saw him?" Wesley ambled over.

"I did. But he had little to say. Only that they didn't find Abby."

Wesley looked at Briley. "What's wrong with you, sourpuss?"

Tilly didn't give her a chance to answer. "Don't mind her. She's put out because she has a homework assignment to tell a story about the history of Old Town."

"That doesn't sound so bad." Wesley sat down at the table with her.

Tilly wiped her hands on a kitchen towel. "Honey, I'm sure we'll find someone."

Schuyler almost smiled when she said, "Sophie knows two ladies who have lived in Old Town a long time. I could share them with you."

Briley brightened a little. "Really?"

"Absolutely," I said. "Would you like to meet them? I bet they won't stop talking. I'll just make a couple of quick calls."

Minutes later, I reported, "Francie and Eunice are thrilled. Here's Eunice's address. I predict that you and Schuyler will have fun with them." I extended my hand to give Briley the slip of paper.

Wesley snatched it out of Briley's hand. "I'll drive you over."

"Dad, please!" Briley seemed embarrassed.

"Wesley, you coddle them too much. This is Old Town and they're not babies," said Tilly. "You two walk over there. And here." She handed them a white bakery box tied with a red gingham ribbon. "Some of the apple cupcakes I baked yesterday. Don't forget to thank these ladies for being so generous with their time!" Tilly ushered them out the back door as quickly as she could.

She closed the door and said, "This is the best thing for Schuyler. It will get her mind off Mia for a little while."

Wesley frowned. "I don't mean to be impolite, Sophie, but Tilly and I don't even know these women!"

"They're little old ladies, Wesley. Not ax murderers." Tilly got back to work creaming butter and sugar.

"Tilly thinks I'm overprotective." Wesley leaned against the kitchen counter where

Tilly worked.

"Get used to it, Wesley," Sophie said. "In just a few years they'll be off to college."

"Would you care for some tea, Sophie?" asked Tilly.

"I need to get going, but thanks for asking."

"Thanks for bringing Schuyler home. How did she seem?"

"Remorseful. Now she wishes she had been more loving toward Mia."

"Mia told me there was a time when she thought she would never have a child, but then Schuyler came along." She paused. "I have to think of her exact words, because I could relate. She said, 'Schuler is so precious to me. I want to shrink down to fairy size and sit on her shoulder to make sure everything goes well for her.' "

I laughed. "Except for shrinking, that's pretty much what she did, according to Schuyler."

"I guess a lot of parents feel that way. Wesley and I have talked about this. He feels like Mia did. But I was on a set most of the time. My mom was always there hovering over me. And when she wasn't, the studio teacher was. I never had time to just be a kid and hang out. I don't want Briley to feel that way. I want her to have friends, and fun, and make a few mistakes along the way so that she'll learn."

Wesley paled. "I don't want her making the mistakes I made."

I hoped he was talking about silly things kids do. But I wondered if he meant something else. Something bigger, like murder.

"Not anything major." Tilly laughed. "I think it's part of growing up to not be perfect all the time. We can't shelter them from everything. I want Briley to be confident in her own abilities. Little things like letting them walk over to see a couple of old ladies will build their confidence. They can do that!"

Wesley tapped his fingers on the counter. "I still don't like it. Maybe I should tail them in my car!"

Tilly cracked an egg. "You'll do no such thing. They have good heads on their shoulders, and they're together. They'll be fine."

"Briley wants to be Miley Cyrus for Halloween," said Wesley. "I wish she were back in the Little Mermaid phase."

"I know!" Tilly added the spices to her cake batter.

I would have added more cinnamon. I felt as if I were channeling Abby, again.

At that moment, I spied a roll of red gingham on a shelf. "Is there any significance in red gingham?" I asked Tilly.

"I love anything gingham. To me it's a sign of home, of cozy, lazy days with family. Nothing pretentious, nothing fancy, just the comfort of a country home."

"So it's sort of your trademark?"

"I guess you could say that." Tilly pulled back and looked at me curiously. "Is there something wrong with it?" She gasped. "Oh my! Does it mean something else that I don't know about?"

I laughed. "If it does, I don't know about it, either. I was thinking that you should use it on the cover of the cookbook in some fashion. It would be a fun way to market anything else you might make. Like if you decide to sell jam, for instance, you could put some red gingham on the jars somewhere."

"I love that idea! I'll tell the producer of my TV show, too. Maybe they can use it as a logo somehow."

CHAPTER 19

Dear Natasha,
My niece is getting married and moving into her first home. I would love to surprise her with a housewarming gift of spices and herbs. Which ones would you recommend for a novice cook?

Proud Mom in Boring, Oregon

Dear Proud Mom,
What a thoughtful gift. I would recommend ghost chili powder, cayenne pepper, saffron, licorice root, cloves, and turmeric. Your daughter will be ready to create delicious dishes.

Natasha

I walked home feeling like a traitor. I didn't think Natasha was capable of sharing a TV show with someone else. She always had to be the star, the center of attention. And it would be a miserable experience for Tilly because Natasha would constantly correct her. But why couldn't they each have a TV show?

That evening, I ate leftover chicken and dumplings for dinner. Neither Natasha nor Wolf called me, so I assumed Charlene's condition hadn't changed and that no one had found Abby.

I settled in with a good book and relaxed. But I double-checked all the doors before going to bed. For all we knew, a crazed killer had attacked Charlene and was still roaming the streets.

My neighborhood was quiet and calm when I walked Daisy on Thursday morning. I decided to treat myself to breakfast at The Laughing Hound. Who knew? Maybe I could pick up some news there.

After feeding Daisy and Mochie, I hopped in the shower and noted with dismay that steam from the shower was beginning to loosen the tape where the tiles were missing. I would have to make that a priority as soon as I finished the cookbook for Tilly. I blew my hair dry and pulled on stretchy black jeans, a wine-colored sweater set, and gold hoops. I doubled a black, white, and red plaid scarf and pulled both ends through the loop. I let it hang loosely, but it made all the difference in the outfit.

With Daisy and Mochie contently snoozing, I walked down to the Laughing Hound.

Brittany made a beeline for me when I entered the restaurant.

"Bernie found the most recent receipt from Fred Conway," she whispered. "He lives a few blocks from here on Princess Street."

"How did you find out his address?" I asked. Wolf wouldn't have shared that, would he?

Brittany's face flushed, but she seemed very proud of herself when she said, "On my way to work this morning, I saw Wolf get out of his car and walk up to a house. I may have lingered a little bit to see who answered the door. It was Fred."

It was exactly what I would have done. I grinned at her. "Excellent work! Now maybe we can find Charlene's relatives and learn more about her."

"I have to get back to my tables. Bernie and Mars are eating on the private terrace upstairs."

"Thanks, Brittany." I knew exactly where it was and quickly found the two of them. I took one look at Mars's plate and teased, "You're eating eggs Benedict without me?" It was one of my favorites.

Mars's plate hadn't been touched. That wasn't like him at all. Something was wrong. Mars shoved his plate toward me. "Help yourself."

I sat down next to him and ate. "It's good. What's your problem?"

Mars's gaze met Bernie's.

"Uh-oh. What's going on?" I asked.

Mars sucked in a deep breath. "*I* have been fired."

I nearly choked on the eggs Benedict. Bernie poured me a cup of coffee from the carafe on the table. When I caught my breath, I asked, "By Wesley?"

Mars nodded. "It's the first time in my entire life that I've been fired. No one fires me. I can't believe this."

"Maybe it's for the best," I said.

Mars shot me an annoyed look.

"Wesley wouldn't have fired you if something underhanded wasn't going on. It might be a good thing that you're no longer involved with him. I was over there yesterday, and your pal Jericho was calling the shots."

"Interesting," he muttered. Mars's entire demeanor shifted from dejected to suspicious.

I could tell that he felt better already. "They're sitting around watching the news and complaining about the fact that Wolf hasn't been in touch. In fact, Jericho tried to talk me into getting information for them from Wolf, like a spy. Can you imagine?"

"Yeah, well, I might have done that, too," said Mars. "It's frustrating not to know what's happening."

"Mars! You know perfectly well that Wolf wouldn't tell me anything."

"Not unless he wanted you to know," observed Bernie. "Wolf's a smart guy."

"I heard you found Fred Conway's receipt," I said.

Mars picked up a fork and began to eat the other half of the eggs Benedict. "I can't imagine what the deal is with Wesley. I'm having trouble imagining that he was having an affair with Abby."

"He was about to jump out of his skin when I was over there. In my most humble opinion, he's overreacting for someone who barely knew Abby."

"Firing me is certainly proof of that. But why did he want me out of there? That's what I don't understand."

Bernie said, "You don't suppose that Abby overheard something and was onto them?"

Mars stopped eating. "That would make sense."

"No, it wouldn't!" I swiped a napkin from

207

Mars. "What about Mia? Did she overhear something, too?"

"Why not?" asked Mars. "They both hung out with Tilly. That's entirely plausible. Maybe Mia went over to Abby's house to discuss whatever they overheard."

"You realize that you're incriminating your former client," I pointed out.

"Or Jericho," said Mars. "He's sleazy enough to do something underhanded."

"By the way, we have another problem. It sounds like Tilly has been asked to take over Natasha's TV show."

Mars coughed. "She'll flip out. She's already crazy upset about her sister. This is going to kill Natasha."

"Is Mercury in retrograde?" asked Bernie. "It feels like everything is going a bit awry." He sipped his coffee quietly. "Correct me if I'm wrong, but doesn't Natasha have a lot of fans?"

"That's been my impression," I said.

Mars groaned. "Does she ever. They're rabid! They treat her like she's the Queen of Sheba. When we were dating and they saw her in public they would rush to her to fawn over her."

"Then why don't we stage a protest of some kind? We can pick a time and date and announce it on Facebook and Twitter. I bet we can fill the restaurant."

"Bernie! What a great idea. And you pretend that you don't care for Natasha," I said.

"It doesn't mean I'm a fan. But I hate to see her lose the show." He grinned when he said, "Besides, if she doesn't buy Mars's share of that house, I'll never get him out of *my* house!"

I was most intrigued about the way Bernie put that. He had told us that he was taking care of the mansion for the absentee owner of the restaurant. I'd had my doubts and suspected Bernie might have bought the house. I wasn't sure why he would want to hide that fact from us, but for the time being, I would let him keep his secret.

Between the two of us, Mars and I had cleaned our plate and managed to finish off the coffee. We thanked Bernie for breakfast and he promised to quietly put together a protest of Natasha's firing. Mars and I left. We were walking home when Mars's phone buzzed.

It was impossible not to overhear what was happening. Wolf had called him.

When he hung up, Mars said, "Wolf wants to speak with me again. That can't be good."

"Are you worried?"

"Not particularly. I didn't murder Mia,

209

and I have no idea where Abby went."

Back in my kitchen, I pulled carrots and onions out of the refrigerator to cook Tilly's carrot pumpkin soup. It wasn't difficult to make, but when I had tasted it at her house, I definitely thought it needed herbs to perk it up.

While I sautéed the onions, I thought about Charlene and wondered where she had lived. The police must have checked out her home. What did Charlene do for a living?

The rich aroma of sauteed onions wafted up to me. I added thyme and sage, and the scent took on a new and delicious note. I spooned in mashed pumpkin and added chicken broth and sliced carrots. Now all it had to do was simmer.

I had so many questions about Charlene. How could I find out more about her? Charlene must have known other people in Old Town. So far Fred Conway was the only link.

I retreated to my office and made a few discreet phone calls. No one knew Fred Conway. That didn't mean anything. Maybe he wasn't the kind of guy who joined clubs and was involved in galas and events. I Googled his name and the street he lived on. By a complete fluke, I discovered Fred's exact address in a small mention because he had attended a public meeting where he revealed his address to make a comment. I couldn't just show up at his doorstep, could I?

CHAPTER 20

Dear Sophie,
My husband and I have an ongoing battle about the refrigerator. Where does one store the meat? He says it goes into the vegetable crisper (which he learned from his wacky mother), and I say it goes in the main part of the refrigerator. What do you say?

Aggravated Wife in Defiance, Oklahoma

Dear Aggravated Wife,
Meats and highly perishable items go in the main section close to the rear and the walls, where it's coldest. Greens and veggies are best off in the middle, where they won't get too cold.

Sophie

Of course, I could visit Fred. His girlfriend was dying. There was nothing more appropriate than swinging by with food. The soup smelled heavenly, but I didn't want to carry soup over to his house. I looked through Tilly's recipes until I found the recipe for apple fritters. I had apples in the fridge and the recipe sounded delicious. The rest of the ingredients were basically pantry items. It was one of the recipes that had the strange code on it.

But first I phoned Natasha. To be honest, I was feeling very guilty for being so nosy. I reasoned that Fred's girlfriend had been beaten and he was probably eager to find her assailant — unless of course, he had attacked her. Another excellent reason to involve Natasha. There was certainly safety in numbers. In addition, Natasha had every reason in the world to want to meet Fred and learn more about the woman who was so closely related to her.

When I told Natasha that I planned to pay Fred a visit, she immediately said she would like to come. We agreed to go around two in the afternoon.

I peeled and sliced the apples, thinking that the fritters probably needed a little something more. But I would reserve judgment until I tasted them. I dredged the apples through the batter. I made a note on the recipe: *Add cinnamon.* The oil was heat-ing nicely. I checked the temperature with a thermometer. It was time to add the apples. They sank initially, but immediately rose to the surface. I turned them over as they became golden, then scooped them out and set them on a paper towel to absorb the oil.

As soon as one was cool enough to eat, I tasted it. Why hadn't I tried making apple fritters before? They were delicious. But I thought they needed just a little something to dress them up. I placed them in an aluminum container that Fred wouldn't have to return.

Then I pulled out a small pot and melted butter with dark brown sugar. When the sugar had melted, I turned down the heat and poured in some heavy cream and bourbon. I dipped a spoon into it. The sauce hit enticing autumn notes.

Quickly, before I forgot, I wrote down the ingredients and the amounts. We could add that to Tilly's apple fritter recipe if she liked the sauce.

I poured some of the sauce into a disposable bowl with a lid and placed it in a bag with the apple fritters. I stashed the leftover fritters and sauce in the fridge.

Natasha arrived right on time carrying a big bag of her own. She had dressed head to toe in black. I was relieved she hadn't worn a hat with a veil.

I grabbed my smaller bag. "What are you bringing him?"

"My Coca-Cola cake."

"I hope someone else drops by with savory dishes."

We walked over to Princess Street. Fred lived in a Federal-style house with a typical brick exterior and tall windows. It had a flat roof, as did many of the neighboring homes. I walked up the front steps and gently banged the door knocker in the shape of an owl.

I could hear footsteps coming toward the door. There were a couple moments of silence.

"Mr. Conway," Natasha called out. "I would like to speak to you about Charlene. I'm her half sister."

The door opened about four inches. Fred peered at us. We must have looked okay to him, because he swung the door wide to admit us.

But now I was hesitant. I couldn't swear to it, after all it had been dark, but I thought he might be the man I saw leaving through Abby's gate. I let Natasha take the lead.

She held out the cake to him. "I can't tell you how broken-hearted I am about Charlene's condition."

Fred took the cake but appeared puzzled. I understood what Brittany meant when she said he was plain. I was short, but he only had me by five or six inches. Natasha towered over him. His waistline bulged over the belt he wore. He was bald in front. A horseshoe of mousey brown hair ringed his head.

"It's a Coca-Cola cake to help you through this difficult time."

I waved at him. "I'm Sophie Winston. I brought apple fritters with a bourbon sauce."

"Are you from a church or something?" asked Fred.

"Didn't Charlene mention that she had found her half sister?" asked Natasha.

"Uh, yeah. She did say something about that. Come in, please." He showed us into the living room.

It was furnished nicely if somewhat sparsely and was immaculately clean. We sat on a blue sofa.

"Do you have any pictures of Charlene?" asked Natasha. "I'd love to see what she looks like under all those bruises."

Fred's shoulders sagged. He stared at the floor. "I hadn't given it any thought before, but Charlene was the one who took photos on her phone. I don't think I have any pictures of her. I wonder what happened to her phone. Maybe the police have it. Do you know what happened to her?"

Natasha coughed. "I hoped you knew."

He shook his head, obviously not a big talker. "They asked me a lot of questions, but they didn't tell me much."

"What did Charlene do for a living?" Natasha asked.

"She had started a home business. She cooked for five families and delivered the food to them on weekdays. Sort of like having your own chef, except much cheaper."

"She was a chef! Like me!" Natasha clasped her hands to her chest. "I bet we are a lot alike. What else can you tell me about her?"

Before he could speak, I said, "I'll just pop the food into your refrigerator so it won't go bad." I was up on my feet and in the kitchen snooping before he could protest.

On a pad under a wall phone, someone had written *Griselda Smith, Tacoma Park, Maryland.*

I had the fridge door open when he rushed into the kitchen. "Um, I guess I should offer you something."

"Oh no! Don't be silly. I hope we're not imposing. Natasha is devastated. She was looking forward to meeting her sister."

"Yes, I see."

I placed the items in his refrigerator, noting that he had an ample supply of cheeses and cold cuts. A bottle of milk looked lonely, but I expected that was for his breakfast cereal. Mustard, mayo, and an assortment of foreign beers filled the rest. No fruit. No veggies. I guessed that might be typical for a single man.

Like the living room, the kitchen was spotless. Not a dirty dish in the sink or a crumb on the floor. I followed him back to the living room, but not before catching a glance of the dining room, which was set up with a dining table and chairs. The crystal chandelier gave it an elegant touch. There was no hutch or buffet or painting on the wall.

When we returned to the living room, Natasha asked, "Is Charlene's mother alive? I'd like to meet her."

"Yes." He didn't offer any more information.

I tried to hide my surprise. Why did I think that Griselda was probably related to Charlene? Maybe he didn't feel right giving out the mother's information to a couple of nosy women he'd never met before.

A long-haired white cat with blue eyes sauntered toward us with the attitude of a feline who thought she owned the place.

"What a beautiful cat!" I exclaimed.

Natasha recoiled. "She won't jump on me, will she?"

"No. She is a very well-mannered cat."

The cat wound around my legs. I reached down and rubbed her ears. "And what do you do?" I asked.

"I work from home fixing people's software problems."

"That's interesting. So I can call you if I run into a snag?" I asked.

"It doesn't exactly work like that. I work for companies, and they send people my way."

"Too bad. How did you meet Charlene?"

"In the grocery store. The guy in the cheese department didn't know if they had smoked Gouda. Charlene was next in line. She saw it in the open case and handed it to me. We had coffee and . . ." He tailed off as if we knew the rest. Or maybe as if there was no more.

While Natasha peppered Fred with additional questions, I gazed around the room. It was remarkably devoid of knickknacks, which didn't surprise me much. In my experience, a lot of single men spent their money on gadgets rather than decorative items. But there was something empty about his house. Almost as if it were a transitional place, not a home where he intended to stay.

"Natasha," I said, "I think we've taken enough of Fred's time. Again, I'm so terribly sorry about Charlene."

He saw us to the door. After we stepped out, we heard a bolt lock snap closed inside.

Alma Riddenhauer was gardening across the street. She held a rake in one hand and motioned to us with the other. Alma and her husband had been fixtures in Old Town for a long time.

We crossed the street, and she hissed, "Fred is the quietest neighbor I've ever had. For a long time, I thought he was a hermit."

"Do you know his girlfriend, Charlene?" I asked.

Alma nodded knowingly. "I think he clobbered her."

Natasha gasped. "Really? Why?"

"First of all, I don't know what a sweet thing like Charlene would be doing with Fred. Second, he's just too quiet."

That hardly pointed to violence. I sighed. Gossip. Sometimes there was a tinge of truth, but Alma's reasoning wasn't grounded in facts. "Why would he want to hurt Charlene?" I asked.

"He never says a word. He's completely inhospitable. Honestly, I work outside all the time —"

"It looks beautiful," Natasha interjected.

"Thank you, sweetheart. I don't know what's come over Old Town. It was always such a nice place. But we've had two bags of lime stolen from our yard. Now who would do that?"

"Lime?" asked Natasha.

"Yes, darling. Lime is the reason all our plants look so beautiful."

"Are you saying Fred stole them?"

"I doubt it. Have you taken a close look at his yard? He could do with some lime. But he never comes over for a chat. He might wave or say hello, but that's all. He's definitely not from the South, I can tell you that for sure. He probably has a lovely mama, but she didn't teach him a thing about manners."

"Maybe he's shy," I suggested.

"Well how long do you get to be shy before you talk with your neighbor?" Alma asked. "It broke my heart to hear about Charlene. She sure didn't deserve what he did to her."

"I hope you've reported all this to Wolf," said Natasha.

Alma snorted. "Ha! There's another man with" — she drew an imaginary zipper across her lips — "a closed mouth. He

221

wasn't interested in what I know."

"When did you see Charlene last?" I asked.

"On Friday evening. I saw her under the streetlights. She came running down the outside stairs of his house and dashed along the street that way." Alma pointed in the direction of Abby's house. "I said to my husband, I said, 'She's finally running away from him. Good for her. She deserves a nice man, not an ice man.' He got a big kick out of that!"

Natasha looked at me, her eyes huge. "We were just talking to her assailant!"

I doubted that. He was cold and kind of odd, but that didn't mean he had beaten her. Besides, she had suffered a serious attack. She was in no condition to run along the sidewalk. Whatever happened to Charlene had occurred after she left Fred's house.

"Look at him," whispered Alma. "He sits up there in that bedroom and watches people go by on the street. Gives me the chills every time I see him."

Unless I missed my guess, that was a lot. "Do you keep an eye on him?" I whispered.

"Of course I do. I don't know what will become of him now. Charlene was the only person I ever saw him with. He never puts out a Christmas wreath or anything for Halloween. I can't imagine why he would want to harm Charlene, though. She was as sweet as she could be."

I thanked Alma and tugged Natasha away. "I can't believe you let me go to see Fred today. He could have attacked me, too!" she complained.

When I thought we were out of earshot and Alma wouldn't hear, I hissed, "Just because a guy is a weird loner doesn't make him violent."

"He didn't seem very upset about what happened to her."

That was certainly true. "Maybe he was numb. Or he's torn up inside but doesn't know how to show his feelings."

"Or maybe he really doesn't care because he's the one who beat her!" Natasha ended her sentence in a shriek. "We cannot allow him to get away with the murder of my half sister. I never had a chance to know her or teach her how to cook —"

"In the first place, she's not dead yet. And second, she cooked for a living, Natasha. One has to assume she was good at it."

She ignored me. "I never babysat for her or celebrated a holiday with her or went to lunch or shopping with her." Natasha stopped walking and grabbed me by the shoulders. "This is the only thing that I will ever be able to do for her. *You* have to find her assailant!"

Chapter 21

Dear Natasha,
Are there herbs that can bring me luck? I've hit a rough patch and need some good luck.

> Sad Sack in Nowhere, Colorado

Dear Sad Sack,
Mint, poppy seeds, and cinnamon not only are good for your health but will bring luck your way!

> Natasha

I did not care for the way Natasha emphasized that *I* had to find Charlene's killer. "Griselda Smith of Tacoma Park."

"Who's that?" she asked.

I shrugged. "He had written that name on a pad in the kitchen."

"You were snooping?" She sounded aghast.

"It was right out in the open. It might be

an aunt."

"It doesn't matter. Let's find Griselda."

"Now?"

"Before he harms her, too!"

There wasn't a good reason not to check out Griselda. We stopped by my house and Googled her. As soon as I saw the web page for her business, I wanted to shield Natasha from it, but it was too late.

In a deadpan voice, Natasha said, "She could be my mother."

Griselda's website was all about herbs and stones and how they could bring a person health, wealth, and luck. Even the photo of Griselda was eerily reminiscent of Natasha's mom.

I jotted down the address, and we headed for my garage. "Are you sure you want to do this?"

"Sophie, there are few things that I have wanted more." Natasha slid into the passenger seat. "Let's go."

We left Old Town behind and headed north to Tacoma Park. Before long we arrived at a funky store called Strawberry Moon. Someone had painted the building in a rainbow of colors.

"It's making me dizzy," Natasha muttered. "She may be worse than my mom."

We stepped out of the car, and Natasha

double-checked the address. "I know it's not wrong, but a girl can hope."

"It appears that your dad was attracted to free-spirited women."

Natasha groaned. "Thank you for putting it so kindly."

I hung back and let Natasha enter the store first. She grabbed my arm and pulled me inside. If the exterior was colorful, the interior was overwhelming. Like walking into a kaleidoscope. Gauzy, breezy clothes in bright colors hung on racks. Kites in the shapes of fish, birds, and bugs dangled from the ceiling. Bottles of herbs lined shelves behind a long counter.

A middle-aged woman wearing her hair in a long braid looked up. "May I —" She stopped speaking and whispered, "Who *are* you?"

"Natasha Smith. You've probably seen me on TV. I have a show —"

The woman with the braid opened a door and shouted, "Griselda! There's someone you need to see out here."

"Lonnie, I am not working today. How many times do I have to tell you that?" The woman who spoke was medium height with white hair that stood straight up from her head. It was at least three inches long. I wondered how much gel she had to use to get it to do that. She had styled it so that it looked tousled and unkempt. "Who are you?"

Natasha repeated her name and the information about her TV show. "Are you Griselda Smith?"

The white-haired woman looked fearful.

"I believe you may have been married to my father," said Natasha.

As we watched, Griselda dropped to the floor in a dead faint.

Natasha and I rushed behind the counter.

Lonnie, the woman with the long braid, tapped Griselda's cheeks.

I propped her up and held her to prevent her from falling back.

"Griselda! Take two of these." The woman with the braid handed her two tiny pellets.

"What's that?" I asked.

"Ignatia. It calms people. It's especially helpful when they have experienced a death in the family. Griselda hasn't been able to reach her daughter in days. She's quite fragile at the moment."

I could feel Griselda supporting herself. She sat up. With Lonnie's help she stood and faced Natasha. "I am not fragile," she snapped. "Anyone whose daughter goes missing would be upset."

"It's perfectly understandable," Natasha

murmured. "I'm heartbroken that I have to tell you Charlene is in the hospital."

I feared Griselda would faint again, but she shrieked instead. "Where? What's wrong with her?"

Natasha teared up. "She suffered a terrible attack. She's unconscious."

"I have to go. I have to go to her! Lonnie, I'm packing an overnight bag. Get the name and address of the hospital." Griselda disappeared into the back of the store.

"I'm devastated that I never got to talk with Charlene face-to-face," said Natasha. "We spoke on the phone, but she was injured before we could meet."

"I'll say this, the two of you sure look like sisters. Come on over here." She motioned to Natasha to follow her to a wall full of photographs.

It wasn't hard to pick out Charlene. Her resemblance to Natasha was uncanny.

To the woman with the braid, I said, "Hi. Sophie Winston."

"Lonnie Bayfort."

"I gather Charlene told her mom about the DNA test she took?"

"Griselda was completely against it. She's so angry with Amos for leaving them." She leaned toward me and said under her breath, "It's been decades. I don't think

229

she'll ever get over it."

"How did it happen?" asked Natasha.

"He just walked out one day and never came back. After spending years looking for him, she finally decided he must have died. Then one day someone recognized his photo on the wall over there. We think he's still alive, but heaven knows where he might be."

"That sounds exactly like what he did to me and my mom." Natasha's face flushed with anger.

"Do you really have a TV show?"

"Yes. And a newspaper column, too. Do you recognize me now?"

"No. You just look a lot like Charlene. There are so many cable shows these days, you know? Griselda hasn't had a TV in years. I don't know how she does it. She refuses to buy a cell phone, too. She's stuck in the past."

"Did you ever meet Charlene's boyfriend, Fred Conway?" I asked.

"Don't bring up his name to Griselda. She's certain that he's no good. He's a bit of an odd duck, isn't he? Charlene brought him around a couple of times. He was always polite enough, but he gave me the creeps."

"Did Charlene ever mention someone

230

named Abby to you?"

Lonnie shrieked. "Yes! Charlene was so excited about Abby. They met at an advanced class on French pastries."

Finally, a connection that made sense. "Did they do other things together?"

"I believe they became fast friends."

She was happy to gossip, which I appreciated. I tried to pull as much information out of her as I could. "I'm a little surprised that Charlene was interested in Fred."

"We were, too. She's such a pretty woman. You'd think she could have her choice of gentlemen friends. Of course, she has her mother's moxie. Griselda is thickheaded and opinionated, which can be hard to take sometimes. But I'll let you in on a little something."

"Oh?" I leaned toward her.

"Charlene was about to break off their relationship."

"Are you certain about that?"

"I was standing right here when she told Griselda. She slipped a topaz into Charlene's pocket when she wasn't looking. They're supposed to bring courage to the wearer."

I reeled from that information. "Did you tell the police?"

"Of course! Griselda hasn't been able to

work since Charlene stopped answering her phone. She's been hanging out in the back pretending to take inventory, but I know she's just trying to keep herself busy so she won't have to think about Charlene. I've been crying myself, but I try not to do it in front of Griselda. I love Charlene as much as if she were my own child. She is the sunshine in Griselda's life."

Natasha huffed. "Well, now I'm just mad. I used to be sad about my dad, but I'm angry with him now."

She wiped away tears viciously.

Griselda reappeared rolling an overnight case behind her. She stopped in front of the wall of herbs and selected a number of them, which she placed in an old-fashioned doctor's bag. "Got that hospital information?"

Lonnie handed Natasha a pad of paper and a pen. Natasha wrote it down and tore off the sheet, which she carried over to Griselda.

Griselda wrapped an arm around Natasha. "The next time your mother comes for a visit, I hope you'll bring her up here. I'd like to meet her. We have a lot in common. And if you learn anything about who mugged my Charlene, I hope you'll tell me."

Griselda hugged Natasha and kissed her

on both cheeks. She took Natasha's hand, dropped something in it, and closed Natasha's fingers over it.

"Thank you, Griselda."

I said goodbye and left the store, noting that no customers had visited while we were there. I hoped they weren't having financial difficulties.

When I started the engine, Natasha opened her hand and smiled.

"What is it?"

"A piece of topaz. For courage, I imagine. Isn't that what she gave Charlene?"

Natasha was uncharacteristically quiet on the drive home. It wasn't until I stopped my car in front of her house that Natasha said, "I think Fred is the one who beat Charlene. But I don't know how to prove it."

The trouble was, neither did I.

I took Daisy for a long walk that evening. She needed to get out, and I needed to think and wrap my head around all the things that had happened. It was a cold night. I pulled my fleece jacket closer and could smell smoke from fireplaces. It was a familiar and cozy scent that evoked memories of fun times with friends and family around a crackling fire.

Meanwhile, I was out in the cold, pondering murder.

Daisy wagged her tail cautiously, as if she wasn't certain about something.

She stopped before a young woman who sat on brick steps.

"Schuyler?" I asked.

"Hi, Sophie," she patted Daisy.

"What are you doing out in the dark?"

"I was supposed to meet up with a guy, but I guess I've been stood up."

Ouch! I remembered that kind of hurt. "What time was he supposed to be here?"

"An hour ago." She snuggled deeper into her hoodie.

"You must be freezing."

"It's not that bad."

"Does your dad know you're here?"

"Please don't tell him! He thinks I'm at Briley's house studying for a biology test."

"We could walk you home."

"Thanks. I know he's not coming, but sometimes I like to get away for a little bit."

"How about a hot chocolate?"

"That would be great."

"Come on." The three of us strolled to the coffee place where Mars had asked me to work for Tilly. I ordered two hot chocolates and one carrot pupcake for Daisy. We sat down at a table and warmed our hands on the hot cups.

"I gather you don't particularly want to go home."

"It's not really like that. I just need to take a break now and then. My dad says I was everything to my mom. I appreciate that, but it's weird now that she's gone. My dad's an obstetrician, so he's always having to go deliver babies. No wonder my mom wanted me around all the time. She was lonely. Was your mom that way?"

"No. But I remember being your age and wishing I had more freedom to do things on my own. Aren't you afraid hanging out in the dark?"

Schuyler shrugged. "What's there to be afraid of?"

I didn't want to scare her. On the other hand, maybe she needed a little fright so she would realize that bad things could happen to her when she was wandering around in the night. "Your mom was murdered, Abby disappeared, and another woman was brutally attacked."

"I heard about that. My dad says they were probably using drugs and didn't pay their bills."

"You knew Abby."

"Sure. I met her at Briley's house."

"Did she seem like a drug user to you?"

"No. She was really nice to me. I don't think my dad ever met her. What do you think happened to her?"

"I wish I knew. Did she ever say anything to you about being scared of someone or worried about something?"

"No. She was always cheerful. The last time I saw her, she helped me put my hair up in a messy bun and said I looked very grown-up."

CHAPTER 22

Dear Sophie,
Some of my friends are into dinner parties. It seems like they all received gorgeous china as wedding gifts and they bring it all out. I need to reciprocate, but my dishes are mismatched and I can't afford to buy an entire set of fancy china for a dozen people. What do I do?
Hopelessly Mismatched in Dish,
Texas

Dear Hopelessly Mismatched,
You're in luck. It's trendy to mix and match dishes. All you need is a set of one dozen plain white plates. You can get a good deal on them at some of the big box stores, restaurant supply shops, or even at yard sales. I get some of my best buys at yard sales! Now all your mismatched salad, soup, and dessert

dishes will look intentional.

Sophie

By ten o'clock on Friday morning, I had walked and fed Daisy. I popped open a can of chicken with cheese for Mochie. I could see bits of yellow, so maybe there really was cheese in it. He settled by his bowl and ate with gusto.

Anticipating warmer weather, I wore a simple white shirt with khaki trousers. I grabbed my bag and headed for Tilly's house.

Television vans still clustered in front of Tilly's home. I wondered what they expected. Did they think Wesley would come outside and make some kind of incriminating statement?

A handful of reporters jostled around me as I made my way to the front door.

Tilly let me in. "It is so hard for me not to yell at them! I thought the paparazzi were bad when I was a kid, but they've got nothing on these people."

On our way to the kitchen, we walked by the living room where Wesley, Jericho, and another man appeared to be meeting.

In the kitchen, Tilly said, "I guess this is the last recipe. I have to say that a week ago I was in despair and never imagined we would be able to catch up and complete this on time."

"I'm glad I could help. What are we cooking today?"

"I thought I'd make my famous garlic mashed potatoes with meatloaf for lunch. That should improve Wesley's mood."

I tried to sound casual. "Is he upset about Mia's death?"

"That, too. Someone has been hacking into his computer and releasing information. And he's not the only one. It's a dire situation. He's reached the point where he's afraid to put anything in an e-mail."

Tilly got to work, and in minutes I was measuring and jotting down notes.

When the meatloaf was in the oven, I helped Tilly set the table in the dining room. She used teal Lenox French Perle Groove dishes against a brown tablecloth. Even though it was only lunch, she fussed about a centerpiece and left the dining room in search of one she liked better while I added the flatware, napkins, and aqua glasses that matched the dishes.

The dining room was located next to the living room. I felt certain the gentlemen could see me through the French doors, but that didn't prevent them from continuing their lively conversation.

"Look," said Wesley, "I feel terrible about it. He's a nice guy, and he's good at what he does. He never steered me wrong."

"I don't know what you're so worried about. It all happened before the Internet. It's highly unlikely that anyone will find out." It was Jericho's voice.

I glanced over at them, trying to keep my head bowed so it wouldn't appear that I could hear their discussion.

"We have to locate Abby. Once she shows up, no one will be digging around anymore." Wesley sounded angry.

"How do you suggest we do that?" Jericho asked in a voice tinged with sarcasm.

"I still feel lousy about this." Wesley sat on the sofa, leaning forward and rubbing his hands together.

I realized suddenly that they might not know I was in the dining room. It appeared that the angle of the doors blocked their view of most of the room. I could hear them just fine, but I couldn't see them unless I moved very close to the table.

"You had to do it. He would have taken you down. This way when he's investigated, you remain in the clear and he takes the fall. You're the good guy because you got rid of him as soon as you realized there could be a problem."

240

I backed up against the wall. At that moment, I knew they were going to blame Mars for whatever had happened at Abby's house that fateful night.

CHAPTER 23

Dear Sophie,
I am the worst at arranging flowers. My family teases me about my centerpieces. I never know what to do to dress up the table. Do you have any easy suggestions?
Hopeless Flower Arranger in
Centreville, Virginia

Dear Hopeless Flower Arranger,
Here's one of my favorite quick fixes. Buy a couple of small but beautiful blooming potted plants at a nursery. Wrap the containers in foil. Pop them into a pretty soup tureen or basket. They'll fill it up, and people will rave about how lovely they are.
Sophie

They were throwing him under the bus, sacrificing him to protect Wesley from something. But what? I wasn't clairvoyant, but everything fit together. Wesley's way out of this mess was to place blame on someone else, and Mars was his target. Could he have arranged for Mars to meet Abby? Had Wesley and Abby known each other before Mars worked for Wesley? Just how long had this scheme been in progress?

I probably would have been thrown out, too, if Tilly hadn't been so desperate to finish the cookbook. I bolted from the dining room before they could realize I was there.

Tilly sallied forth through the kitchen carrying a tray that contained three smallish pumpkins. She had used them as vases and bunched golden mums in each of them. It was delightful. Casual enough for lunch and elegant in its simplicity.

Lest anyone was paying attention, I made sure I spoke from the kitchen as she placed it on the table. "You should make some centerpieces for the book. You have a knack for putting together tablescapes."

"Do you really think so? A photographer will be coming next week to photograph me for the cover. Maybe we should take it in here. What do you think?"

Wesley opened the French doors to the dining room.

"You have a beautiful dining room," I said. "Why not?"

"Why not what?" asked Wesley.

Tilly launched into an excited recitation of our conversation, demanding opinions from Jericho and the third man about the best background for the cookbook cover.

It was somewhat amusing, because I had a hunch none of the three men had ever bought a cookbook.

Wesley followed Tilly into the kitchen. "It smells wonderful in here. How's the cookbook coming, Sophie?"

"We're getting close to wrapping it up." I packed up my notes and discreetly bowed out for the day.

Tilly was in her element, fussing with the presentation of the meal on platters. "See you tomorrow," she sang.

I let myself out the front door, deeply disturbed by what I'd heard. What had happened that night? Where had Abby gone? And why was Wesley so worried about it all?

The reporters didn't bother to approach me this time. I guessed they were used to seeing me come and go.

I strolled home by a store that featured a gorgeous sink in their show window. It had been painted with an intricate design of flowers. It would have been overwhelming had it been larger, but it might be perfect for my main floor powder room. What

244

would be a better focal point for a tiny bathroom?

I stepped inside and inquired about it.

The saleswoman raved, "Isn't it wonderful? That one is sold, but it was made by a local artist, Maury Ipswitch. He probably has more if you want to check with him. I'm itching to buy it myself, but we just finished renovating our bathroom and I can't bring myself to throw out a perfectly good sink."

"How much does he charge?"

She quoted a price that was higher than most sinks but might be doable. I thanked her and headed home.

A crowd of reporters lurked outside of Bernie's house. What on earth was going on? I ran toward my own home, planning to call Mars the minute I stepped inside.

But to my surprise, I found him sitting on the banquette in my kitchen with Daisy on one side and Mochie on the other. I hadn't seen Mars look so miserable since Natasha had tried to put his mother in a home. I moved Mochie and wedged in next to him, wrapping my arms around him as if he were a kid who'd had a bad day.

Daisy's ears perked. She barked and ran to the kitchen door. I scooted out of the banquette. A man's face peered through the

245

glass in the door. He cupped his hands around his eyes.

Daisy stood guard at the door. I opened it. "May I help you?"

"Ken Publiski, Channel 81 news. I'd like to ask Mr. Winston some questions."

"Then I suggest you go over to Mr. Winston's house." I closed the door and locked it.

Ken appeared confused.

I shot a glance at Mars and waited for Ken to leave. When he walked out to the sidewalk, I motioned for Mars to stand. I quickly propelled him into the den and pulled the curtains closed.

My small den had three interior walls and a sliding glass door. With the curtains drawn, it was very private. I pulled the curtain aside an inch and peered out. No one was there. "Have you eaten?"

"Who can eat?"

"Mars, it's not that bad."

"Are you kidding? The cops are asking what I did with Abby's body! Why would they think I killed her?"

Okay, that was far worse than I expected. He was probably the last person who had seen her alive.

I hustled to the kitchen and prepared two mugs of hot English breakfast tea. Maybe that would help his nerves. I double-checked to be sure I had locked the kitchen door before carrying them into the den.

"Let's go over this. Abby went to Tilly and Wesley's house that Friday. According to Tilly, it was somewhat chaotic. You were there for lunch, right?"

"Yes." Mars sounded very crabby.

"Who else was there?"

"That's not going to help."

"Indulge me."

He groaned. "Wesley, a couple of his staffers — Ian Culver and Stu Jericho, Tilly, Abby, the two girls, and Mia."

"Thank you. Did you notice what Abby was doing?"

"No."

He wasn't being helpful. "Did she talk with anyone?"

"You think Wesley had something to do with her disappearance." Mars watched me.

"I don't know." I did know that Wesley planned to blame Mars, but I didn't think this was the time to mention that. Mars was usually very level headed. Right now he was very upset. I would have to find the right time to tell him what I had overheard. There was no point in depressing him further right now.

"You asked her to dinner that night."

247

"Yes! Yes, I did." Now he sounded defensive. "That doesn't mean I made her disappear."

"Chill a little, Mars. What I'm getting at is whether Wesley saw or overheard you asking Abby out."

"Oh." Mars looked away as if he was trying to recall the events. "Yeah. Yeah, I think he or Stu might have been around then."

"Just to be clear. Who met Abby first? You or Wesley?"

"You think Wesley set me up?" Mars sat up straighter. It was like someone had given him a shot of energy.

"I'm not sure. You're the one who always says we have to look at the facts. I'm sorry, but I have a feeling Wesley is up to something."

"And it involves Abby?" Mars shook his head. "No, I introduced them. I recommended Abby."

"How did you meet her?"

"It was at a party. A cocktail party . . . Wait a minute. Wesley was there. They could have set me up. Maybe he did know her already." He scratched the back of his head. "But that doesn't make sense. What would be the point?"

"To murder Mia?"

"That's ridiculous!" cried Mars.

248

"I agree, except it's the only logical reason to make you the fall guy. They needed to get rid of Mia for some reason, so they banked on the fact that you were taking Abby out that night. Did Abby ask you to walk her home?"

"I don't think so. It's just what a gentleman does."

"It puts you at the site of the murder and likely makes you the last person who saw Abby. Did you go into her house?"

Mars yanked at his collar as if it had suddenly become too tight.

"Did you spend the night there?" I tried to sound academic about it.

"No! I walked her to her front door, gave her a little kiss, and walked home."

"Mars, this is no time to be bashful. It's okay if you went into her house. You're a single guy. Abby is a single woman."

"I'm embarrassed because I *didn't* go inside. A cool guy would have. The truth is that I just wasn't that interested in her. I liked her but there wasn't a special attraction. And she was a little bit boring."

I bit back a grin. He didn't have to confess anything to me. "Do you see what I'm getting at? They'll say you murdered Mia and that Abby fled out of fear."

"Why did they murder Mia?"

It was a very good question. "I don't know. I haven't been able to figure out what Mia was doing at Abby's house that night."

"That flies in the face of your theory. I'm not buying it."

"Okay, then, let's go back to facts." I thought for a moment. "We've got nothing. Two women — one is dead, and one is missing."

"How about this?" Mars stretched his arms while he spoke. "Abby saw Wesley murder Mia and is in hiding because she's afraid of Wesley."

"Same problem. What was Wesley's motive? Do you think it's possible that Charlene was injured at Abby's house? They were friends."

I picked up the phone and called Wolf.

"Oh swell," muttered Mars.

I had expected to get his voice mail, but Wolf answered the phone.

"It's Sophie, Wolf. Do you recall telling me that you found the blood of a third person at Abby's house?"

"I do."

"Could you check it against Charlene Smith's blood?"

There was a long silence. "And why exactly would you think Charlene had been at Abby's house?"

250

"Natasha and I met her mother yesterday. I'm surprised that no one notified her that Charlene was in the hospital."

"It's not my case, Sophie. I don't know what to tell you about that."

"It turns out that Abby and Charlene were friends."

"That's not exactly overwhelming evidence that Charlene was at Abby's house that night. What are you getting at? You think Abby tried to murder Charlene, too?"

"That hadn't occurred to me. But Wolf, I think I saw Fred Conway coming out of Abby's gate."

"You think you saw him or you're sure it was him?"

"It was dark."

"Sophie, call me when you have facts. I have an investigation to pursue."

He hung up.

Mars snickered. "You're lucky he let you ramble as long as you did."

"Okay, smarty-pants. Let's take your scenario and substitute Fred Conway for Wesley. Charlene breaks up with Fred and flees to Abby's house. Fred follows Charlene and tries to murder her. Abby witnesses the murder and is in hiding from Fred."

"That actually makes sense," said Mars. "Except for one major oversight. You forgot

251

about Mia being there."

I sagged against the back of the sofa.

"Let's put motive aside. What if, according to your scenario, Fred arrived at Abby's house. For some reason, three women couldn't prevent him from murder and mayhem and he's at fault for everything. Then what is Wesley so worried about?" asked Mars.

"An excellent question." He was correct. Nothing fit together. I had been premature in suggesting Wolf check the blood against Charlene's. "You're in a better position than I am to know what Wesley's problem is. I overheard Wesley and Stu speaking today. They definitely mentioned something that Wesley is afraid will be made public. Stu told him not to worry, but Wesley was angry."

Mars looked at me with wonder. "Are you certain?"

"Absolutely. I'm sorry to tell you this, but they're going to put the blame on you."

"Blame for what? I haven't done anything."

"My best guess is that your date with Abby put you in the right place for something. If it's any consolation, Wesley feels pretty bad about it."

"They're covering up. It's a classic deflec-

252

tion move. They're going to blame me for Mia's death in order to move attention away from something else. Oh ho!" Mars finally smiled. "You can be my spy."

"Oh no. I would make a lousy spy."

"There's nothing to it. You're over there every day. Just see what else you can pick up. Mind if I use the computer in your office?"

"Of course not. What are you up to?"

"I'm not sure yet. But there must be something in Wesley's past that everyone missed. Everyone except Stu. If he could find it, so can I."

253

CHAPTER 24

Dear Sophie,
I usually cook for my husband and myself, so I rarely use an entire package of bacon. I hate to waste it. What's the best way to use it up?
                    Baconista in Bacon, Missouri

Dear Baconista,
Go ahead and cook the entire package of bacon. Crumble up the leftovers and freeze them. Now you can pop them into any dish without having to cook more bacon!
                                        Sophie

Mars spent the night at my home to avoid the press that camped out in front of Bernie's house. Saturday morning I found Mars bleary-eyed, still looking at the computer screen in my home office.

"Good morning. Did you get any sleep at

all last night?" I asked.

"Not much. I conked out on the sofa for a while, but then I thought of something and got back to work."

"Can I make you some coffee?"

"Yes, please!"

I retreated to the kitchen and put the kettle on. After the water boiled and sat for a moment, I poured it over coffee grounds in the French press.

Before letting Daisy out in the yard, I peeked outside to be sure the gate was closed and that no reporters lurked around. I could see a couple of diehards at Bernie's house, but my yard was peaceful and safe for Daisy.

At that moment a car pulled up in front of Francie's home. She stepped out and waved at me before opening the passenger side. Eunice squabbled with Francie about needing her help. I left Daisy inside the fence and hurried over.

"Good morning, ladies!"

"Will you tell Francie that I don't need her help getting out of a car?" Eunice grumbled.

I figured she didn't want my assistance, either. "Could I carry something for you?"

Francie left Eunice to her own devices and popped open the trunk. "That suitcase is pretty heavy. And then there are the cats."

"Cats?"

"In the back seat."

I peered into the car. Sure enough, Eunice's cats looked back at me from their carriers. I took them into Francie's house two at a time. When they were all safely in the house, I lifted the suitcase that weighed next to nothing and a laptop computer.

"Don't drop that!" Eunice shouted.

"What's going on?" I asked Francie.

"We're doing what you suggested. There's a contractor at Eunice's house right now putting in a main floor bathroom and converting the dining room to a bedroom. He's also installing an elevator!"

"Ouch. That must be expensive."

Francie waved her hand as though it was nothing. "Not as much as going to an old folks home. He's also putting in wheelchair ramps, just in case. Smart guy. He thinks ahead."

"Eunice is staying with you for the time being?"

"If we don't kill each other," Francie quipped.

Eunice had managed to step out of the car. She stood erect with her cane in her hand. "Sophie, I love Briley and Schuyler! They've been by to visit every single day."

256

"They're coming to my house this afternoon," added Francie. "Such a shame that sweet Schuyler lost her mom at a tender age. Eunice and I are trying to help her work through this terrible time."

I swelled with joy. Who'd have thought that would happen?

"Can I bring over some breakfast?" I asked.

"Nope." Francie held up a bag from Big Daddy's Bakery. "We already picked it up. But you can carry that heavy bag into my downstairs bedroom."

"Don't drop that computer," cautioned Eunice again.

"What's with all the TV crews?" asked Francie.

"They're after Mars because he was the last person known to see Abby."

"So?" asked Francie.

"I guess they're hoping there will be a development and they don't want to miss it." I carried the suitcase to the guest bedroom in the back of Francie's house. Duke, the golden retriever, accompanied me.

The bedroom was small but very sweet. Francie had painted it a soft blue that matched two curtains featuring red and brown birds. I placed the suitcase on a white luggage rack and stared at it. It was brown leather, definitely a few decades old. I wasn't sure they made luggage like that anymore.

But something was bothering me about it. I looked at the blue walls and remembered the blue suitcase that an elderly man had pulled out of the water. What was his name? I doubted that the suitcase had any connection to Abby or Mia, but it was worth a phone call to him. Maybe he had found something interesting inside.

I stopped in Francie's cozy dining room, where they were unpacking their breakfast. It also served as a home library. Francie and her husband had installed walls of bookshelves around the room.

"I met a guy at the river the other day and I'm trying to remember his name. I'm pretty sure the first name was Sam, but I can't remember his last name."

Eunice said, "The only Sam I know was a guy I worked with. We used to call him Sam Bambam."

"Bamberger! That's it. That's the guy."

"He's a doll," said Eunice. "Too bad I wasn't with you. I'd like to see old Sam again."

"Do you have his phone number?" I asked.

"Isn't he a little bit old for you?" Eunice

raised her eyebrows.

"He found a suitcase in the Potomac. Now I'm wondering what he found inside."

They looked at me blankly. It took a minute to sink in.

"I wonder if any of Abby's luggage is missing." Eunice's mouth pulled tight.

"Maybe Benton would be able to tell," I said. "He must know what her luggage looks like. It probably has nothing to do with Abby, but we should check."

"I'll contact him right after we have breakfast."

"Would you like to join us?" asked Francie. "We have plenty."

My hand flew up to cover my mouth. "Mars! I was making him coffee. I forgot all about him."

I flew out the door and over to my house.

Mars was in the kitchen drinking coffee. "Where have you been?"

I explained about Eunice while I popped a loaf of frozen bread into the oven and started frying eggs and cooking bacon.

Mars gazed out the window. "I wonder where Wesley and Stu were the night Mia died and Abby left."

"Didn't you keep track of Wesley's schedule?"

"Whoever killed Charlene did it after eight

259

o'clock at night. Wesley didn't have an evening engagement that night. Think you could ask Tilly what he was doing? I'd like to know if he has an alibi."

"Do you think they could have planned it together?" I asked. "Tilly made sure she had an alibi. She probably knew Abby was going out to dinner with you, giving Wesley time to sneak into Abby's house and wait for her. I bet they planned an alibi for Wesley, too."

"Better put on more eggs. Bernie and Nina are on their way over."

I pulled out another frying pan and poured some oil in it to heat.

Mars opened the kitchen door for them. "Fried eggs okay with you guys?"

"I smell bacon." Nina made a beeline for the kitchen island and poured two mugs of coffee.

"Are you ever coming home?" Bernie handed Mars a laptop computer.

"As soon as the press leaves."

"They're asking me if you murdered . . . let me get this straight, *Why did Mars murder his former employer's lover?*"

"Now they think Wesley had an affair with Mia? That sounds awful. At least it wasn't Mia I went out with. Why aren't they pursuing her husband?" asked Mars. "Don't answer that. I know how it works." To Bernie and Nina, he said, "Wesley and Stu are trying to place blame on me."

"Would they be wicked enough to make up evidence?" I slid eggs onto plates and Bernie carried them over to the table.

"What do you mean?" asked Mars.

"They could claim one of them saw you leaving Abby's house late at night. Or tell Wolf that you confessed to them and that's why you were fired," I said.

Mars looked a little green.

I removed the bread from the oven, and Nina took a deep breath. "There's just nothing better than bread!" she said. "Except maybe bread that's still warm from the oven." She found a serrated knife and a bread board while I retrieved butter, apple butter, and blackberry jam from the fridge.

When we sat down to eat, I noticed that Bernie had a pad of paper and a pen. "What's that about?"

"Mars always tells us that we have to stick to the facts."

Nina picked up a slice of bread and slathered it with apple butter. "Well, I think Abby is dead."

"That is not a *fact,*" pointed out Bernie.

"It sort of is. No cat lover would have abandoned her cat like that. The cat dishes were gone. The carrier was in the middle of the living room, which indicates to me that she was planning to take him with her. But she didn't, ergo, Abby is deceased."

"That's quite a theory," said Bernie. "But as you may recall, I have three cats and the mere appearance of the cat carrier is sufficient to cause all three of them to vanish instantly. How do you know that her cat didn't hide from her?"

Nina flashed him an annoyed look and chomped down on the piece of crusty bread.

"Who else besides Mars is a suspect?" Bernie ate a bite of egg.

Mars hid behind his coffee mug and looked upset. "Wesley and Stu Jericho."

"Motive?" asked Bernie.

"Unknown. But they're hiding something, or they wouldn't have fired me."

"Abby?" I suggested. "We don't know much about her relationship with Mia, but maybe they had an argument?"

"Considering that Abby disappeared, I suppose we have to add her to the list," Bernie said.

"What now?" asked Mars. "How do we prove any of this? I have suggested that Sophie spy on Wesley and Jericho."

"Isn't it funny that they want me to get information from Wolf?" I asked.

Nina laughed. "You're a double agent!

Will you provide them with misinformation?"

"Ha ha. So not funny. I am not Benton Bergeron."

"Benton!" Bernie scribbled his name on the list. "Of course, he's a suspect. I forgot all about him. Is he a spy?"

I told them about his odd behavior of picking up a soda can out of the trash.

Bernie's eyes grew. "You're serious, then. He really is a spy."

"No way," Mars grumbled. "Soph, if he were a spy, you never would have seen him do that."

"But what if Sophie is right? A spy would know how to kill someone," said Nina. "Aren't they trained to do that? Like in the movies?"

We gazed at one another. Clearly, we didn't know.

"In any event, we need to keep an eye on Benton." Bernie placed a star by his name.

My door knocker sounded at that moment. I jumped up and went to the door but noted that Daisy didn't bark. When I opened it, Duke barged inside, followed by Eunice, Francie, and Sam Bamberger, who carried the blue suitcase he had caught.

CHAPTER 25

Dear Sophie,
I'm divorced and retired. It's just me in the house, so I don't keep a lot of food around. I buy what I think I'll eat in the next few days. But people keep dropping in on me. If I knew they were coming, I would stop at the bakery for something to serve them. How do I handle this?

Lousy Hostess in Sweet Home,
Oregon

Dear Lousy Hostess,
Cupcakes and cookies are the friend of every hostess. Bake them and keep them in the freezer. Frozen cookie dough can be baked quickly for a treat. Cupcakes, complete with frosting, are even easier. At room temperature, they will thaw and be ready to serve in forty-five minutes.

Sophie

"We thought we'd come over and open the suitcase in front of you." Francie paused in the foyer and peered in the kitchen. "I hope we're not interrupting your breakfast."

Sam shook my hand. "I never thought I'd see you again!"

"I'm glad you kept the suitcase. Did Eunice explain why we'd like to see it?"

"I had a hunch. When I heard that lady was in the freezer, I wondered if it could belong to her."

"Did you find a name inside?" I asked.

"Nope. Clean as a whistle. Maybe she didn't know she should put her name inside the suitcase, or maybe she took it out on purpose."

Francie frowned at him. "Why would a person do that?"

He tilted his head. "Because she didn't want anyone to know the contents belonged to her?"

I ushered Eunice and Sam into the living room. Leaving the two of them to catch up, I hurried back to the kitchen to make more coffee and tea.

I reached into the freezer and pulled out my favorite harvest cupcakes with caramel frosting that I had baked and stashed away so I wouldn't gobble them all up. I set them on a two-tiered tray and carried it into the living room. Nina followed me with a tray of mugs, napkins, sugar, and milk. I retrieved the coffee and tea, and it felt like an impromptu party.

When we were settled, Sam pulled on gloves and opened the suitcase with all the fanfare of a special gift.

"I took the items out to air-dry. Mostly it's just clothes." He unfolded the skirt I had seen when he first opened the suitcase at the park. He removed each item with reverence. But it was when he took out a long-sleeved blue jean dress with a tie belt that Eunice moaned.

"It's Abby's. I know that dress for sure. It was one of her favorites."

Nina said, "It's not an unusual style. I bet they sold hundreds of those dresses."

"Keep going, Sam," said Eunice. "Maybe there's something else I'll recognize."

Sam continued to remove clothing. For the most part it was T-shirts, jeans, and skirts. Nothing that would be readily identifiable.

"Can't they get DNA off these clothes?" I mused. "If they can establish Abby's DNA through items in her home, then we would know if the suitcase and contents belong to her."

Sam nodded. "You're exactly right,

266

Sophie. But they're so behind in testing for known crimes that I don't think anyone could get them to do that kind of test. If the suitcase had blood on it or was found at the crime scene, that might be different. Even if they established that this suitcase belongs to Abby, it wouldn't mean anything. It could have been in the river for months. Long before the last time she was seen."

"But why would that happen?" Francie peeled the paper off a cupcake. "I can't say that I have ever been inclined to pack my clothes in a suitcase and throw it into the Potomac. The mere thought of it has never entered my mind."

"Mine either." Nina settled back in her chair. "We have to talk Wolf into dragging the river. Or at least sending a diver down where you found the suitcase. What if Abby is down there?"

"Then things will look far worse for me," muttered Mars.

I was still stuck on what Sam had said. He was probably correct about no one bothering to check DNA on the suitcase. It was common sense, really. But there was something about the confidence with which he had said it. "Sam, are you a retired police officer?"

"Oh my, no! I worked for the government."

In Old Town, most people meant the federal government when they said it that way. I eyed Eunice, who was busy snuggling with Mochie. Hadn't she said that she worked with Sam? I was about to ask but decided I might get more information if I could catch her off guard and out of the presence of so many people. I hadn't known that she worked at all. I thought she was the proverbial heiress who spent her days concerned with philanthropy. It was certainly a curious development but had nothing to do with the matter at hand.

"Look at the time," exclaimed Francie. "We'd better get home." She smiled at me. "We can't be late for Schuyler and Briley."

"They are such a delight." Eunice looked like a new person. Getting out and being with people had already made a difference in her.

"And now we're getting Sam Bambam involved in their project."

Sam had packed everything back into the suitcase with care. He carried it with him. "Thank you for your hospitality, Sophie. I wasn't sure I would see you again, but I'm glad I have."

"Me too, Sam. Watch out for Francie and

Eunice. Don't let them drag you into trouble," I joked.

"It's too late," he whispered. "They already have."

Nina and Bernie helped Mars and me clean up the kitchen. Before long they were off to who knows where, and Mars settled in the den with his laptop. Eager to finish the cookbook project, I took the recipe pages to my computer.

It hadn't occurred to me before then that Abby must have the originals on her computer. And Abby, wherever she was, had taken her computer with her. I hated to have to re-create everything. I quickly checked to see if I could scan documents and make them editable. It turned out to be possible. I wasted an hour scanning all the recipes, but once it was done, all I had to do was add cute stories about them as though I were Tilly.

I phoned Tilly to ask if I could come over to chat. She readily agreed. I slid my laptop and wallet into a bag.

On my way out, I checked on Mars. He was lying on the sofa with his knees bent and the laptop propped up against his thighs. Mochie snoozed on the back of the sofa, and Daisy had curled up on the other end of the sofa near Mars's feet. I felt a little bit left out! "I'm going over to Tilly's."

"Great. I want you to pay particular attention to any names they mention. Oh! If you can, start the video on your camera to record them. Just be sure to turn the screen away so they won't know it's on."

"Excuse me, but isn't that illegal?"

"Sophie, they're trying to blame me for a murder I had nothing to do with. Isn't *that* illegal?"

I got his point. "I should be back in a couple of hours." I walked to the kitchen door.

"If they catch you, tell them you must have hit *video* by mistake."

I made sure the door was locked behind me. Wesley and Jericho weren't going to catch me, because I had no intentions of illegally taping anyone. I strolled along wondering how Charlene was doing when I spied Benton Bergeron very deftly placing something into an aged brick fence and hiding it by shoving a partial brick back into the hole.

I could hardly believe my eyes. He didn't see me and briskly walked away toward a lamppost, which he casually scraped with his right hand at hip level. If I hadn't been watching him so carefully, I would never have noticed what he did.

While I wanted to stop and search for the loose brick in the fence, I hurried to catch up so I wouldn't lose sight of Benton. I took my eyes off him when I passed the lamppost. He had left a horizontal white mark on it. It appeared to be chalk. I touched it with my finger. It felt like chalk and smeared. What was he doing?

When I looked up, I'd lost sight of him. Gazing around, I hurried forward.

"Hi, Sophie!" Benton smiled and stepped out of a recessed doorway that led to a restaurant. "It's nice to see you again."

271

CHAPTER 26

Dear Sophie,
I write a cooking blog. I'm having such fun with it. I love taking photos of the dishes I create. But my family teases me unmercifully about the photos of casseroles. I bake a lot of casseroles! How can I make them look good?

Southern Cook in Bean Station,
Tennessee

Dear Southern Cook,
Take the photograph of the entire casserole before you serve it. Place it on a pretty tablecloth and use coordinating colors. I vote against photos of casseroles once they have been served. They tend to fall apart. While they taste delicious, they're no longer very pretty.

Sophie

Chills ran through me. Benton had caught

me. He knew perfectly well that I was following him! "Nice to see you, too."

It was broad daylight on a busy street. Unless he put a gun to my head and forced me into a dark alley, I should be fine. I pretended nothing was amiss. "I'm sorry Mars dragged me off so quickly after Natasha's party."

"Me too. Was it the emergency he claimed?"

"Sort of. It was about Abby. We thought they'd found her."

His expression changed. "Really? Why didn't anyone notify me about this?"

I waved my palms at him. Maybe Wolf didn't want him to know they had found her phone. "It . . . wasn't her." That was actually the truth. I may have said it in a manner that was misleading, but I couldn't help that. "You haven't heard from her?"

"Not a word. They took the crime scene tape off her house. But she hasn't been in touch with me. I was watching you and Mars at Natasha's party. I wish Abby and I could reach that stage and be friends. Our divorce wasn't hateful. But I guess we both carry some baggage. You know how it is."

Did I? Hadn't Abby said something to Tilly about people being products of the past? "What kind of baggage does Abby have?"

"Old stuff that happened over a decade ago. Life leaves scars on everyone. They're just not always visible."

How was I going to get him to tell me? "I heard she was from Wisconsin. Does she still have relatives there?"

"I don't think so. Maybe distant cousins. She was an only child, and her parents passed when she was quite young. It was truly tragic. Very difficult for her. I think we probably stayed married longer than we should have because she felt very much alone in the world."

"How sad for her."

"Indeed. Where are you off to?"

Warning flags waved in my head. Was he going to try to sneak up on me? "On my way to a job."

"Oh. I shouldn't keep you then. How about dinner tomorrow?"

"Tomorrow?" I choked out. "I'm kind of tied up this week. Maybe another time?"

"Are you and Mars getting back together?"

Had he been spying on my house? Maybe he got that idea at the party. "No. Nothing like that. I'd better get going." I took off at a good clip and walked down the block toward a restaurant I knew well. I strode in as if it was my intended destination. Of course, I tried to surreptitiously look back at him when I entered. He was following me!

I ducked farther into the restaurant, hoping he wouldn't dare come inside. He didn't. I sighed with relief when I saw him walk past. Of course, two could play this game. I peeked out of the door. Had he darted into a store to wait for me to pass by?

Ha! I could deal with the likes of Benton Bergeron. I doubled back and took a side street toward Tilly's house. The coast appeared to be clear the whole way.

Tilly opened the door with a smile. "I have to thank you for setting up Briley and Schuyler with your friends. I don't know what kind of magic they worked, but Schuyler is almost back to her old self. Wesley is still leery, of course, but he's such a worrywart about everything."

I followed Tilly to the kitchen, glancing at the living room on the way. There was no sign of Wesley.

While I settled on the sofa and pulled out my laptop, Tilly brought pumpkin lattes and spiced cookies to the coffee table.

For the next two hours, I asked her about

the origins of various recipes. She told me tales about her grandmother and various aunts who all loved to cook and bake.

"Grandma Peggy was a hoot. She always said what she thought. There was no talking behind anyone's back with her. One day, she came right out and told my aunt Alice that she made a lousy pumpkin cake. There was stunned silence in the room. But Aunt Alice was very much like her mother, Grandma Peggy, and right there in front of us she challenged Grandma Peggy to a pumpkin cake contest. My mom had that same streak in her, and she joined in the fun. Suddenly it seemed as if the whole family was in on the contest. A month later, we all met with our cakes. We brought in outsiders who wouldn't recognize our cake dishes and hadn't been involved in the testing that went on in our homes. It was one of the most fun parties we ever had. The judges voted and, wouldn't you just know, Grandma Peggy won! After that, she was always the champion baker in the family, a title that she pulled out quite frequently lest we forget."

"Your grandmother and aunts sound delightful. It must be hard for you to live so far away from them."

"It is. There are times I'd like to fly down

to Texas, but a lot of them aren't there anymore. We've scattered throughout the country. I come from a family that always celebrates with food. Doesn't everyone? I try to keep that up in my own little family now. When Briley gets an A on a difficult test, I make her favorite mac and cheese. And to tell you the truth, Wesley and I have been to so many fund-raisers and wonderful events that it's a treat for us to stay home with family and gather around the table for a delicious meal. We can take our time and laugh together and hear what mischief Briley has been up to. Don't write this, but it's so much better than a piece of dried-up chicken breast at a function."

"Do you want a little introduction to each of the recipes or just some of them?" I asked.

"I think using them on selected recipes will have more impact. And we want to leave room for photographs, of course."

"Okay. I can't believe I'm saying this, but I think we're about to wrap up my part of this in the next couple of days. I'll add your wonderful stories and bring the pages over to you. You can make any changes you like. I promise I won't be offended. Massage them to sound like Tilly. I'll edit the pages, and you can take it from there with the food stylists and photographers."

Tilly frowned at me. "What does the stylist do?"

"I believe they re-create the recipe so it can be photographed. They focus on making it appear fabulous."

"I've heard of that. Oh no! They are not using motor oil on my food!"

"I don't think that's the norm, although I understand they use some unconventional methods to make food look great."

"Like what?"

"They might use a red jelly to give something a reddish glaze, or maybe soy sauce can add to the browned look on a roast. Things like that. You'll have to take it up with your stylist."

Tilly looked me in the eyes. "I didn't know how to put this, but I want you to know that I'm devastated that Wesley fired Mars. We're both very fond of Mars." She leaned toward me and whispered, "I don't trust Stu Jericho, and I have said as much to Wesley. He wanted Mars out for some reason, and it troubles me no end."

I didn't say anything.

"Wesley hasn't been himself. He's not sleeping, and he barely eats. It won't do him any harm to lose a few pounds, but I feel like there's something very bad going on.

He's been so short-tempered, which is very unlike him. It started when Abby left and has grown progressively worse, especially after Mars was fired."

"Do you think Jericho is giving him bad advice?"

"I wish Wesley would talk to me about that."

"Could Jericho have had anything to do with Abby?" I wondered if I should ask what I wanted to know. Maybe this was the right time to put it out there. "I know Abby was dating Mars. Is it possible that she had something going on with Wesley?"

Tilly didn't react the way I had expected. There was no shock, feigned or otherwise. She didn't protest or cry. "Don't think I haven't considered that possibility. Abby was very fond of Wesley. A lot of people are. He's an extremely approachable and affable person. It's what makes him a good politician. Everyone feels like they know him. But I have wondered if Abby's interest in Wesley got out of hand. I don't relish the thought. Mia warned me about it. I thought she was exaggerating. But now I'm not so sure."

"Have you asked him?"

"Asked him what? 'Dear, did you have an affair with Abby and murder her to get rid of her or did you pay her off?' "

I chuckled. "That wasn't quite what I had in mind, but it would certainly get his attention!" She'd told me before, but I wanted to see if she stuck to her story. And specifically, I wanted to know where Wesley was that evening. "What did you and Wesley do the Friday night that Mia was murdered?"

"Abby left here around four in the afternoon. She was agitated. Oh my. Do you think she and Wesley had a fight? Right under my nose?"

I tried to steer her back to Wesley's whereabouts. "What else happened?"

"There was a football game that night, so I drove Briley and some of her friends." Her words slowed as if she was mulling something over while she spoke. "Wesley wasn't interested, but I thought it was important for at least one parent to keep an eye on them. Afterward I took them all out for pizza and burgers. I love hearing them chatter. They're at that age where they think they're grown up and they know everything. It was at least eleven or so by the time we got home."

"Was Jericho still here?"

"No. But neither was Wesley. He came home about fifteen minutes later."

"Oh?"

Her eyes met mine. "That means he has

no alibi." She shook her head vigorously and covered her eyes for a moment. "No. I'm sure he was with someone. I shall ask him tonight. Wesley had no reason to kill Mia. That's ridiculous."

"I'm sure you're right," I said as soothingly as I could, even if I wasn't as convinced as she wanted to be. "I'll give you a call when I'm done with these pages."

I walked home feeling sad for Tilly. She was a lovely person, but she had some sort of major problem with Wesley. I hoped they would sort it out and that it didn't involve murder.

I passed my own house and went straight to Francie's side door.

"We were just talking about Abby," she said. "Come join us."

Eunice sat at the long farmhouse table in the dining room that was part of Francie's kitchen. Her laptop was open in front of her. "I know that was her dress. Do you think we could ask Benton to look at the contents? He might recognize other clothes."

I slid into a chair at the table. "I believe he would agree to that. But . . . there's something weird about Benton."

CHAPTER 27

Dear Natasha,
My little boy complains about the sandwiches I make for him to take to school. He says the bread is always soggy. How does one avoid that?

Billy's Mom in Toast,
North Carolina

Dear Billy's Mom,
Spread both slices of bread with mayonnaise or a dressing. The fat keeps any water inside from being absorbed by the bread.

Natasha

Francie leaned toward me. "Do tell!"
I explained about seeing him pick a soda can out of a public trash can. "And today he hid something in a brick wall, and as he walked along the street, he marked a lamppost with chalk."

Eunice laughed as if I'd told her something very amusing. "That's called a dead drop."

"That's what Wolf said."

"Sure. You leave a message for someone, but you never actually interact with that person. Though I must say I'm surprised you noticed him doing that. He'll be caught in no time if he's that poor at his job." Eunice lay a finger across her lips. "Shh. Let's not mention that to him, shall we?"

"Why Eunice Crenshaw! You little sneak. How do you know so much about spying?" I leaned back against the chair, beginning to form my own suspicions about her.

"I read a lot."

"About spies?" I asked.

"That and other things. Sophie, sweetheart, Washington is full of people who know secrets and have boring covers. We are silly with spies in this town. There must be at least ten agencies in Washington with spies. The CIA is loaded with employees. Not to mention all the embassies and consulates that belong to countries all over the world. And don't forget the foreigners who are spies with no diplomatic cover, leading normal lives like they're Americans. They can be quite difficult to spot."

"You seem to know a lot about this,

Eunice. Where did you and Sam work?" I asked.

Eunice smiled. "It was a long time ago. We were so young and eager." She lifted her forefinger and waved it. "Here's how you recognize a spy. First and foremost, with a few exceptions, they won't be eye-catching people. Your friend Natasha, for instance. We know she's not a spy because she does her level best to draw attention to herself. A spy will live quietly and be somewhat plain in the sense that they don't wear fancy watches or drive Ferraris."

"That makes sense," said Francie.

"They are often gone for long periods of time, so you won't find them involved in anything that could tie them down like the PTA or a condo association. Sometimes they need to leave quickly. Oh! And you'll *never* see them on Facebook. No cutesy shots of them at the Eiffel Tower or eating fondue in Switzerland."

"You and Sam worked for the CIA." I said it straight to her face.

"We've been retired for decades. And we weren't in the clandestine service." She was silent for a moment. "Most of the time, anyway. I was young when I applied as a secretary. It was all very exciting."

"Then you think Benton is an inept spy.

284

What was with the chalk? Why did he do that?"

"You leave a chalk mark on something so the other person knows you've left a message in the hiding place. Chalk washes off quickly and easily. Sometimes two marks have a special meaning. I'm glad you told us about this. Now I understand the divorce. Those long absences can put a real strain on a marriage."

"What if Abby learned something she shouldn't have known?" I speculated. "We have to tell Wolf. Maybe Benton killed Abby to save his job or to stop her from revealing information that she might have learned."

"Wolf might already know. It depends on what Benton's cover is and whether he's an operations officer."

"What do you mean?" asked Francie.

"Some employees can admit that they work for the CIA. There are a lot of accountants, and human resource employees, just like in other big companies. But if he's an operations officer, what you think of as a spy, then he'll have a very good cover and even the police may not realize who he really is. Poor Abby. I hope she's hiding somewhere, but as the days go by, I fear the worst."

Francie snorted. "If the murderer meant

to kill Abby, why didn't he put her in the freezer, too?"

"Not enough room?" suggested Eunice.

"Eunice," I said, "something bad happened in Abby's past. Benton sidestepped me when I asked about it, but he said it left scars. Did she ever tell you about an incident?"

"Maybe she was a spy, too?" Eunice smiled. "Francie, we really must invite Benton for tea and a suitcase examination. Perhaps Wolf could come as well."

"I think you'd better invite Wolf for your own safety if you do that. And me too." I stretched. "I'm off to finish up these recipes for Tilly."

"Did you ever unravel her code?" asked Eunice.

"It irritates me every time I see a recipe with the code on it. If we ever find Abby, that's the first thing I'm going to ask her about."

I left Francie's house through the back door. When my garage was built, we had installed a gate in the fence between our houses. I used it now to go home.

I let myself in and Mars bolted into the kitchen. "Oh, it's you."

"And I'm pleased to see you, too. What's going on?"

286

Mars yawned. "The Internet is a scary thing. I finally got onto the dark web. There's a lot of creepy stuff on there."

"You think Wesley is involved in the dark web?"

"I don't know yet. Did you know the dark web was started by mathematicians that worked for the government? That sounds so innocent, doesn't it?"

"Mars, what did you and Abby talk about on your date the night she vanished?"

Mars sat down at the kitchen table with me. "Just stuff. She talked about Benton a lot. You know how people are when a divorce is still fresh. Their lives were tied up with their spouses for so long that that's all they talk about."

"Did she say the kind of things I would say about you? Or that she feared him? Or that he grows orchids?"

"Regular stuff. I don't think she was over him."

"Then she wasn't afraid of him."

Mars stared at me. "She was jumpy. We ate at The Laughing Hound and, unlike you, she absolutely definitely did not want dessert."

I couldn't help smirking. "Your waitress said that's the sign of a bad date."

"She's probably right. Neither of us tried

287

to escape through the back deck or anything, but she was distant."

"That was your second date. How did the
first one go?"

"Do I detect a note of jealousy?"

"No! I'm trying to figure out what was
going on with Abby."

"We met for coffee. No big thing. No pressure. It was okay or I wouldn't have asked
her to dinner."

"So she was jumpy. Did you ask her if
something was wrong?"

He was getting irritated with me. "No, I
didn't ask her. I, uh . . . if you must know, I
thought she didn't like me."

"Maybe that's why she didn't ask you in
for coffee when you walked her home. Do
you think the killer was already there?"

"If he was, I did not see or hear him. Abby
unlocked the front door, thanked me for
dinner, and that was it. I went home. You're
worse than Wolf. I still don't understand
what you're getting at."

"Abby was agitated at Tilly's house that
day. And then she was jumpy at dinner. So
obviously something was wrong."

"And that would be why she left. This is
nothing new, Soph."

"I wish she had told someone about it."

"Maybe she shared it with Charlene."

I shot him a dirty look. "Someone who is conscious."

"What would *you* do if you were afraid?"

That was an interesting approach. "I guess I probably wouldn't leave unless I thought my life was in danger. I wonder why she went out to dinner with you."

"Thank you so much. You flatter me so. Because I'm a charming and interesting guy."

"Uh-huh. I meant, if she was so scared that she felt the need to flee, then why did she waste time going out to dinner with you?"

"More flattery. I can hardly take it."

"Be serious. She must have thought she was safe with you in a public place. But when she got home, or maybe during dinner, she decided to flee. Or did she know she would have to murder Mia? That would make me very nervous."

"Great. You think I was supposed to be her alibi?"

"I wish she had left us a message. Are you sure she wasn't trying to tell you something during dinner? You can be kind of obtuse."

"I beg your pardon? I was gracious and gentlemanly."

"You're sure she didn't write something

on a napkin and shove it across the table to you?"

"I think even one as obtuse as me would notice *that*."

"Did you check your pockets?"

"Yes! I do that after every date in the hope that my companion left a love letter. Sophie! You're throwing around wild and crazy ideas."

"I'll be right back." I hurried to my office and fetched the recipes. On my return to the kitchen, Mars was peering in the refrigerator.

"Is there anything in here that I can heat up? I haven't had lunch."

"Neither have I. There's some sliced turkey from the deli."

"Perfect." Mars picked up a bottle. "Sparkling apple cider. Is this alcoholic?"

"No."

"Great," he said. "I have a lot more work to do. What are you looking for?"

"Maybe Abby did leave a message, but I haven't been smart enough to figure it out. Eunice said the codes on the recipes look like the kind where two people use the same book to decipher them."

"Why do I think Wolf wouldn't let us into Abby's house to look through all her books? And who would she have left the message for? There would have to be another person who would understand and know where to look," said Mars, irritation creeping into his tone.

"Like Wesley?" I asked.

His eyes met mine briefly before he returned to his earnest task of building sandwiches so thick with turkey, cheese, tomatoes, and lettuce that we wouldn't be able to bite into them. "Does Wesley know about the codes?" he asked.

"I haven't said anything to him, but I asked Tilly about them. She could have told him."

"A book." Mars gestured toward me. "If it were you, what book would you use as a key?" He brought the sandwiches to the table with two tall glasses of sparkling cider.

"One that wouldn't attract attention. A book I could carry with me without raising eyebrows or causing people to notice me. Like an Agatha Christie book."

"Swell, she wrote dozens of books. How would we ever figure out which one it was?"

"Abby would have to use a book that Wesley had access to," I mused.

Our eyes met. "Tilly's cookbook," we whispered simultaneously.

"It's perfect. She could leave messages in it for him and no one would notice. Except . . ." I tried to recall what Tilly had said. "I think she took it home with her each day. It was only that last day that she left it there. Because she knew she wasn't coming back, or so Wesley could read the message she left for him?"

Mars bit into his sandwich and grabbed the cookbook pages. He glanced at the list of codes I had written. "We used to do this for fun when my brother and I were kids. Okay, how does it work? What does the first letter stand for?"

"If I knew that, I would have already unraveled the code."

"There are no page numbers."

I bit into a sandwich. Either it was pretty good, or I was way hungrier than I thought.

"*GPP251,*" he read aloud. "Does that mean anything to you?"

Clearly it didn't. But as I swallowed, a thought came to me. "Grandma Peggy's Pumpkin Bundt Cake. GPP."

Mars flipped through the recipes. "Got it! So if the numbers are a guide, then the first two would be the line? And the last number would be the letter? No. That doesn't seem to work."

"Oh, this is going to be tedious."

"Maybe not. According to your list, there are only twelve codes."

I examined the list of codes. "Hold everything! Look, the last numbers go from one to twelve. Maybe that's the order of the letters? Go to line one."

"I'm there."

"What's the fifth letter?"

"That would be P. So according to your theory, P would be the first letter in the message."

"Right." I put my sandwich down. "What's the next one?"

"R P C one four two."

"Roasted Parmesan Chicken."

"That would give us an E."

"PE? Oh gosh. I hope this doesn't have anything to do with Grandma Peggy!"

We worked our way through the letters. The result was PEYTONPOULON.

"What's that supposed to mean?" Mars squinted at the letters.

"Maybe something on the Internet can descramble it."

Mars borrowed my laptop and typed PEYTONPOULON into the Google search bar. "It's a name!"

CHAPTER 28

Dear Sophie,
I read recently that a guest should never bring anything to a dinner party. That goes against everything I was taught. Is that the new rule?

Party Pooper in Five Forks,
South Carolina

Dear Party Pooper,
It is always gracious to bring a hostess gift to a dinner party. Wine is the most conventional item. Whatever you bring, even if it's your favorite wine, do not expect your hostess to serve it. He or she may have a carefully planned menu with specific wines chosen for the dishes being served. An exception would be if you have severe allergies or other food issues. It can be smart to bring a dish you can share with the others.

Sophie

"There are a bunch of articles about Peyton Poulon." I jumped to my feet and looked over his shoulder. I read aloud. *"A young woman who contacted police in the belief that she might be Peyton Poulon is not the missing girl. DNA has confirmed that the young woman is not the biological child of Hannah and Kurt Poulon. Peyton was abducted at age two from the home of her babysitter, Abigail Jensen."*

"Could that be our Abby? Or does this mean Abby is actually Peyton?" Mars opened a new tab and searched the name Abigail Jensen. A grainy newspaper image of Abigail Jensen came up immediately."

"Is that her?" I asked, returning to my sparkling cider.

Mars huffed. "I can't believe this. It's definitely her. She looks older now, of course. Abigail Jensen is Abby Bergeron. She kidnapped a child!"

"It said the child was stolen from her home," I corrected.

Mars read aloud. *"Abigail Jensen was arrested yesterday for the abduction of two-year-old Peyton Poulon, who has been missing from a suburb of Milwaukee. Peyton was in the care of Jensen at the time of her disappearance. Anyone with information on the whereabouts of Peyton is requested to notify* the authorities."

"Arrested? I think we now know what that burden from her past was."

"The next one says, *'Abigail Jensen is out on bond in the matter of the disappearance of Peyton Poulon. Hannah and Kurt Poulon, Peyton's parents, have issued the following statement. 'We live with the hope that Peyton is still alive and well. If she is in your care, please return her to her loving family. If you have any information at all as to her whereabouts, we beg of you to notify the police immediately. An anonymous hotline is available.'* "

He continued, "Finally, there's one that says, *'Police have dropped all charges against Abigail Jensen in the matter of the kidnapping of two-year-old Peyton Poulon due to lack of evidence. The case remains open, and police continue to investigate.'* "

"So she got off! Maybe she didn't do it. But why would she write Peyton's name in code?"

"She was obviously trying to alert someone. But why write the code? Why not tell someone?" asked Mars. "She could have told me at dinner. That would have been a lot more interesting than her stories about Benton."

Mars shook his head. "This is crazy. The

code is probably meaningless and we're reading something into it that was never intended. Plus, it's stupid to leave a message in code. Most people would have thrown these codes out. Who would have noticed them besides the next ghostwriter?"

"It wasn't the best choice, but maybe she thought Benton would see them. There *is* a chance that he's a spy."

Mars laughed. "Will you stop with that? He's not a spy."

"I told you about the Coke can in the trash."

"That was strange but I don't think it means he's a spy. But I'll grant you that he clearly likes to play games." Mars sat back and mused. "He's quite sociable. I enjoyed his company at Natasha's dinner."

"I'm going to call Wolf." I pulled out my phone and pressed his number on the keypad.

He answered right away.

"I think Abby may have left a message."

"Like a note? You're just now finding it?"

"It's complicated. I think you should see it."

"I'll be by shortly."

I cleaned up the kitchen and made a pot of coffee. When he didn't show up right away, I busied myself by creating an apple tart using store-bought puff pastry. While it baked, I whipped sweetened cream to spoon on top of each slice.

Mars sat at the banquette, concentrating on a computer search.

Wolf arrived just as I was taking the tart out of the oven. He took a deep breath. "I smell cinnamon."

"You've timed your visit perfectly," I said, getting out vintage dessert plates and matching coffee cups, which were white in the center with a scalloped blue edge.

I placed a slice on each plate, poured the coffee, and brought it all to the table with a bowl of sweetened whipped cream. I added napkins, dessert forks, spoons, cream, and sugar.

"It's not often I receive this kind of service when investigating a murder," said Wolf.

"I'm surprised you came at all after Sophie's ill-thought-out request to check the blood in Abby's house against Charlene's blood," said Mars.

I sat down to join them.

Wolf's mouth twisted to the side. "Turns out I may have been hasty about that. We did the comparison in a four-hour DNA tester that we're trying out, and Sophie was right. They're a match. Unless Charlene bled at Abby's house some other time, it's likely she was present when Mia was murdered."

Mars's eyes met mine.

"Do you think Charlene murdered Mia?" I was having trouble wrapping my head around that development.

"Last night your theory was that Fred Conway beat up Charlene and that Abby is in hiding." Mars ate a bite of the tart.

"To be honest, it complicates matters." Wolf held his coffee cup and looked at me. "Where's this message you found from Abby?"

Mars and I showed him the codes Abby had written and explained how they worked. "And it spells out *Peyton Poulon,* who was kidnapped at age two while she was in Abby's care."

Mars opened his laptop and turned it so Wolf could see the screen.

Wolf laid his fork on his dessert plate. Silently, he read the brief articles about Abby being arrested and released. He ate the rest of his apple tart and gulped coffee.

His phone buzzed. He glanced at it and grinned. "There are a lot of sleuths in your neighborhood."

"Nina or Francie?" I asked.

"Both." Wolf looked from me to Mars. "Think you two can keep this under your

299

hats for the time being? If, and I emphasize *if,* Abby discovered Peyton and her kidnapper living among us, we don't want said kidnapper to find out and bolt. And there's the issue of the kid finding out. We would need a DNA confirmation and a psychologist to break the news to her. This isn't something we can blab about. Understood?"

Mars held his palms up in the air. "No problem here."

"Sophie?" asked Wolf.

"Of course. The kidnapper did a great job staying under the radar for thirteen years. We don't want that to happen again."

"I'm sorry to run, but I need to check out a few things and I have to stop by Francie's place. Good work, you two!" He rose from his chair. "Thanks for lunch."

He wasn't looking as tired anymore. Peyton Poulon, whoever she was, had invigorated him. "Do you think they would mind if I came with you?" I asked.

"Probably not. It's something about a suitcase."

We left Mars in the kitchen and departed through the French doors in my living room. Outside, we used the gate in the fence that surrounded my house.

Francie opened the kitchen door, where we found Benton Bergeron looking bereft.

He sat at the farmhouse-style table between Eunice and Sam. The suitcase lay on
top of the table, open wide so the contents
could be seen.

Eunice introduced Sam to Wolf. I hung
back, staying quiet so I wouldn't interfere.

Benton said bluntly, "It's hers. There's no
question."

Wolf eyed the clothes. "How do you
know?"

"I recognize some of the contents. And I
carried this suitcase for Abby many times.
The silk scarf was a birthday gift from me
several years ago."

Eunice reached over and clutched Benton's hand. "I'm sorry, Benton."

"Sorry for what?" asked Wolf.

I was surprised by his question. Didn't
the suitcase in the water confirm that
something terrible must have happened to
Abby?

Benton licked his lips. "It's not good news
in any event. Either Abby threw her suitcase
in the river or someone else did. Either way,
it won't end well."

"Why would Abby throw her suitcase in
the river?" asked Francie.

Wolf remained mum. I thought he was
watching Benton.

Sam finally said, "Perhaps it's not as

301

ominous as you think. She might have meant to throw us off. To make it look like someone else did it so she could start a new life and we would all assume that she was deceased."

A tragic silence filled the room.

I tried to break the gloom by asking a question that had been on my mind. "Benton, Tilly told me that she overheard Abby asking if 'the squirrel had landed' on a phone call. Does that mean anything to you?"

He bowed his head for a couple of minutes as if he was composing himself. "She was talking to me. It was a silly joke between the two of us. We watched a movie once where someone used the line 'the eagle has landed' and we laughed about it. We thought in our lives it would have been a squirrel. It was just a silly thing we said. My nephew had returned from a math competition in Florida. So in this case, he was the squirrel who was back home."

Wolf excused himself to make a phone call. He returned quickly. "Please refrain from touching the suitcase or its contents. A crime scene investigator will be by this afternoon to collect it. Thank you for assisting us in this case. I'm glad you didn't throw the suitcase out, Sam. Good call."

I left with Wolf through Francie's front door. He was solemn as we stepped outside. Just before I turned left to my house, Wolf said, "Be careful, Sophie. Someone went to great lengths to prevent us from knowing about Peyton."

He was right. Just because we had unraveled Abby's message didn't mean we should let our guard down. When I walked into my kitchen, the dishes had been washed and put away, and Daisy pranced around me, letting me know that she was due for a walk. I grabbed the halter and was in the process of fastening it when Mars whooped from the den.

Daisy and I flew in to see what was going on.

Mars was grinning ear to ear. Mochie, who was curled up next to him on the sofa, had opened one eye.

"I found the connection between Jericho and Wesley. It took a little digging, but I'm onto something now."

"Does it involve Peyton?"

"No." He scowled at me like I had ruined his fun. "But they went to the same college at the same time *and* they were fraternity brothers."

CHAPTER 29

Dear Sophie,
My family loves to eat Chinese takeout
with everyone trying all the dishes. But
it grosses me out when my brother licks
his chopsticks and then sticks them in
the carton to serve himself more food.
Eww. I say he should use a serving spoon
for that. Don't you agree?
                Smart Sister in China, Texas

Dear Smart Sister,
Tell your brother that the thick ends of
his chopsticks are for helping himself to
food. The thin ends are for eating.
                                        Sophie

"Gosh, I'm sure that's illegal," I said drolly.
"Don't you see? That's why I'm sitting on
your couch and Jericho has my job. Jericho
knows Wesley's secret."

"Do you think Jericho is blackmailing Wesley?"

"It wouldn't surprise me. Don't underestimate Mars Winston. I will get to the bottom of this."

"And I shall take Daisy for a nice long walk. Thanks for doing the dishes."

I locked the kitchen door behind us when we left. As we strolled I noticed a lightpost with chalk on it. I slowed down, not wanting to be too obvious. Was there another person marking posts in Old Town? Or was that Benton's handiwork again?

A teenage boy walked past me. He glanced back and grinned. I didn't think he was smiling at me. He had a sweet boyish face with brown eyes. A curl of his unruly golden brown hair flopped onto his forehead. He turned around and ambled along the sidewalk.

I was enjoying the fall decorations. It seemed as if everyone was eager to leave summer behind. Daisy and I crossed the street and watched the same teen boy pause to eye the decorative pumpkins and dried cornstalks.

He walked up to a gatepost. A tall urn, very much like Nina's, stood beside it.

I stopped walking to observe him.

He stared at the urn briefly before lifting

a small yellow pumpkin. He snatched something from the urn, replaced the pumpkin, and strolled away.

I debated whether to shout at him. Part of me thought I should stop him, but part of me wondered what a flower urn could possibly hold that he would want.

Before I could decide, he rounded the corner and disappeared.

I hurried forward for a better look at the urn. It had a wide top. Two plants of orange mums filled the back, and on the front, straw acted as a support for the small pumpkin he had lifted. It was distinctive because of a thick and curiously curling dried vine attached to the top. I raised it. Nothing was underneath it. I flipped over the pumpkin. It looked perfectly ordinary.

I replaced the pumpkin and gazed around. Nothing appeared to be out of place or unusual. What was that about? Daisy and I walked to the corner. Numerous people went about their business, but there was no sign of the boy.

Still wondering what he had been doing, I strolled over to Eunice's house. The front door was open, so Daisy and I walked inside. The area to my left, formerly the dining room, looked like a demolition zone. I was pleased to see they hadn't ripped out the beautiful old moldings.

"May I help you?"

The man's voice came from behind and startled me. By the time I turned around, he was already squatting to pet Daisy.

"I'm Sophie, a friend of Eunice's and Francie's. I hope you don't mind. I saw the door was open and thought I'd check on your progress."

He rose to his feet and shook my hand. He had a firm grip but rough hands that let me know he did a lot of the work himself. He wore his hair cut short. Muscles strained against the short sleeves of his shirt. "Cal Simons. They said you might stop by. You're interested in renovating a bathroom?"

"I am. Maybe you could come by sometime and have a look?"

"I'd be happy to do that."

He pulled a tiny well-worn pad from his pocket and wrote my address. "As you can see, we're converting the dining room into a dual-use room. Eunice can use it as a bedroom and bathroom if she prefers to live on one floor. If she decides to sleep upstairs or sell the house, it can be used as an office or a dining room."

I followed him into a framed area.

"This will be the bathroom with a shower she can roll a wheelchair or a walker into."

I was doubtful. "Won't the water splash out?"

He grinned. "They made this great material that compresses under wheels but pops right back up to keep water from running out. She can have shower doors if she wants, but I usually recommend curtains for my elderly clients. They're easier to keep clean, and doors can get in the way. They're difficult if you're in a wheelchair."

"Sounds like you've done this a few times."

"I think my name is being passed around among older residents. I love these old houses, but they're tough if you can't negotiate stairs."

"Francie mentioned an elevator?"

"We're waiting on approval for it." He motioned for me to follow him. "I think we can fit it right here. She wouldn't lose too much space. I hope it works out. It would give her full use of the house. No more sleeping in the recliner unless she wants to nap there."

"I'm very impressed."

"So is Francie. She wants me to come over and enlarge her first-floor bedroom with a bathroom like Eunice will be getting."

"I have a feeling you'll be spending quite a bit of time on our block this fall."

"I might. You haven't even seen the best part."

He led me through the kitchen and out to the back patio. "We're getting rid of the stairs and creating an elevated deck so Eunice can come outside and get some fresh air without being afraid of falling. See where the deck box is?"

"Behind the two chairs?"

"Exactly. Right about there, it will serpentine downward to the garage and gate so she can get to her car, or someone like Francie can come to pick her up and go out on the town. And it will all be smooth concrete. No more uneven brick to trip on. Francie plans to plant some perennials that won't need much attention around the sides. Life will look a little different for Eunice when we're done here."

I shuddered to imagine what it would all cost. But it would restore Eunice's way of life and enable her to live in her beloved home for many more years. No one could put a price on that.

When I left, I looked forward to hearing Cal's ideas for my bathroom. He seemed like a knowledgeable guy.

Daisy and I continued our walk, this time in the direction of Fred's house. I didn't want him to think I was snooping, even though I was. I should have asked Benton for tips on how to look innocent while spying. I observed Fred's house from the corner, far enough away not to seem intrusive. We crossed the street, and when we reached the alley behind his house, we turned and ambled along as though we were simply out for a walk. Which was actually the truth. I didn't expect to see anything of particular interest.

A fence enclosed his backyard and I couldn't see anything. But I could see the second story of his house. It was unremarkable, as plain as the interior.

It wasn't as though I had expected to see anything sinister. Not everyone was warm and fuzzy, I reasoned. Maybe he was just a private sort of guy. I wondered if he had been over to the hospital to see Charlene.

We walked home, and the minute we entered the house, Mars yelled from the den, "Do you know there are tiles missing in your shower?"

"Yes, thank you. I am aware of that." I removed Daisy's halter and refilled her bowl with fresh cold water.

Mars strolled into the kitchen and poured coffee into his mug. "Do you need a loan?"

"Are you offering?"

"Sure."

"If I recall correctly, I'm getting a nice little paycheck from Tilly."

"So you are. Unless Tilly and Wesley are in the slammer for stealing Peyton-slash-Briley."

The thought hadn't even entered my mind. "I guess I'd better hustle and finish up. I'm going to run by the hospital to see how Charlene is doing. I should pick up some groceries. What would you like for dinner?"

"Chinese. I never get Chinese anymore because I'm always at The Laughing Hound. I'll order and pick it up."

That suited me. "Sounds good. I'll see you later."

I walked out to my hybrid SUV and drove over to the hospital. I recognized Natasha's car in the parking lot and peeled in next to it. Inside, I asked for directions to Charlene Smith's room.

I found it easily, but seeing her brought back memories of my former boyfriend who had been badly injured. No one else was in the room. Charlene's face was swollen and bruised but not bandaged. I thought that might be a good sign.

I knew her mom, Griselda, had been there. Small stones lay beside her pillow. I recognized amethyst and tiger's-eye. There were also pink and black stones.

Her left leg was in a cast and propped up on a pillow.

I touched her hand. "Charlene?" I said softly. "It's Sophie Winston. I'm a friend of Natasha's."

She didn't react in any way. I took her hand and held it in mine. "A lot of people miss you. Natasha has always wanted a little sister. Want to hear something funny? Your mothers are so much alike!"

"That's what Natasha tells me." Griselda spoke from the doorway. Natasha stood behind her.

"How's Charlene doing?"

"Believe it or not, much better." Griselda checked the monitor attached to Charlene. "When I arrived here, they told me I'd better say my goodbyes. Of course, I brought my own medicine. They can tell you stones and herbs don't make a difference, but they do."

"Has Fred been to visit?" I asked.

"He has," said Griselda. "I don't like him any better, but he has come by."

"He brought the beautiful pink roses." Natasha leaned over to smell them.

"That was thoughtful. They're beautiful." A vase of lilies and gladiolas sat next to them. "Who are the other flowers from?"

"Mia's husband," said Griselda. "He even came by to see Charlene. Why didn't she meet a nice man like him? I still don't like that Fred. He can bring all the roses in Old Town and it won't change a thing. He has the evil eye." Griselda tossed a handful of something in the air.

I was certain the nurses appreciated that! "Have the police told you anything?"

"I think they've forgotten about her." Griselda yawned. "I apologize. Natasha and I are taking turns staying with Charlene."

Natasha did seem tired, but oddly calm.

"You two must be exhausted," I said.

Natasha moved to the other side of the bed. "I promised her I would stay. There's nothing else I can do for her."

"That's not true," said Griselda. She turned to me. "Charlene's apartment building is going condo. She'll have to buy or move. It's not the best timing for either of those choices. Natasha has offered to let her live in an apartment over her garage."

"That's wonderful! It's a very cute place. I'm glad she's in good hands." I said goodbye and drove home.

The piquant aroma of Chinese food drifted to me as soon as I entered the house. Mars puttered around the kitchen. I noticed he had closed the curtains over the sink.

"Feeling paranoid?" I asked.

"It's those crazed reporters. I don't want them seeing me from the street."

Mars had set the table with chopsticks and my square Adelaide dinner plates. I had to admit that the blue on white toile-like pattern of lush flowers, branches, and birds had a decidedly Asian look.

"Dinner's ready. I worked on it all day." He poured white wine into Spode Blue Italian wineglasses. The pattern and color coordinated with the dishes surprisingly well.

"You won't believe what happened." Mars gestured for me to sit down at the table.

I gladly slid into the banquette and helped myself to Kung Pao Chicken. I peeked in another container. "Is this Peking Duck?"

"Only the best for you."

I sipped my wine. "What's your big news?"

"It's all over the news shows. Remember how Wesley's computer was hacked? Today someone released an e-mail he wrote that outs two American spies. It is such a huge breach. This will follow him his entire life. When he dies, the media will call him the congressman who outed undercover agents of the United States. I'm not sure he can get reelected now."

Even I recognized the significance of that. "Does that mean they hacked into his system again?"

"Probably. As far as I can tell, it's all happening very fast. Someone hacks into the computer, and the next day it's on the news."

"Can't they track it? I thought all computers had identifying numbers."

"They do. But hackers are very clever. It's a shame that smart people use their skills that way."

I rolled the duck into a steamed pancake. "Was Benton one of the agents who was outed?"

"I didn't see his name. I hope those two can get to safety."

"Wait a minute. Could Abby be a spy?" I gazed at Mars.

"She writes cookbooks."

"What if she doesn't? What if that was a cover? She was married to a guy who is probably a spy. Maybe the whole thing was a setup to get her into Wesley's house and inner circle."

"That's so crazy!" Mars pulled out a pad of paper and a pen. "We have to get back to what we know for sure."

"Mia was murdered," I said. "And Charlene was there. Someone, maybe Mia's murderer, must have beaten her at Abby's house, because Charlene's blood was found there."

CHAPTER 30

Dear Sophie,
What do you bake when you need something in a big hurry? I'm always stumped. It seems like everything needs to bake for a long time or has to cool before it can be frosted.

Always in a Rush in Ding Dong,
Texas

Dear Always in a Rush,
Coffee cake. Most only need a glaze. Even if you take the time to put a crumble on top and still add a glaze, they are remarkably quick to make.

Sophie

"Excellent. Those are facts. We're on the right track now. Charlene must have managed to escape, though I can't imagine where she was before you found her."

"Maybe she passed out somewhere?" I

guessed. "The pain from trying to drag yourself along with a broken leg has to be excruciating."

"Abby is gone," said Mars. "Either she's dead or she ran away to hide from someone."

"And it's worth noting that Abby sort of ran away from her life in Milwaukee. I bet a lot of people there still remember her as the babysitter who was caring for Peyton Poulon when she disappeared. She didn't have that hanging over her when she moved away."

"I feel a little bit better about our lousy date now that I know she was preoccupied with thoughts about Peyton's kidnapper. I wish she had told me about it. If she had, maybe none of this would have happened," said Mars.

"Why were Mia and Charlene at Abby's house? Did they not know she had gone out to dinner with you?" I asked. "Or did she send them a come-rescue-me-from-this-horrible-date text?"

"Ha ha." There was no mirth in Mars's tone. "But that's a very good question."

I turned my chopsticks to the thick end, dipped them into the takeout carton and helped myself to more duck. "It is also a fact that Abby left a message about Peyton

Poulon."

"And we have confirmed that Peyton was kidnapped when she was only two years old."

"Did you do any more research on Peyton?" I asked.

"No, the outing of the spies got my attention. I went back to researching Wesley's background."

"Don't tell me you think he's a foreign agent or something," I said.

"Probably not. But there's something bad in his past, and I'm determined to find it."

"The kidnapping of Peyton Poulon?" I asked.

Mars sat back and rubbed his forehead. "Do you think that's possible? How old would Peyton be?"

I hated to tell him. "Around fifteen, I guess."

"Do you know how old Briley is?"

"Fifteen."

"Oh boy. That would be the end of everything for him." Mars shook his head. "You were worried that he'd had an affair with Abby, but this is so much worse!"

"Maybe it's Schuyler. Or one of their friends. I've been assuming that whatever happened to Abby started at Tilly's house. But we don't know that. She could have received a phone call from someone that morning. Or she could have seen a girl she thought was Peyton the night before, or when she walked to work."

"Or on TV, for that matter," Mars added.

"Or maybe what happened at Abby's house had nothing to do with Peyton. Maybe it was completely unrelated."

"You're speculating again."

"Make a new list of suspects. Everyone who had anything to do with Mia or Abby."

"Including Wesley?"

"Of course. And add Fred Conway. I've got nothing on him at all. His neighbor doesn't like him because he doesn't stop and chat with her. And he brought beautiful pink roses to Charlene."

"A killer for sure," Mars uttered sarcastically.

"Someone beat Charlene, and the boyfriend is always the top suspect," I pointed out.

"But that flies in the face of your previous theory," argued Mars.

"I'm sticking to the facts like you always tell me to. I miss having Nina and Bernie here."

"Me too. But we can't say anything about Peyton. There's always a chance that she's at the root of Mia's murder. Do you think

Wolf is calling the cops in Milwaukee?"

"I would imagine so."

"I have a bad feeling that we now know why Wesley has been so nervous."

"Do you think he murdered Mia?"

"Whether he killed her or someone else did, I'd put money on Briley being Peyton Poulon. If he or Tilly was involved in the abduction, that would be disastrous. I don't know the penalty for kidnapping, but I'd guess they would spend the rest of their lives in prison, even if they didn't murder someone. *Something* must have happened that caused Abby to make the connection." Mars made a note on the pad. "I'll see if I can find anything that places Wesley in the Milwaukee area around that time."

"What if Abby somehow discovered that Schuyler was Peyton Poulon?"

"And how would she have learned that?" asked Mars.

"Just indulge me for a minute. Oh! Maybe Abby confided to Mia about Peyton's kidnapping. Or maybe Abby figured out that Briley is actually Peyton and she confided in Mia."

"I'm indulging you, but that's all just speculation. And if Abby thought something like that, why would she confide in Mia?"

I pursued my line of thought. "Mia goes

to see Abby to talk about what to do. Wesley, who has no alibi for that evening, follows Mia, waiting for an opportunity to kill her so she won't spill the beans. Abby and Charlene have the opportunity to escape while he's murdering Mia."

"An interesting scenario, Sophie. And one could easily substitute Jericho for Wesley."

"Why do you continue to believe that Jericho killed Mia when it's probably Wesley?"

Mars leaned back in his chair and sighed. "Even though Wesley fired me and is trying his level best to point a finger of guilt at me, I like the guy. You said it yourself. Jericho is hanging around there running the show. And I know for a fact that he's a sleazebag."

I skipped past his obsession with Jericho. "Unless . . . what if Schuyler is Peyton, and Abby murdered Mia for abducting her?" I asked.

"I almost wish that were the case. But Wesley has been so edgy that I suspect Briley is Peyton. Have you ever met Schuyler's dad?"

I gasped. "How could I have overlooked him? Schuyler says he's an obstetrician and quite dedicated to his work. Oh no! I never even thought to bring them a dish. How very impolite of me!"

322

"I would bet that Tilly has been keeping them well fed."

"Maybe so." I glanced at the clock. "Do you think it's too late to stop by their house with a dessert?"

"Can you bake two?"

"You're always so subtle, Mars. Maybe I could whip up a blueberry crumb cake for their breakfast tomorrow."

Mars carried the dishes to the sink. "Sounds delicious. Bet it would make a great midnight snack, too."

While he rinsed the dishes and put them in the dishwasher, I preheated the oven and doubled my recipe for blueberry crumb cake.

An hour later, I drizzled the two cakes with a lemon glaze and packed one to take to Schuyler's house. I peeked in the den before I left. Mars was on the sofa glued to his laptop. Daisy looked up at me and gently flapped her tail. Mochie slept next to Mars, upside down.

"I'll be back soon."

Mars didn't even look up. "Okay. We'll guard the fort."

I stepped outside the kitchen door and returned immediately for a jacket. It was definitely a transitional time of year. How did the temperature drop so fast? Wearing a

323

dark green quilted barn jacket, I ventured forth.

There weren't many lights on in Schuyler's home. Especially not compared to Tilly's house next door, where it seemed that lights glowed in all the windows.

I knocked on the door and heard footsteps approaching. A short man with a remarkably round head opened the door. "May I help you?"

"I'm Sophie Winston. I've been working for Tilly and met Schuyler at Tilly's house. I just wanted to drop this off for your breakfast and to let you know how very sorry I am for your loss."

"Oh. That's very kind of you. Won't you come in?"

I stepped into a grand foyer. Mia had kept it somewhat simple, with beige walls and a table for flowers in front of a mirror. An arched opening led to an impressive staircase.

He led me into a formal living room. A chandelier hung from the ceiling, and the fireplace had an elegant marble surround. The furniture was prim, the kind that forces you to sit up straight and mind your manners.

"Pierce Hendrickson," he said, holding out his hand. "I believe Schuyler has mentioned you. She's out on a date."

"A date?"

He gestured to me to sit down.

I placed the coffee cake on a table.

"Do you think she's too young?" he asked.

"I have no idea," I said. "They grow up so fast these days."

"Tilly seemed to think it was okay. It's a group thing, I think."

He seemed lost, as if he had landed on a planet he knew nothing about. "Mia took care of those details. Don't get me wrong, I couldn't love Schuyler more if she were my own, but I don't know anything about teenagers." He forced a wan smile. "They really should come with instructions."

A chill came over me. "Schuyler isn't your daughter?"

"Oh, she is. I adopted her a long time ago. She's not my biological daughter. She's Mia's child by a previous husband. Schuyler was five when I married Mia. She was such an adorable child! And now" — he took a deep breath — "I guess it's just the two of us."

"I'm so sorry. I still can't believe Mia is gone."

"Me either." He looked away. "It's, uh, life-changing. I've been wandering through my days in a haze, unable to comprehend why anyone would be so brutal. Every night I lie in bed wondering why Mia went to that woman's house. I was at the hospital delivering a baby." He looked at his hands. "One life was snuffed out and another one began that night."

Pierce looked at me. "I never realized how much Mia did around here. I was so focused on my job that I find myself at a complete loss. Everyone has been so kind." He paused briefly as though he was trying to hold himself together. "I actually had to look for the coffee. Mia always had it ready and waiting for me. She took such good care of Schuyler and me."

Tears ran over his cheeks. "I'm sorry." He sniffled.

"Don't be silly. It's quite understandable. Grief takes time."

"I'm not the handsomest guy in the world. When I met Mia, I couldn't believe she was interested in me. How did I land a beauty like her? She could have had any man she wanted. That auburn hair of hers cascaded around her shoulders and gleamed like it had been touched by gold. She turned heads everywhere we went. And I knew people were always wondering, *what does she see in that guy?* I felt like the luckiest man on the planet."

I ached for him. Had no one let him talk? Had his colleagues and friends been too busy telling him how they felt? I let him ramble in the hope that it was cleansing for him.

"I just don't understand why she was taken from me." He winced and mashed his eyes shut. "When I think what that person did to her. She must have been so scared. And then, the freezer. What kind of demented person does that?"

He tried to smile but his lips quivered. "I'm sorry. You're the first person who hasn't run off or told me what to do. Death is an awful thing. None of us know how to handle it. I can only hope that the police find the monster who killed my angel."

"I know Wolf personally. You couldn't ask for a better investigator."

"He stopped by here, too. He wanted to know where I was on Friday night. I never would have hurt a hair on Mia's head. She and Schuyler are everything to me. I can only hope that I don't mess up Schuyler's teen years."

As I listened to Pierce ramble, I couldn't help drawing a distinction between him and Natasha's father, who abandoned both of his daughters. Pierce was a shambles at the moment, but I could see his kind heart and his desire to do the best for Schuyler.

"Can I offer you some tea?" he asked. Before I could answer, he giggled halfheartedly. "I don't even know if we have any tea. I do know that we have wine."

"Thank you, but I should get going." I found a pen and paper in my purse and wrote down my name and phone number. "If you should need anything, I hope you'll give me a call. Even if you only need to talk with someone."

He glanced at my name. "Thank you, Sophie. I might just take you up on that."

In spite of the chill in the air when I left his house, I walked back over to Abby's house. It was dark and silent. I opened the gate to the passageway along the side of the house and ventured to the back patio. In the quiet night, I tried to imagine what had gone on there. Mia hadn't escaped the killer's wrath, but Charlene, beaten as she was, had somehow found the strength to get away. Had she dragged herself through the passageway? The gate to the alley was much closer. I walked over to it and gazed at the latch. Lying on the ground, I pretended I couldn't use my legs and reached for the latch. I was able to hit it with my fingers. The gate opened. I scrambled to my feet and stood in the alley. Which way?

If Charlene knew where Natasha lived, then she might have headed in that direction. But she probably needed to hide from the killer. She must have been terrified that he would find her.

Eunice's house would have been the closest. I repeated the action of lying on the ground to see if I could open the gate latch. No problem. The gate swung inward.

If I had to hide, I would have tried to get inside Eunice's garage. It would have been hard for Charlene, but I thought she could probably have opened the door.

I gazed around Eunice's patio for any other possible hiding places. Except for the deck storage box, there really wasn't anyplace. I walked over to it and tried the latch. It opened easily.

CHAPTER 31

Dear Natasha,
I live in a small townhouse with a lovely little patio. But I have nowhere to store my patio furniture over the winter. I can bring the umbrella in, but there's no room for all the fluffy cushions. Where do you keep yours?
No Room in Mosquitoville,
Vermont

Dear No Room,
Deck storage boxes are the answer. The better ones are waterproof. They've improved over the years and no longer look like eyesores. Some can even double as extra seating or as tables.
Natasha

In the darkness, I couldn't see what was inside the box, but it was so heavy that I couldn't push it. A vile smell wafted out, faint but revolting. I pulled my phone out of my purse and turned on the flashlight. At first glance, it looked like sand. Sort of a dirty white powder.

Could Eunice or a friend have dumped sand in her deck storage box? Perhaps to keep it stable? So it wouldn't move around when a strong wind came through?

The dreadful smell caused me to think otherwise. I turned off the flashlight and called Wolf's number.

When he answered, I said, "I'm at Eunice's house. I may have found Abby."

I closed the top while I waited, mostly because the smell made me gag. I sat in one of Eunice's garden chairs and stared at the box. Why hadn't this occurred to us? She had been right here with us for an entire week. The killer had put Mia in a box, so it only stood to reason that he or she had sought out another box in which to place Abby.

Eunice's poor hearing and refusal to wear her hearing aids would have prevented her from hearing anything the killer did when he entered her backyard.

Wolf arrived quickly. He opened the deck box and pulled his head back. "I'm sorry to say I know that smell. I believe you're right." He made a phone call, and shortly thereafter more police arrived along with crime scene investigators. I remained silent and watched them work. No one thought to kick me out, and I wanted to know for sure if Abby was in the box.

After taking photographs, they began to scoop out the sandy material. A woman lay at the bottom.

I left at that point. I knew who it was. They would have to check her DNA or have someone identify her, but it didn't make sense for it to be anyone else.

I dragged home feeling sad. Part of me had hoped she was alive and in hiding from the killer. She must have been afraid of someone to bother to leave a note in the recipes. One of them must have kidnapped Peyton and murdered Abby and Mia to keep Peyton's true identity secret. But which one?

I thought we could write off Schuyler's dad, Pierce. That left Wesley and Jericho.

Mars met me at the door when I arrived home. "Where have you been? I was beginning to think Schuyler's dad murdered you, too."

"I found Abby."

Mars stared at me in shock. "Do you want a drink?"

"A cup of tea would be nice."

"Only you would drink tea after finding a corpse. Where was she?"

Over hot tea and blueberry crumble cake, I told Mars everything that had happened. "You kept asking me what I would have done. When I went over to Abby's house, I tried to envision what might have happened. Where did Charlene go? How did she manage to elude the killer? It seemed like there were only two places to hide. Charlene could hide in either the garage or the deck storage box. When I opened the box, a horrible odor wafted out. I called Wolf."

"No one noticed the smell?" asked Mars.

"Wolf said the container was probably airtight to be waterproof. I didn't look at her. I imagined her beginning to look like a mummy. They haven't confirmed that it's Abby, but . . ."

Mars gave me a funny look. "That does away with a lot of our theories. Someone killed two women and beat up a third one. He took the time to stuff them into boxes, which I find curious."

"What do you mean?"

"It's just an interesting choice. One would hide the bodies to eliminate evidence, right? Wouldn't it have been more logical to drive their bodies out to the countryside and leave them? Did the killer think no one would notice? Was he was buying time to get away?" Mars speculated.

"He took Abby's suitcase and dumped it in the river." I gasped as things began to line up. "And he drove to Reston, where he left her phone at a mall —"

Mars finished my thought. "So it would look like she was still alive. He thought it through. Maybe he even planned it carefully in advance. This was one cool character."

"You know who we've been overlooking? Benton."

"How does he figure into the Peyton Poulon kidnapping?"

"I don't know. But if he's a spy, hasn't he been trained to be cool and calm in adverse situations?"

"Good point. But I don't see the motive. And if he was really a spy, why would he kidnap a child?"

"Because his wife couldn't have one?" I suggested.

Mars winced and rubbed his eyes. "I grant you that he might have been able to pull off the murders. He would have been smart enough to get rid of Abby's phone and computer, but unless he kidnapped Peyton to sell her and Abby knew nothing about it . . . ." Mars shook his head. "I don't see

334

that. What about Mia's husband?"

"He's a really nice man and he's devastated by Mia's death. It sounds like he relied on her heavily and now he's lost without her. One little interesting tidbit, though. Schuyler is not his biological daughter. She was five when he met and married Mia."

"Assuming he's not lying, I guess that counts him out."

"Did you make any progress while I was out?"

"I did. The Internet is a wonderful, amazing, and scary place. Turns out that there was a hazing incident at the university Wesley and Jericho attended. And it involved their fraternity. None of the newspaper reports cite Wesley or Jericho, but you know how these fraternity things are. I'm willing to bet one or both of them were involved."

"What kind of incident?"

"Alcohol-related, naturally. One of the kids took a bad fall and broke his neck. One day he was a baseball star, and the next day he became a paraplegic for life."

"No! How tragic. The poor guy. But I don't get it — how does this impact Wesley?"

"It's only a guess, but I assume Wesley and/or Jericho were among the instigators. I don't think any politician could survive something like that becoming public knowledge."

"Kind of weird that the people doing opposition research haven't discovered that," I said.

"Not at all. I had to connect the dots. If I hadn't had some kind of suspicion or hint of wrongdoing to track down, I don't think I would have figured it out."

"So you're saying you're better at opposition research than the people who do it for a living?" I teased.

"Let's just say I was more determined to find the dirt."

I went up to bed, but I couldn't sleep. I kept imagining the horror that had unfolded at Abby's house. Had the killer been inside waiting for her when Mars walked her home? And why had Mia and Charlene been there? Why couldn't three women overpower one killer? I sat up. Maybe there had been more than one killer.

At two in the morning, I tiptoed downstairs to get a melatonin gummy to help me sleep. I had barely entered the kitchen when I saw the dark outline of a person looking in the window of the kitchen door.

CHAPTER 32

Dear Natasha,
My aunt is in the hospital. I would love to send her flowers, but she has allergies. What can I bring her to brighten up her stay?
            Out of Ideas in Scrabble, Virginia

Dear Out of Ideas,
How about a game to play? Or a special snack, like a milkshake, with the doctor's okay, of course. Or maybe a mirror and some makeup or nail polish. I know that's what I would want!
                                    Natasha

He moved away, but my heart still thumped. And then I heard him tapping on the door to the sunroom.

I shot through the kitchen to the den. I didn't dare turn on a light. "Mars! Mars, wake up. There's someone outside."

"Hmm? Not now, Sophie."

The rap on the door came again, louder this time.

Mars sat up. "What is that noise?"

"Someone is at the door," I whispered.

"Don't answer it! What time is it?"

"Two."

"Sophie, Sophie?" I could hear the man outside hissing my name in a loud whisper.

"See who it is, but don't open the door," said Mars.

I pulled my robe tighter and padded to the door in bare feet. I flicked on the outside light, which I hoped would blind him a little and give me an advantage. It was Wesley.

I opened the door.

"I'm so sorry to wake you, Sophie. I thought you might know where Mars is staying."

"I'm right here, Wesley." Mars emerged from the shadows, and I saw him tuck the Taser he had given me years ago in his pocket. So that was why he wanted me to see who it was. He needed time to get the Taser.

I stepped aside so Wesley could come in.

Mars whispered in my ear, "Good job not opening the door."

I ignored him. "Wesley, could I offer you some coffee or hot apple cider?"

"Whatever you have on hand is fine. Don't go to any trouble for me. I apologize for waking you. I've made such a mess of things. After the way I treated you, I'll be lucky if you even speak to me, Mars."

"Why don't we go into the living room?" Mars led the way while I hurried to the kitchen. I could hear him closing curtains.

I poured apple cider into a pot to heat and fetched the apple brandy that Nina had used. In a matter of minutes, I had three mugs on a tray with napkins, plates, forks, and little slices of the blueberry crumble cake.

I carried it into the living room and set it on the table. I figured they would throw me out, but neither of them said a word when I sat down and listened.

"I guess you saw the e-mail that was released naming two operatives," said Wesley. "It's all over the news. I don't think anyone missed it. Have you seen Twitter? I'm being attacked on the national news, and there are people calling for my resignation!"

"This was from someone hacking into your computer?" Mars sounded completely calm, as though this wasn't the worst thing that could happen.

"Yes. The thing is that I never wrote it."

"Are you sure?" asked Mars.

"No way. Not only didn't I write it, I don't know who those people are. I've never even heard of them."

Mars sipped his brandied apple cider. "You're saying that not only were you hacked, but someone is releasing phony e-mails and claiming they came from your computer?"

"Right. I feel terrible. Those two people have been put in danger. But I had nothing to do with it!" Wesley's nostril's flared and his chest heaved.

"What do you think happened?" asked Mars, who was completely in his element and not even slightly flustered.

"I have no idea. Unless it's Jericho." Wesley breathed heavily. "You warned me about him, but I didn't listen. I should have realized something was up when he said I had to let you go. I'm really sorry. I should have shown Jericho the door."

"But you had a long association with him. So you trusted him," said Mars.

"He's blackmailing me." Wesley didn't take his eyes off Mars.

To Mars's credit, he didn't shame Wesley or act in the least bit put out. "Does this have anything to do with the hazing incident?"

Wesley's face went completely white. "How do you know about that?"

"I figured Jericho was up to no good, so I did a little research."

"It was the single worst thing I have ever done." Wesley shook his head as though he still couldn't believe it.

Mars raised his eyebrows. "You were at fault?"

"No. But I was there. I could have stopped it. I could have done something instead of standing by. They never should have moved him. I knew that. The outcome could have been different for Robbie."

I looked over at Mars. I could understand Wesley's feelings of guilt.

"Jericho has extorted money from you? He threatened to release this information?" asked Mars.

"Exactly. But it gets worse. I couldn't believe what happened. It was one of those moments when you wish you could reel back time and change the outcome. I couldn't do that, so I send Robbie a check every month. I don't know how far it goes with all the medical expenses he has. I've done it for years, since I got my first job. I feel like he's my obligation, like he's part of my family."

I wasn't following him at all. I didn't know

a single other person who would have been so generous. If anything, that should improve his standing politically, not hurt it! But what did I know? I gazed at Mars but couldn't gauge his reaction.

"Does Jericho have anything else on you?"

"No. There is nothing else."

"Are you absolutely certain? This would be the time to come clean. I don't want to take on one mess only to find there's another one that you didn't tell me about."

I admired Mars for being so calm.

"No, I swear," Wesley insisted.

"What about Abby's murder?" asked Mars.

"They found her?" Wesley's eyes went wide.

"Sophie discovered Abby's body. If you had anything to do with it, then you won't need to worry about a hazing incident from your college days."

"I did not have an affair with Abby. And I most certainly didn't murder her. I liked Abby. Why would I harm her?"

I wanted to believe him. I could understand why Mars liked Wesley. He seemed like a nice guy.

Suddenly, Wesley faced me. "Did I hear Jericho ask you out?"

"Yes."

"You didn't tell me about that," Mars exclaimed.

"Yes, I did. He wanted me to get information out of Wolf and report back. I told you that."

"That's not the same as asking you out on a date," Mars protested.

I chuckled. "It is when that was what Jericho really wanted."

Wesley snickered. "You two sound like Tilly and me. I wonder if Jericho asked Abby out. Maybe she turned him down and he saw her going to dinner with you, Mars. Jealousy is a powerful motivator."

My eyelids were getting heavy, and I was wondering if I could excuse myself and slip up to bed.

Fortunately, Mars said, "We're going to have to handle this very carefully. You cannot let on to Jericho that you have been in touch with me. Think you can manage that? If he gets even a whiff of what's going on, we're toast."

"I'll do my best," Wesley promised.

"I'll make some calls in the morning regarding that e-mail. And I think that, properly handled, we can go public about the hazing so it won't be hanging over your head anymore."

"I don't know how to thank you. Mostly

343

I'm grateful that you're taking me back as a client." Wesley took a deep breath and appeared much relieved.

"We'll work it out."

I said good night and headed upstairs, leaving Mars to see his client to the door and clean up the living room.

I slept in on Sunday morning. When I finally made my way downstairs, I found Wolf, Nina, and Bernie in my kitchen with Mars. The kettle was whistling, and Bernie was turning pancakes on the griddle. The scent of bacon hung in the air.

"Looks like a party," I said.

"Wolf came by to confirm that it was Abby whom you found." Mars delivered a plate of pancakes to Wolf.

"Benton Bergeron came in to identify her." Wolf poured maple syrup over his pancakes.

I plucked a slice of bacon from a platter and munched on it. "At least we found her. Any leads on her killer yet?" I asked.

Everyone turned to look at Wolf. He shook his head and ate a forkful of pancakes.

"I heard about it on the news this morning," said Nina. "What I don't understand is why no one smelled anything."

Wolf took a sip of coffee. "Lime. The killer

poured lime on her. It's for agricultural use but well known for absorbing strong odors."

I nearly dropped the teakettle. "Fred!"

Wolf stopped eating. "What's this?"

"Natasha and I went to visit Fred Conway. When we left, Alma Riddenhauer was out in her yard, and we stopped to chat. She told us that two bags of lime had been stolen from their yard."

"Alma, cute little old lady? Always wears sunhats. Her husband is too old to be out in the yard with a chain saw but that doesn't stop him?"

I smiled at Wolf's description. "That's the Riddenhauers. But you'll have to be careful so Fred doesn't see you. He lives on the other side of the street. I have a feeling the Riddenhauers spy on him all the time."

Wolf continued eating. I snagged the next plate of pancakes and gave Bernie a big smooch on the cheek. "Thanks for fixing breakfast!" I sat down on the banquette with my friends.

"Do you think Fred could be the killer?" asked Mars. "I've never met the guy."

"Don't go jumping to conclusions. Just because bags of lime are missing doesn't mean the killer stole them," said Wolf. "And frankly, the Riddenhauers might well have misplaced them. I'll look into it, though."

When everyone except Mars left, I threw on a comfy sweater and soft jeans and hustled to my office to finish up the details on Tilly's cookbook. I hoped to bring it over to her the next morning.

But while I should have been working, I looked up Peyton Poulon. There were hundreds of articles. Most of them had a lot of comments. There were multiple theories about who had taken her. Apparently, the parents themselves had been suspects. Pictures showed Kurt and Hannah Poulon as a traumatized young couple. Hannah was crying in most of the photos. Hannah's brother and a neighbor had also been suspects. I found myself almost hoping that Briley or Schuyler was their missing baby. I couldn't imagine their pain. How could a person cope with that kind of loss? Did they still get up in the morning and think of Peyton first thing, wondering if she was dead or alive? Were they numb? Or had they somehow come to terms with her absence just so they could move on and live their lives?

I read through article after article. Abby had been babysitting while Kurt and Hannah were at work. She had put Peyton down for her nap and left the bedroom. When she returned to the room, Peyton was gone.

346

Abby had searched the house and the backyard. When she couldn't find Peyton, she called the police, Hannah, and Kurt, in that order.

Peyton had been wearing a pink-and-white-striped shirt and pink shorts with bows on the sides. And then I read the one sentence that told me which girl she was.

CHAPTER 33

Dear Sophie,
My sister says the word spice means hot.
I think it means something that isn't an
herb. One of us is buying lunch depend-
ing on your answer. Hope it's not me!
Smarter Sister in the Nutmeg State,
Connecticut!

Dear Smarter Sister,
You are correct. Herbs are from the
leaves of plants. Spices come from the
other parts of plants, like berries, bark,
and roots. The word does not imply
anything about the heat a spice imparts.
Enjoy your lunch!
Sophie

*Peyton has a distinctive port-wine stain
birthmark on the back of her neck in the shape
of a heart.*

Schuyler was Peyton. I had mistakenly

thought the heart on her neck was a tattoo. I would have felt sorry for either of them, but somehow it seemed wrenchingly sad that Schuyler had lost Mia, the only mother she had known, and now was likely to lose the man who had been a father to her. It boggled my mind to imagine what she would go through. How could a person cope with the discovery that she wasn't who she thought she was? Traumatic didn't begin to cover that kind of experience.

The shock and suffering to Schuyler aside, it also meant Mia had stolen her. Another fact that would come as a blow to Schuyler.

There was no other possibility. If her father, Pierce, didn't meet Schuyler and Mia until Schuyler was five, something Wolf could undoubtedly confirm rather easily, then it could only have been Mia who abducted her.

But Mia had been murdered.

I thought back to Tilly's description of Friday at her house. She said the girls were around and were trying out messy buns. That must have been when Abby saw Peyton's birthmark on Schuyler's neck. If she babysat for Peyton regularly, she would have known exactly what it looked like. Abby would have been in shock when she realized that the baby stolen from her thirteen years ago was miraculously standing before her.

Mia must have been there and seen Abby's reaction. She knew she had finally been caught.

And Abby had been sufficiently fearful to have written Peyton's name in code on the recipes. Then she went to dinner with Mars. I understood better why she might have done that. She probably found some degree of safety in his company and might have needed time to process what she should do next.

But how had both Mia and Abby ended up dead? If Mia went to Abby's house intending to murder or confront her, then Abby would be dead, unless she fought back and overcame Mia's attack on her. One of them should still be alive. And how did Charlene fit into the equation?

I tried to focus on the recipes, but my mind always wandered back to Mia. Tilly had called her a helicopter mom. It all made so much sense. Mia wasn't an overprotective mother. She was making sure that no one recognized her daughter as the missing girl from Milwaukee. All those years of homeschooling had a purpose, and it wasn't education.

Had Mia managed to enter Abby's home?

Was she hiding there waiting for Abby's return?

I walked through the sunroom to the den. "Did Abby have a key to unlock her door when she came home after your dinner together?"

He looked up at me and his forehead crinkled. "Um, no. She fumbled in her purse and finally used a key that she keeps under a rock in case she locks herself out."

Mia could have used that key to gain entry to the house, or she could have stolen the key from Abby's purse while Abby was working at Tilly's. "Thanks."

"What's going on?"

I explained the birthmark on Peyton's neck. "Mia kidnapped Peyton. I'm sure of it."

"Then why is she dead?"

"There's the rub. I don't know."

"Clearly there was a fourth person present," said Mars. "One who killed two women and hid their bodies. He probably thought Charlene was dead and went into a panic when he couldn't find her. That fourth person was the only one who walked away unscathed."

"It had to be Fred. He knew where to find lime in the middle of the night."

"Why did he kill Mia and Abby?" asked Mars.

I collapsed on the cushy armchair. "I don't even know if he was acquainted with them. Although Abby and Charlene were friends. She probably mentioned Abby to him. Did you notice that Wesley didn't mention anything about Briley last night?"

"I wondered about that. Either he feels secure about the fact that Briley is his daughter, or he doesn't know about Peyton yet. It feels kind of strange to know something that will change the lives of people in Wisconsin whom we have never met. I wonder if the police have informed them that there's a possibility Peyton has been located."

Changing the subject I asked, "What if someone followed Mia?"

"Her husband and Tilly have alibis. That leaves Benton, Wesley — whom I believe we can eliminate — and Jericho."

"And Fred," I added.

"And Fred, who probably didn't even know two of the three women."

Frustrated, I went back to work on the cookbook. In the early afternoon, I made a quick white chili with chicken breasts and great northern beans, as well as Tilly's recipe for iron skillet corn bread.

I poured half the chili into a bowl to take to Francie and Eunice for their dinner and added half the corn bread. It was early for dinner, but they could warm them whenever they felt like eating.

Mars was sniffing the air when he emerged from the den. "I'm getting hungry."

I latched Daisy's halter on her. "I'm taking some over to Francie. I won't be long."

"Isn't that what you said yesterday when you found Abby's body and were gone for hours?"

I didn't think I had said that, but I understood his point I threw him a look and left through the backyard.

When I arrived at Francie's house, she had company. Benton opened the door.

"Thank you. Looks like you're having a party over here."

It was a strange assembly of people. Francie and Eunice, of course. Sam the fisherman. Benton the spy. Briley and Schuyler. They all went silent and gazed at me.

I was pleased to see Schuyler looking bright-eyed. Maybe it was good for her to get out and be with people instead of sitting at home and thinking about Mia.

On the table in front of them were two laptop computers and one desktop computer.

353

I tried to joke about it. "Briley and Schuyler, don't tell me you're doing schoolwork on a Sunday afternoon."

Eunice said quickly, "It's due soon. We're going to make sure that they both get As in that class."

If Benton hadn't been there, I might have bought her explanation. But I couldn't think of a single reason that Benton would be involved in their study of Old Town many years ago.

"Everything was so different when I was a young bride," said Francie with a smile.

I could feel the tension. They were all waiting for me to leave. Had Schuyler suspected all along that she wasn't Mia's child? Could she remember a previous life or had she been too young? Were they researching missing children?

"Well," I said uneasily, "enjoy your dinner."

Daisy and I left immediately, but when I was outside, I could hear the chatter and giggles. I turned around and saw Sam Bambam wiping his face like my visit had been a close call.

They were definitely up to something.

It was too early to eat dinner. I strolled toward Eunice's house and spied Wolf's car there. Instead of walking along the street,

Daisy and I cut through the alley. It really wasn't very far to Natasha's backyard from the alley.

There was no yellow crime scene tape on the gate, so I opened it and looked inside.

Wolf spotted us right away. He was standing in the middle of the patio. "You can't come in yet."

"No problem. I'll be glad when they renovate back here and it looks fresh and different. The memory is a little gruesome. I do have a question for you, though."

"What's that?"

"Did the autopsies show how Mia and Abby died?"

"They were both strangled."

"Then the same person probably killed both of them?"

"I don't know that one could draw that conclusion. Plus, in both cases a ligature was used. But not the same ligature."

"Did you find the material that the killer used?"

"No. Whoever cleaned up the crime scene did a fairly thorough job."

"But you know this because the pattern on the necks don't match?" I guessed.

"Exactly."

"Was either one of them beaten like Charlene?" I asked, hoping he would keep giving me answers.

"Mia took a punch to the face."

"Are you as confused about this as I am?" I asked.

Wolf smiled. "I hope not."

That was reassuring. Maybe he was onto something.

I thanked him and closed the gate. Daisy tugged me toward the end of the alley, where a squirrel raced up a tree.

We weren't far from Fred's house. I wasn't sure why I kept coming back to him. But as we walked, I realized that he fit Eunice's description of a spy. He was somewhat plain, as was his home. He was quiet and didn't draw attention to himself. I knew nothing of his travel habits, but I thought it was sort of funny that such an ordinary fellow fit the description of a spy.

As I approached his house, Georgia Beckworth, a local florist, waved at me. I had used her services many times for events. I stopped for a moment to chat with her.

"I can't believe what's going on in Old Town," she whispered. "Two women dead? I trust Wolf, but I hope you're looking into this case, too. It's just horrible. Mia was a customer of ours. I'm just horrified by what happened to her. Why would anyone do such a thing?"

"Wolf's working hard to figure that out."

"And poor Charlene! Fred is just sick about her condition. I hope she pulls through."

"I saw the beautiful roses he sent her. I imagine they came from your store?"

"They did. He was darling. So precise." She held up her forefinger. "They must be pink and there must be thirteen. I told him an even dozen was traditional, but he said, no, no, no. That's for funerals. It must be an uneven number, so she'll get well. Isn't that adorable?"

"I've never heard that."

"It's a Russian custom. We send flowers for a few Russians who live around here. They always insist on an uneven number of flowers unless it's for a funeral."

"Russian? Is Fred Russian? I don't recall that he has an accent."

"His English is perfect. I think maybe his parents came from Russia. We're all superstitious, aren't we? We say we're not, but we won't walk under a ladder." Georgia giggled.

"Do you know Fred well?"

"We don't socialize with him if that's what you mean. He's a good neighbor, though. Very quiet and polite."

I smiled. "That's not what Alma Rittenhauer thinks."

"Isn't she a hoot? It drives her crazy that he's not more chatty. But some people aren't. I think he's just an introvert."

I took a chance. "Did you happen to notice if he was home on Friday night a week ago?"

"Why, Sophie Winston. I don't spy on my neighbors like Alma does." She pursed her lips. "But I did hear Charlene leave. I gather from the neighborhood scuttlebutt that she was through with Fred." Georgia wrinkled her nose. "He's a nice-enough fellow but a little boring. I can't say I blame her. He hardly ever leaves his house!"

"You heard her leave? Was she yelling?"

"You're just like Wolf. He asked the same thing. I wouldn't have called it yelling so much as Fred calling her name from the front door. I looked out to see her run by. And he followed at a slower pace a few minutes later. But he's not the one who beat her."

CHAPTER 34

Dear Natasha,
I love cilantro. I'm so glad you use it in your recipes. Unfortunately, my husband and his family act as if I'm insane for using cilantro. They claim it's a genetic thing. Oh, sure. Everyone has a genetic thing these days. Are they making this up?

Fed-Up Wife in Bat Cave,
North Carolina

Dear Fed-Up Wife,
Normally, I would agree with you. But their claim is true. To some people, cilantro tastes like soap, and it appears to be a hereditary condition. Sorry! Offer the cilantro on the side.

Natasha

"How do you know that?" I asked.
"Sophie, he's besotted with her! I know

359

jealousy is a powerful emotion, but I would bet my ears that he never harmed a hair on Charlene's head."

"Do you think he knew Mia?"

"Honey, I don't know. But I don't see how he can know many people since he almost never leaves his house."

It was interesting getting two differing views on Fred from his neighbors. But it was even more interesting that Fred had left his house minutes after Charlene broke up with him. At least, that was what everyone suspected she had done.

I thanked Georgia and walked along the sidewalk, right by the entrance to Fred's house. It was as quiet and boring as Fred himself, until I spotted a cop I knew sitting in a car. He gave me a funny look when I walked by. And he was dressed in plain clothes, not a uniform. I thought better of rapping on the window and asking what was up. I just kept walking.

Our path home took us by Bernie's house. A few members of the press still hung out. I guessed Sundays weren't hot news days. We crossed the street and entered our house through the kitchen door.

"Mars?" I called as I took off Daisy's halter. I joined him in the den. "Want to hear something weird?"

"Always."

I told him about the odd conglomeration of people at Francie's house.

He shrugged it off. "Maybe they all like one another."

"Benton had to identify Abby's body last night or this morning. I would like to think if you had to identify my body that you would be too broken up about my death to be partying."

"I might open a bottle of champagne. Would that be okay?"

"Actually, I think that would be lovely. Sort of a celebratory send-off."

I washed my hands at the kitchen sink. A car outside honked its horn, and I saw a white cat run across the street, narrowly avoiding death.

I ran out through the front door. The poor cat seemed traumatized. I feared that if I went to the cat, it would run back into traffic. I moved toward it at a glacial pace. When I was about six feet away, I sat down.

It watched me with intelligent blue eyes. I would have sworn it was the same cat I met at Fred's house. I had hoped she might inch toward me and come close enough for me to catch her, but she did the opposite. She ran directly at me.

I scooped her up and held her tightly as I

walked back to the house. When the foyer door was safely closed, I released her. This wasn't a stray who had been out in the world fending for herself. Her long fur was immaculate. It might even have been brushed. She was well fed, too. This was someone's cat who managed to sneak away.

She sniffed around, eventually following me into the kitchen, where I offered her some of Mochie's food. She ate very daintily.

Mochie was most curious. I thought he might hiss at her, but he was a true gentleman, interested yet polite to his new friend.

She wasn't wearing a collar.

I picked up the phone and called Wolf. "Do you have a phone number for Fred? I think his cat is here."

There was a long moment of silence. "Did you just walk by his house?"

"Yes."

"What were you doing there?"

"Walking Daisy."

I could hear him making a tsking sound. "Sophie, stay away from there. We're trying to get a search warrant, but there's some kind of hang-up."

"So I was right! He killed Mia and Abby!"

"I don't know that."

My mind was racing. "What if he's the

362

one who released Abby's cat? Wolf, I hate to tell you this, but I think Fred has fled! He just did the same thing with his own cat. You can't be on the run with a cat carrier."

"He's the one who flung the collar that landed in the holly tree?" Wolf speculated.

"Could be."

It wasn't the best choice to simply let a cat run free, but he had bothered to consider the fate of the cats and had let them go, which indicated some consideration for their welfare.

"Is it just me or is it weird that a person who would bother to release a cat would batter his girlfriend and murder two women?"

"I'm not aware of any studies correlating affection for cats with a propensity not to commit murder," said Wolf drily.

"Very funny. Good luck getting your warrant."

We said goodbye and hung up. But two seconds later, it dawned on me that if Fred were really fleeing town, he might stop at the hospital to see Charlene one last time.

I called Wolf back, but his phone rolled over to voice mail. I left a message.

"Mars! I'm going to the hospital. I think Fred might be there."

"What?"

"I don't have time to explain. I'll see you later."

Mars grabbed the car keys off the hook in the kitchen. "I'll drive. You can explain on the way."

Traffic seemed maddeningly slow. I explained to Mars that someone had let out Abby's cat, and now I thought Fred had done the same with his own cat. It was a sign that he wasn't coming back.

"I'm taking you to the hospital so you can single-handedly, without a gun or any training, capture a man who killed two women?"

"I called Wolf," I protested. "I'll text him, too, since this traffic is holding us up."

"Let me get this straight. You think that Fred is going to the hospital to say goodbye to Charlene, even though he knows the cops are onto him?"

"In the first place, he might not know that. And yes, I fear that he's going to say goodbye for the last time before he vanishes, or even worse, could be he's planning to complete the job he didn't finish. She's the only one who can positively identify him as the murderer."

"Oh. Now I feel *much* better about your plan."

"Mars, I can at least notify hospital security and the nursing staff to be on the lookout for him."

"That makes more sense."

He slowed to pull into the parking lot, a gigantic four-story labyrinth.

I opened the door and hopped out. "I'll see you at Charlene's room." I slammed the door and ran for the hospital entrance. I really didn't know what I would find. A besotted man like Georgia had said, or a fleeing murderer intent on finishing the job. At the front desk, I asked for the security office. The woman pointed me to a long hallway. At the end of it was a glass window with the word SECURITY on a sign above the window. I rapped on the glass.

A man appeared behind the glass panel and listened to me with a bored expression. "Ma'am, if you're afraid of this Fred fellow, I can walk you to your car."

"He's not a danger to me. He tried to kill one of your patients."

"I believe we would have been informed of that." He turned away and tossed a candy wrapper in the trash.

"Don't you understand? I think he's here now."

"Uh-huh." He smiled indulgently like one would at a silly child. "Then you should probably call the police."

His total lack of interest was aggravating

me. "I have! But they're not here yet. Shouldn't you go up to her room and make sure she's okay?"

"What's the patient's name?"

"Charlene Smith."

He didn't bother to write down her name or look on the computer for her room number. "Yeah, okay. I'll check it out." He walked away and poured himself a cup of coffee.

Aargh! I gave up and rushed to the elevator. I gazed around before I stepped out on the third floor. I didn't see Fred. My heart pounded in my ears as I made my way along the hall to Charlene's room.

I took a deep breath before I peeked inside her room.

Fred was there!

CHAPTER 35

Dear Sophie,
I would love to send flowers to my former mother-in-law who is in the hospital. But she's terribly allergic to them. Hospital rooms are simply ghastly, and flowers would brighten up her room. Are there any hypoallergenic flowers?
                    Hopeful Ex-Daughter-in-Law in
                                        Rose, Kansas

Dear Hopeful,
How about roses? Tulips and hydrangeas are also wonderful choices. Talk to your florist about it. People ask them this question all the time!
                                                Sophie

I jerked away and stood outside the room with my back against the wall. I could hear Fred talking softly. He could probably hear my heart pounding.

I pulled out my cell phone and texted Wolf again.

Fred is in Charlene's hospital room right now.

What was I going to do if he started to beat her or if he strangled her like he did the other women? I looked around for a weapon. Was there anything I could smash over his head? The hallway was unbelievably void of objects. There wasn't even a trash can. I walked back a few rooms, glancing in open doors. I found an unoccupied room. The flimsy plastic trash can would bounce off Fred's head.

Why was everything mounted on the wall? Probably so people like me wouldn't rip them off and bash them over someone's head. Ah, but someone had left a step stool behind. It was lightweight and not very large, but it was better than nothing. I carried it along the hallway and paused outside of Charlene's room.

I strained to hear what he was saying.

"You will not see me again, Charlene."

I lifted the step stool over my head and barged into the room shouting, "Nooooo!"

Fred blinked at me. "I knew you were trouble." He walked toward me slowly. "The apple fritters were delicious, but you and your friend Natasha were the only people

368

who pretended to care about my welfare."
He looked up at the step stool that I brandished over my head. "Were you planning to disable me with that?"

"Yes. The legs are made of iron," I lied.

He snorted. "They look like aluminum. An empty syringe with air in it or a knife would have served you better. Perhaps you should make note of that for your future endeavors."

Future endeavors? At least that wasn't a threat. "Move away from Charlene."

His eyes widened. And for the first time I saw him smile. "You are here to protect Charlene? From me?"

"You tried to kill her."

He stared at me without emotion. "Quite the contrary. I killed her attacker. I *saved* Charlene. But she vanished, and I could not find her. I feared she was dead."

"Oh, please!" I cried. "How dumb do you think I am?"

"No, it is true. And I don't think you are dumb. Nosy, perhaps. Alas, your presence here, not to mention your boldness in wielding such an alarming weapon, leads me to believe that the police cannot be far behind." He edged backward and leaned over Charlene.

I hastened to the other side of the bed,

still wielding the step stool. "Don't touch her!"

He ignored me. "My lovely Charlene. I will carry you in my heart until the day I die. I am sorry I must leave. I had hoped to be here longer, but sometimes the unexpected happens and it is not in my control to fix it. I have no regrets. This is the end."

I sucked in a noisy breath of air. "What did you do?" Had he poisoned her? Put something in her IV?

Fred stared at me in alarm.

Where was Wolf? Why hadn't the nurse stopped by? I gazed at the IV. I didn't see a syringe anywhere. I pressed the help button on Charlene's bed. I had to buy time. "I found your cat."

His face softened. "I must leave. I hope you will take care of her. She is a very good cat."

"What's her name?"

"Nika."

Was Mars ever going to arrive? "Don't you want to take Nika with you?"

"It will be a difficult journey. It would not be fair to her. She is better off living in Old Town with a nice person like you."

He wouldn't think I was so nice when Wolf showed up!

"I came to say goodbye to Charlene. When

she awakens one day, would you please tell her that I was here?"

I was confused. It didn't sound like he planned to kill her. "Yes. I would be happy to do that."

"We had an argument. That is the last thing she will remember about me. I wish it could be different."

Footsteps pounded along the hallway outside.

Fred flew toward the doorway.

I threw the step stool at him in the hope of slowing him down.

He turned and came straight toward me. He jammed his hand into his right pocket and withdrew a small weapon. A knife? I had nothing. Nothing to defend myself with. Nothing to throw at him. I thought I was a goner.

And then he swept right by me. The glass in the window shattered, and he jumped out.

Wolf and Mars entered the room, panting.

I breathed a little easier. "He came to say goodbye to Charlene."

The three of us looked out the window. He had landed on the roof of a porte cochere. It was still a long way to the ground.

"Sophie, you stay here and watch him. If

he jumps off, text me which way he's going." Wolf was on the run, barking something into his radio. Mars was on his heels.

I watched as Fred ran across the roof and disappeared. Could he have reentered the building? I texted Wolf and ran for the elevator. I stepped off on the second floor. It was far busier than the floor where Charlene lay.

A couple in the large waiting room squabbled in loud voices.

"Where are my glasses? I had them a minute ago."

"Honestly, Harold. I bought you a chain to put them on."

"I'm not using that thing. It makes me look like an old man."

"You *are* an old man."

I stood quietly, trying to block out their conversation. Doctors and nurses in scrubs walked by me. The security guy from downstairs held a door open to the porte cochere roof and surveyed the glass as though he didn't comprehend what had happened.

A doctor wearing black-framed glasses walked by me with his head down. A surgical mask covered half his face. There was something about him. Something not right. I watched as he walked away from me.

It had to be Fred. And, unless I missed my guess, he was wearing Harold's glasses.

I followed him, texting Wolf and being very thankful for the dictating feature. Fred was headed toward the stairwell.

When he opened the door, Wolf and Mars were waiting for him. Fred turned, ready to bolt, but I was right behind him, and that one-second delay to get around me was all Wolf needed. He had handcuffs on Fred faster than I'd have thought possible.

Fred addressed Wolf. "I know that you believe I have done this to my beloved Charlene, but it is quite the opposite. I saved her from the red-haired woman."

Wolf said calmly, "Maybe we can talk about this at the police station."

To me, Fred said, "You see? A difficult journey lies ahead. I killed the redhead. But only in defense of Charlene."

My head was reeling. "Are you saying Mia, the redhead, is the one who beat up Charlene?"

"Yes. When I arrived, the other woman was already dead. Charlene was on the floor and the redhead was on top of her, punching like a madwoman."

I looked at Wolf.

"Please tell Charlene that I have saved her life. Had I arrived a minute later, she would be dead today."

Mars blinked. "What was Charlene doing there?"

"Her friend, Abby, was leaving town and had asked Charlene to take care of her cat. Charlene was going to pick him up," said Fred.

"But she got there in time to see Mia kill Abby," mused Mars. "Truly the wrong place at the wrong time."

"I can only surmise that this Mia felt she must also kill Charlene because she was a witness to the murder," explained Fred. "It is true that I was forced to kill Mia, but only in defense of Charlene. She would not be clinging to life if I had not intervened."

"Sophie and I will tell Charlene what you did for her. I have to ask you to come with me now, please," said Wolf.

Wolf walked away with Fred. Mars and I returned to Charlene's room, where someone was sweeping up the shards of glass that had fallen inward. Fortunately, the majority were outside on the roof.

"Charlene looks a lot like Natasha," said Mars.

"I think so, too."

At that moment, Natasha and Griselda appeared.

"What's going on?" asked Natasha. "We just saw Wolf with Fred in handcuffs."

We explained Fred's version of what had transpired that fatal night.

"I almost hate to say this, but I believe him," said Mars. "It all makes sense."

"Why would Mia want to murder Abby?" asked Natasha.

Oh boy. We were in a pickle now. But at that moment, I realized that if Abby hadn't left Peyton's name in code, we wouldn't understand what had happened at all. "I think they had an argument."

Mars gave me a subtle thumbs-up.

"What happens to someone who murdered in defense of someone else?" asked Griselda.

"I think that's a legitimate defense," said Mars. "I think they call it justifiable homicide. If the facts line up right for Fred, and it sounds like they might, then he might not even be prosecuted."

"How's Charlene doing?" I asked.

Griselda patted Charlene's hand. "Her internal injuries are mending nicely according to the doctors. They're calling her a miracle. There's hope that she might make a full recovery. But it's going to take some time."

That night, Mars and I made excuses to avoid Bernie and Nina. We hated to do it, but there was no reasonable way we could explain what had happened to Mia and Abby without mentioning Peyton Poulon. We chose to wait a day or two.

At midnight, Wesley arrived for a meeting with Mars. They were still avoiding Jericho. Mars explained to me that it would take a little doing to get everything set up correctly. I accepted that and went off to bed.

On Monday morning, I leisurely cooked fluffy waffles and Southern-style cooked apples for breakfast. Mars dragged in from the den, looking as if he hadn't slept all night.

It didn't stop him from wolfing waffles and apples, though.

I showered, wondering how many more times I would shower before the walls were ripped out. Dressed in a red long-sleeved cotton top, jeans, and a quilted black vest, I tied all of Tilly's recipes in a red gingham ribbon and prepared to leave.

Nika and Mochie had settled in the bay window to watch squirrels. All things considered, they were getting along well.

I walked over to Tilly's house for the last time. She answered the door looking haggard.

"Are you all right?" I asked.

"Someone from the police department is

coming by today to take a DNA sample from Wesley, Briley, and me." She closed the door. "We're just sick about it."

I followed her to the kitchen. Jericho was already there, apparently just hanging out.

"I have coffee. Would you care for some? I'm so distracted, that was the best I could do this morning."

"I'm fine, thanks."

We sat down on the large sofa as we had so many times before. Jericho continued to lurk.

"Apparently a child Briley and Schuyler's age was kidnapped thirteen years ago, and the police think it's one of our girls! I don't understand. Why our daughters?"

"I'm so sorry." What else could I say? Would it be right for me to spring the news that it wasn't Briley? Probably not. What if I was wrong? What if Schuyler had a tattoo like I had originally thought and it was Briley who had the birthmark? Or what if Abby had been wrong?

My blood ran cold. It wasn't impossible that Mia had murdered Abby for some other reason. But I thought that was unlikely.

The best thing for me right now was to be a good listener and be sympathetic.

"They're coming to test all five of us. I

377

had no idea that Pierce adopted Schuyler. But they didn't excuse him from the DNA tests. I'm so nervous! What a crazy thing. Why on earth would they pick these two girls out of the hundreds of thousands of girls their age? Maybe even more. If that little girl was kidnapped, what makes them think she's still in this country? I can tell you I was there when Briley was born. So was Wesley! Neither of us has forgotten the twenty-one hours of labor."

She clutched her hand to her forehead. "As you can see, I'm quite distraught over this whole thing."

"That's certainly understandable. Who wouldn't be? But if you gave birth to Briley, then I'm certain you have nothing to worry about." I inched the recipes toward her on the table to distract her.

"You have been just wonderful, Sophie. So many bizarre things happened while you worked on these! I'm amazed that we managed to get them done at all."

"Would your editor like me to send her a copy via e-mail?"

"That would be so kind of you." Tilly wrote down her editor's name and e-mail address and handed me a check. "I don't know what I'll do without you popping in here every day. Mia's gone and the girls will be back in school, at least I hope they will be."

"I'm sure our paths will cross again."

Tilly gave me a hug. "Thank you for rushing this."

I showed myself out and headed straight to the bank to deposit the check. I did some mental calculations of how much I would have left after taxes. It would be enough to do some serious damage to my old bathroom.

Cal, the builder, dropped by in the afternoon. He suggested a number of different scenarios and promised to work up estimates for me. I crossed my fingers that he was right about the affordability of creating two bathrooms, one off my bedroom and another for guests. A girl could hope.

That evening, Mars excitedly called me into the den. He rewound the program he'd been watching. "Listen to this."

"And in breaking news, the United States is expelling a Russian spy caught right here in Old Town, Alexandria. Authorities say they expect a similar retaliation against one of our operatives in Russia."

"That can't be Fred," I said.

"You bet it is. No messy trial for him. He's going home."

I felt a little bit frustrated that there

wouldn't be a trial. All the details would have been laid out and made clear. And someone would have paid for the horrible massacre at Abby's house. "Do you think prosecutors declined to press charges?"

"No! I think he waved a diplomatic crisis flag, passed Go, and got a get-out-of-jail-free card."

"What's that supposed to mean?"

"Sophie, no one will want to start an international crisis over a guy like Fred."

"That's disappointing. Of course, if he was telling the truth and he only defended Charlene, then I guess he wouldn't have served time, anyway."

"Would you like to come to Wesley and Tilly's house with me tomorrow morning?" Mars asked.

"What's up?"

"Project 'Goodbye, Jericho.' I'm cleaning up Wesley's image. He will be all over every news channel tomorrow."

"I wouldn't miss it."

We were up early the next day. It was still chilly outside when we left, and I was glad I chose to wear a blazer with a scarf around my neck.

The throng of reporters had grown. "How do you feel now that you're no longer a suspect, Mars?"

Mars smiled and spoke directly to the camera. No ducking away this time. "I'm relieved that Sergeant Fleishman was able to uncover the truth. It's always better to let the sun in so the truth can shine."

Tilly opened the door in full makeup and a Texas girl outfit right down to her boots. She called to the press, "Mornin' y'all!"

When we were in the foyer and she closed the door behind us, Tilly sagged. "What a relief all this is coming to an end. I'm brokenhearted about Mia and especially about Abby. But I'm glad to be able to move on."

Tilly had knocked herself out with an assortment of eggs, pancakes, and bacon. Plates, cutlery, and red gingham napkins had been set up on the kitchen island so everyone could help themselves.

"How did the DNA tests go yesterday?" I asked.

"There's nothing to the tests. It's waiting for the results that's scary."

"I hope you get them soon so you can put this behind you."

She whispered, "Briley nearly freaked out. I have assured her that I was present at her birth and I know she's our child, but it's still frightening for a kid to go through."

Briley and Schuyler ate breakfast with us. Jericho hung around Mars as though he was afraid to miss a single word.

Schuyler sat down next to me. "I guess you heard that one of us might have been kidnapped?"

CHAPTER 36

Dear Sophie,
I'm redoing my bathroom and I'm confused about shower floors. What's the best thing to use: tile, stone, marble, or glass?

> Drowning in Options in Bath,
> New York

Dear Drowning in Options,
I know exactly how you feel. While many flooring options look beautiful, you need to consider three main things. How do you clean them? Do they need to be sealed annually? And what size are they? Installers recommend nothing larger than four-by-four inches so that there's enough grout for you to have a secure footing when the shower is wet. Don't forget to consider what hard water might do to the material if that's an issue at

your house.

Sophie

I had to tread carefully. "Kind of scary, huh?"

"I hope it's me!" she said. "It would explain so much. Like why my mom was so weird about things and monitored me all the time. I feel like a traitor for saying this, but I feel so much more relaxed now that it's just me and my dad. I loved my mom, but I always felt like something wasn't right."

"I hope it all works out for you."

"It will. When Dad heard about it, he promised that I can live with him. We're a pretty good team. He's kind of goofy sometimes, but we're managing. You should have seen the two of us trying to figure out the washing machine!" She laughed at the memory. "Dad wants me to see a psychologist to help me through losing my mom and maybe being kidnapped."

"That sounds like a good idea. You've been through a lot."

A moment later she asked, "Do you think my mom murdered Abby? That's what they're saying."

Oh no! I didn't want to make things even worse for her. Her father should be the one telling her about that. But as I looked at her, it dawned on me that she wasn't sobbing. In fact, I would have said she was thriving. I decided it was best to be honest. She'd had the truth hidden from her for too long, and look how that ended. Mars was right about letting the sun shine in. "It appears that she did. Mia was desperate to keep you. She loved you more than anything. It's all a horrible tragedy, but I would guess Mia had been mentally unbalanced for a long time if she thought it was okay to steal a baby."

"That's a good way of putting it. Mentally unbalanced. That's what I've been living with all my life."

"Okay, everyone! Here it comes," said Wesley.

"Good morning, Washington! Congressman Wesley Winthrop is having a good day. He was a person of interest in the murder of Abigail Bergeron, but police have officially announced that Mia Hendrickson of Old Town murdered Bergeron. Hendrickson also died at the scene of the crime. In other news, Congressman Winthrop will hold a press conference this afternoon to announce an initiative against hazing in fraternities."

Jericho looked sick. "You can't do that,

Wesley. Are you insane? If Mars advised you to take this path, then you're falling for his revenge plot. He knows this is political suicide."

"We're just putting a little sunlight on a dark subject, Jericho," said Mars.

"Better start looking for another job, Wesley. Although I don't know who would hire you after the truth comes out." He cornered Wesley. I could hear him whisper, "Come on, man! What are you thinking? This will ruin you. It will ruin both of us."

And that had been the problem all along, I thought. Jericho had been worried that his part in the hazing might be revealed.

Later that afternoon, Nina and I sat in my kitchen and waited for Wesley's news conference on TV.

Wesley walked out to a podium and waved. Mars stood behind him and off to the side a bit.

"Mars looks so spiffy in his suit. I never see him dressed up like that," said Nina.

Wesley spoke. "In my younger years, I was a member of a fraternity in which a horrible hazing accident occurred. My classmate and dear friend was severely injured, changing his life forever. I am proud to say that in spite of being a paraplegic, he is a husband,

386

a father of three boys, and a successful psychologist. For me, there is nothing worse than knowing this didn't have to happen to him. He and countless others have been permanently maimed, and far too many have died because of hazing. My own experience has led me to start a nonprofit foundation to help these individuals move forward in their lives, to give them the financial aid they need for their ongoing medical care, and to rid us of hazing rituals altogether."

"Not too shabby," said Nina.

"Mars did a pretty good job turning a negative into something positive," I said. "I never realized how hard his job is. Everyone has done something stupid in their lives."

Bernie knocked on the kitchen door and entered. He handed each of us a flyer that read

Are you a fan of
Live with Natasha?
The host of your favorite show about all things domestic is about to be replaced by someone else! Help us back up our favorite domestic diva, Natasha, by joining us in a rally to keep
Live with Natasha!
Monday at Noon

The Laughing Hound
Old Town, Alexandria

I was ashamed to admit that I had forgotten all about Tilly replacing Natasha. "This is great, Bernie! I will definitely be there. Is there anything I can do to help?"

"Spread the word."

"I'll take Facebook," said Nina.

"Then I'll hit Twitter." I offered.

Mars moved home that night. The reporters had moved on to other stories, and things calmed down on our street.

A week later I had chosen bathtubs and shower tile. My dream linen closets were sketched on paper. A painted ceramic sink by a local artist had been ordered for the powder room. My head spun with all the details of mirrors, light fixtures, and faucets. And where exactly did I want electrical outlets? It was turning into a much bigger job than I had anticipated, but I had waited long enough and was thrilled that Cal would begin renovation in October.

It also happened to be the day that Charlene was being released from the hospital. Carrying a bouquet of gladiolas, I crossed the street to Natasha's house and cut through the side yard to the apartment over the garage. Natasha had left a key under the mat. No one would ever think to look there!

The fall sun shone in through large windows. I set the vase on the round dining table. I removed platters from the refrigerator, took off the covers, and placed them on the table. I put on coffee and tea and poured sparkling apple cider into a pitcher. I checked the time. People would start arriving any minute.

Nina rushed in. "Doesn't Charlene have a broken leg? How is she going to get up those stairs?"

"It's not ideal. But it's better than having to live with Natasha."

"Will Charlene's mom be staying with her? I thought she had a store in Maryland."

"Her partner will be running the store until Charlene can get around on her own again."

Friends of Charlene's whom I didn't know began to gather with gifts of flowers, balloons, exquisite chocolates, and culinary mysteries to keep her occupied while she healed.

Suddenly there was a commotion at the stairs. I snuck through the crowd that gathered. Charlene was trying to walk up by herself, one step at a time. I was glad to see Bernie behind her, ready to catch her if she slipped.

A cheer went up when she reached the top. Mars had carried her collapsible wheelchair up the stairs, and Charlene appeared glad to be able to sit down and catch her breath.

She chattered and hugged friends. After a bit, people helped themselves to food, and the roar subsided. Wolf arrived, carrying a beautiful rustic bowl filled with moss and colorful African violets. I suspected his wife, an avid gardener, had put it together for Charlene.

One of her friends began to ask questions about the night she almost died, and Charlene told us her story.

"Gosh, it all began with Fred. For months I'd had some suspicions about him. He was immaculate. I never saw anything odd at his house, but he never wanted me to go upstairs. I knew his parents had come here from Russia, and that they supposedly lived near Brighton Beach. But he didn't have any pictures of them around, which I thought was odd. In fact, he didn't like being photographed. One day I sneaked upstairs and saw his computer setup. I guess a lot of people have a number of computers, but it seemed wrong to me." She took a sip of sparkling apple cider.

"That night, I broke up with Fred. He was very upset and begged me to reconsider. It turned into something of an argument, so I told him I had to pick up Abby's cat, Oscar, because Abby was going out of town. That was all true, but it gave me a good reason to leave. I dashed down the street. When I got to Abby's, I went through the passage to the back like I always did. I knocked on the door and looked in through the glass. Oscar was in his carrier, ready to go, and there was a blue suitcase next to it.

"When Abby didn't appear, I opened the door and went inside. I heard a thump and the sound of someone falling down the stairs. I saw Abby crumpled at the bottom of the stairs with a cord around her neck. I thought she was dead. When I looked up, a woman, whom I now know was Mia, stood at the top of the stairs. I screamed and ran for the door. But Mia was faster than me. She caught up to me and literally threw me against the fireplace. I think that's when my leg broke. She started beating me like there was a fury inside her. I thought I would die for sure. I really did." Charlene wiped tears out of her eyes.

"I was in such pain, I tried to drag myself into a standing position, but she kept kicking me. In my head, and my abdomen, and my back. I had almost given up when Fred arrived. He tore her away from me. I could hear them fighting. But I was scared of him. I was afraid of both of them. I knew I couldn't take much more. I didn't realize that my leg was broken. It hurt like the dickens, but at that point everything ached and I was in a panic. I knew I had to get out of there to save myself. I scrambled out the door, trying not to put much weight on my leg. I felt woozy, but I knew I would die if I didn't hide. I managed to make it to the alley but had to keep going. I opened the first gate I saw. The door to the garage was open. I closed it behind me and found a large tarp. I crawled into a corner and pulled it over me in case one of them looked in the garage. And then I passed out."

"You didn't worry about someone following drops of blood?" asked one of her friends.

"Most of my injuries were internal. The only place that I bled was on my head, and most of that was caught in my hair. For the next few days, I would come to and try to get up, but the pain all over my body was so excruciating that I would pass out again. I had no concept of time passing. I didn't know if it was day or night. One time, I thought I heard voices. I was determined to get help. I was finally able to get up on my one good leg without passing out. That was the day I limped to Natasha's house in the dark. By the time I made it through her gate, I was too weak to continue. I collapsed and just lay there in her grass, hoping she would see me."

"I don't understand. Why were you so afraid of Fred at that point?" asked her friend.

"He had followed me! I didn't know what he had in mind. I only knew that Mia had killed Abby and tried to kill me, too. I didn't know who to trust, other than Natasha, a sister I had never met."

Tears streamed down Natasha's face. She hugged Charlene and Griselda. A few minutes later, Natasha sidled up to me. "I probably won't see as much of you now that I have a sister. But I'm always here for you if you need me."

"Thank you, Natasha. I'm here for you, too." I embraced her in a big hug. "I'm so relieved that Charlene survived."

I had a feeling there would be a lot of adjustments ahead. And a lot of arguing. But that went along with being sisters. I suspected I might end up hearing more from Natasha than she expected.

Bernie and Mars caught my eye. Bernie cocked his head to the side, and I knew we needed to leave for the Laughing Hound. Bernie and I snuck away, leaving Mars to coax Natasha to the restaurant.

CHAPTER 37

Dear Natasha,
I was devastated when I heard your show would be taken over by a new host. I watch you every day. No one is more elegant or classy. Could you do some shows on how to dress? I know it's not a domestic diva thing, but your wardrobe is to die for!
                        Plain Old Milly in Old Town,
                              Alexandria, Virginia

Dear Plain Old Milly,
If the show continues, I will certainly do that. What fun!
                                        Natasha

The Laughing Hound was packed. "Who knew Natasha had so many fans?" I asked Bernie.

Across one wall, a huge banner said SAVE *LIVE WITH NATASHA!*

I could see people taking selfies, and someone yelled, "We're trending!"

"Bernie, you outdid yourself."

He just smiled.

A chant went up. "Natasha! Natasha! Natasha!"

Mars timed it perfectly. Natasha walked into the restaurant and broke into sobs. She walked among her fans, hugging them and posing for selfies. She was in her element.

Bernie handed her a microphone, and she stepped onto a podium he had set up.

Everyone applauded. There were more cheers of "Natasha!"

"Thank you. Thank you each and every one. I love you all. I can't believe that you have gathered here today for me! I'm having a serious Sally Field moment right now. You like me!"

Someone yelled, "We love you!"

Natasha clasped her free hand to her chest. "This is truly the best day of my life."

A gentleman I had never seen before walked up to the podium, and Natasha's smile faded. Covering the microphone, she said, "Please don't ruin this for me, Jack."

Jack joined her on the podium. He reached for the microphone. "May I?"

Natasha handed it to him, but she didn't look happy about it.

The voices faded, and the room became silent.

"This week has been an interesting one for us at the TV station. We have received thousands of letters and e-mails regarding Natasha's show. Frankly, I have read enough tweets to last me a lifetime. In light of the public support for *Live with Natasha!* We have decided to continue the show."

Confetti rained from the ceiling while helium balloons rose from the floor. It looked like a New Year's Eve celebration. The cheers nearly drowned out Natasha's thanks.

I gazed at Bernie. "I believe you might like Natasha after all."

"She can grow on a person," he said.

Instead of hugging Natasha, I hugged Bernie.

Jack stepped down and let Natasha enjoy the limelight.

"Excuse me," I said. "What will happen to Tilly's show?"

He looked surprised. "I didn't know word was out about that yet. Not to worry, I think there's room for two domestic divas in this town."

I didn't tell him there were a whole lot more than two.

I left the restaurant and ran into Wolf.

"What's going on in there?" he asked.

I explained what had happened.

"Bernie to the rescue," said Wolf. "He's a good guy."

"I wanted to talk with you. Have you got a minute?"

Wolf grinned. "I figured you would want a few more answers."

"I know Fred released Abby's cat and threw his collar in the tree. But I don't know why he threw the collar."

"I asked him about that. He said if people saw the cat with a collar on, they would assume the cat had a home and that the cat would go back. But Abby was dead. So he reasoned not having a collar would increase Oscar's chances of being taken in by someone, and he threw it in the air."

"What about the suitcase?"

"He thought he should clean up the place. If nothing else, to buy time. So he hid the bodies and threw the suitcase, computer, and telephone in the river. He didn't know what had transpired or why Mia was intent on killing Charlene. And yes, he stole the bags of lime and poured them over Abby's body to keep it from smelling bad. Anything else?"

"Not today."

"See you around, Sophie."

I walked home slowly, considering all the things that had happened. As I approached my house, I saw someone sitting on my stoop. Not a reporter! I thought they all left. It was Schuyler. "Hi, Sophie! I was just about to leave. I wanted you to know that I'm Peyton, which is kind of a cool name. My dad says I can change it if I want to. But I think I might keep Hendrickson. That way, my name will reflect both of my families."

She was taking this way too well. "Peyton Hendrickson. I like it!"

"Mars told me how you unraveled the code that Abby wrote in the recipe book. I wanted to thank you. It's sort of weird to imagine so many people looking for me, and looking out for Peyton, a kid they didn't even know. The shrink says I might have some dark days ahead as everything sinks in. But I think I have so much to be grateful for. Maybe Mia kidnapped me and took me from my real family, but she gave me my dad. And obsessive as she was, she took good care of me. And now I get to have two families. Next week, Dad and I are flying to Milwaukee to meet my birth parents."

"How do you feel about that?" I asked.

"Scared and excited at the same time. They have a room for me! My real mom said every time I had a birthday, and every Christmas, they bought me presents. They're all in my room waiting for me."

"That shows how much they love you. They hoped you would come back to them."

"I don't want to leave my dad. He doesn't have anybody else since Mom died. He and I think that maybe I can live with him during the school year and spend time with my birth family during the summer."

"That sounds like a very reasonable solution."

"They say I look just like my real mom. She never stopped looking for me. How lucky could I be? I think I want to be in the FBI. Did you know that they have a team of specialists who locate and return missing kids? That's what I want to do."

I gave her a big hug and tried very hard not to cry. Peyton was one strong young woman. I had no doubt that she would accomplish her FBI dreams.

That afternoon, I baked a lasagna and took it over to Francie and Eunice. Daisy went along to see her buddy, Duke.

They fussed over the heavenly aroma. I sat down to chat with them.

"We just returned from visiting Charlene and Griselda," said Francie. "They were sitting outside enjoying the sunshine. I think

I'm going to arrange to stay with Charlene for a few hours to give Griselda a break now and then."

"That's very kind of you. I'm sure both of them will enjoy that."

"She was thrilled to hear that Oscar lives with me now," said Eunice. "She really loves cats. But she's worried about Fred's cat called Nika. We went down to the shelter, just in case she was there. But she hadn't been turned in."

"That's because I have Nika."

Eunice's eyes opened wide. "No kidding? You have to tell Charlene. She'll feel so much better. I still can't believe that lovely young woman was practically dying in my garage and I had no idea." Eunice shook her head. "It was bad enough knowing that Fred could place Abby's corpse in *my* deck storage box and I never heard a sound! Francie is taking me to the audiologist tomorrow. I'm getting new hearing aids. I have missed way too much of what's going on around me."

"You haven't missed everything," said Francie with a wink. She turned on the TV.

"What are you talking about?" I asked.

At that moment, someone knocked on the door. Francie disappeared. She returned with Sam, Benton, Schuyler — who was really Peyton, Briley, and the cute teenage boy I had seen acting peculiar on the street.

"Hi, Sophie," said Benton with an engaging smile. "This is my nephew, Troy. I think you know everyone else, Troy."

I greeted him but couldn't help wondering what was going on with the two of them. I held my breath. Why were they all here at Francie's house? It did not escape me that Briley smiled at Troy and beamed. Was this the boy she had a crush on?

"You're just in time," said Eunice. "I'm glad you're here with us to see this, Sophie."

A shiver ran through me. I was leery of Benton, even though he'd been very polite to me.

Everyone talked at once, making it hard to follow any threads of thought. And then, Francie shushed them.

The announcer was saying, "In a joint effort between the CIA and the FBI, agents have been able to track a hacking organization that targeted United States politicians and employees of the federal government. The hacker sent e-mail to their children. When the children clicked on a link, the hackers were able to go through the children's accounts to their parents' accounts, where they accessed passwords. Once they had the passwords, they had complete access to sensitive information and were even able to enter government accounts. I am pleased to announce that the hacker has been apprehended thanks to the diligence of agents and some special assistants."

Briley and Peyton whooped and high-fived. "That's us! We're the special assistants!"

On the TV screen, Wesley stepped up to the microphone. "In recent weeks, there has been a huge outcry, including demands that I resign my position, because of an e-mail that allegedly outed two U.S. agents. That e-mail was phony. It was designed to enable us to locate the hacker. You can see how easily he was able to put it out there. Everyone was convinced that it was legitimate and that I was the source of the e-mail. In fact, I did *not* write that e-mail. Clearly, I would never mention the names of operatives in my communications. And if you look closely at that e-mail, you will find that those operatives are fictional. There are no U.S. operatives by those names. My e-mail and my computer were hacked. But that e-mail was pure fiction, designed as a trap."

Wesley stepped back, and reporters shouted questions.

Eunice clicked mute on the TV remote and turned to me. "One day when Briley came over here to talk to us about Old Town when we were young, she asked me if clicking on a link in an e-mail could have allowed someone to hack into her dad's e-mail. Of course it could, and it did. I called Sam, and together we reached out to old friends at the CIA. They sent Benton over here, and we set up a trap for the hacker."

Benton? I looked over at him in shock. "CIA? So you really are a spy?"

Benton laughed aloud. "No, I'm just a cyber geek at the CIA. Just another ordinary government employee. No undercover work for me."

Really? Should I out him and let him know that I had seen him stashing things around town? I tried to let him know without being too obvious. "I saw you with the soda can."

Troy glanced at Benton.

Benton grinned. "She's onto us, Troy. We're not doing a very good job."

I wasn't following them at all.

"What are you talking about?" asked Briley.

I stared at Benton, wondering how he was going to handle this. Would he confess to being undercover after all? Could spies even do that?

"When Troy was younger and found out that I worked for the CIA, he wished I was a spy. So I started leaving little messages around town for him. It's just all in good fun. You're the first person who called us out on it, Sophie."

Sam shook his head. "You two are going to have to improve if Sophie noticed."

"I left the soda can in the trash," said Troy proudly. "It contained a message telling Uncle Benton what time to meet me to go to a movie the next day."

"The chalk on the lamppost was to let you know something was under the pumpkin?" I asked.

Benton flushed. "Boy, you really are observant. I might start leaving notes for you."

As he spoke, something else clicked with me. "Did you play little games like this with Abby?"

Benton's eyes met mine. His mouth pulled tight, and he nodded.

"So she left the code on the recipes for you. She assumed that if anything happened, you would look for her at Tilly's house and see the codes on the recipes."

"What codes?"

I explained how we figured out Peyton's name. "What I don't understand is why

Abby didn't call the police immediately."

"I wish she had," said Benton. "She might still be alive. But Abby had a history of thinking she found Peyton. She had reported a couple of other girls in the past who weren't Peyton. It was always a huge, horrible scene and so hard on the girls and their families. She had promised me she wouldn't put anyone else through that. To be honest, I thought Peyton was probably dead."

He grinned at Schuyler, "I'm glad you're alive and well. Abby was devastated when you disappeared. It never left her mind. She called Charlene to take Oscar, and then she went out to dinner with Mars, all the while probably trying to decide what she should do. She didn't realize that Mia would move so fast, I guess."

"I'm so sorry that Mia killed her," said Schuyler softly. "I liked Abby."

Francie broke the sad silence. "The girls were fabulous in catching the hacker!" said Francie. "It was so much fun."

"And you'll never believe this," said Eunice. "Guess who the hacker was."

I didn't know any hackers. Unless . . . "Not Fred!"

"He was right under our noses all along," said Francie. "We told Charlene, and she said she had a feeling something wasn't right."

"That's what you were doing over here the day I dropped by. I thought you were up to something."

"We're gonna miss that. It felt good to be involved in taking down a criminal," said Eunice.

When I left Francie's house, I knew what I had to do. I didn't really want to, because Nika had fit into my household so nicely. She and Mochie got along well. But sometimes you have to do what's right. I packed up a litter box and some cat food. Apologizing to Mochie the whole time, I lifted Nika out of the bay window and carried her over to Natasha's guest house.

Charlene cried when I placed Nika in her lap. I handed the litter box and cat food to Griselda, who was obviously a cat lover and couldn't get over Nika's beautiful blue eyes.

"Are you sure it's okay for me to have her?" asked Charlene.

"Absolutely. Fred may have been a terrible man, but he loved you and Nika."

"Actually, I meant Natasha," said Charlene. "I thought she doesn't like animals. She calls them furballs."

"Bernie lived here with three cats. I imagine Natasha will get over it."

Griselda winked at me. "The doctor said a pet might be a good idea. They have healing qualities."

They did indeed. I could hear Nika purring already.

When I left their apartment, I spied Natasha walking across her lawn. I darted out the gate as fast as I could and hoped she hadn't seen me. They were sisters. They would argue and make up and love each other anyway, I reasoned.

I was halfway home when I heard Natasha scream. I smiled. Now everything was back to normal. My sister, Hannah, and I loved each other dearly but there were times when we drove each other nuts. For Natasha and Charlene, the fun was just beginning.

RECIPES

GRANDMA PEGGY'S PUMPKIN BUNDT CAKE
HPS5106

1/2 cup butter (1 stick), melted, plus extra
  for pan
3 cups flour
1 tablespoon baking powder
3/4 teaspoon baking soda
3/4 teaspoon salt
1 1/2 teaspoons cinnamon
1/2 teaspoon nutmeg
1/4 cup vegetable oil
3 large room-temperature eggs
1 1/2 cups sugar, plus extra for pan
1 1/2 cups dark brown sugar
3 cups pumpkin puree
1 tablespoon vanilla
Powdered sugar (optional)

Preheat the oven to 350°F. Grease the
Bundt pan well with butter and sprinkle
sugar in it as you would flour to prevent
sticking.

Melt the 1/2 cup of butter and set aside to
cool. In a bowl, mix together the flour, baking powder, baking soda, salt, cinnamon,
and nutmeg. Set aside. In a large mixing
bowl, combine 1/2 cup melted butter and
the oil, and mix. Beat in the eggs. Add the

411

sugar and dark brown sugar and beat on slow, then gradually increase the speed. Add the pumpkin and vanilla and beat. Slowly add in the flour mixture, about 1/3 cup at a time. Pour the mixture into the greased Bundt pan.

Bake 55 minutes or until a cake tester comes out clean. Allow to rest on a rack about 15 minutes, then loosen the edges and middle and flip onto a serving plate. Optional: sprinkle with powdered sugar before serving. Serve warm or cold.

ROASTED PARMESAN CHICKEN BREASTS
BAC149

1 teaspoon garlic powder
1 teaspoon paprika
1/2 teaspoon salt
1/2 teaspoon pepper
1 1/2 tablespoons parsley flakes
1/2 cup mayonnaise
1 cup panko
1/2 cup Parmesan cheese
4 chicken breasts

Preheat the oven to 375°F. Grease a 9 × 9 inch baking pan. Mix the garlic powder, paprika, salt, pepper, parsley flakes, and mayonnaise in a bowl. Mix the panko and Parmesan cheese in a separate bowl. Dip the chicken breasts into the mayonnaise mixture and then into the panko mixture, covering the breasts completely. Place the breasts in the baking pan.

Bake 30 to 35 minutes until the chicken registers 165° on a thermometer.

MAPLE-GLAZED BRUSSELS SPROUTS WITH BACON
WFM2912

1 pound Brussels sprouts
4 slices bacon, cut into bite-size pieces
1/4 tablespoon olive oil
1/8 cup maple syrup
1/2 teaspoon salt
1/4 teaspoon pepper

Preheat the oven to 350°F. Clean the Brussels sprouts and remove the outer layer of leaves. Place the sprouts on a lipped baking sheet in a single layer. Add the bacon. Pour the olive oil over them and turn to coat. Sprinkle with salt and pepper and turn again.

Bake 25 minutes. Remove the sheet from the oven and turn the sprouts. Pour the maple syrup over them and toss.

GARLIC MASHED POTATOES
GPP251

6 cups chicken stock
3 pounds red potatoes
1/2 cup unsalted butter
3 tablespoons garlic powder
1/2 cup milk
3 ounces cream cheese
1 1/4 teaspoons salt

Pour the chicken stock into a large pot and bring to a boil. As the stock heats, cut the potatoes into one-inch chunks. Cook the potatoes in the chicken stock until the potatoes can be easily pierced by a fork. Melt the butter. As it melts, gradually whisk in the garlic powder. Remove the potatoes from the broth to a mixing bowl. Mash the potatoes with the butter, milk, cream cheese, and salt until smooth and creamy.

CORNBREAD WITH A CORNY TWIST
MGB4143

1 cup milk
1 teaspoon vinegar
1 cup self-rising cornmeal
1 cup all-purpose flour
1 teaspoon baking powder
1/2 teaspoon baking soda
1/8 teaspoon salt
1 large room-temperature egg, beaten
1/2 cup unsalted butter
1/3 cup honey
1 cup frozen corn

Preheat the oven to 350°F. Pour the vinegar into the milk and set aside. In a large bowl, combine the cornmeal, flour, baking powder, baking soda, and salt. Mix well. Whisk the egg lightly into the milk, pour in the honey and mix. Melt the butter in a 10-inch cast-iron skillet and swirl to coat the bottom and the sides. Pour any excess butter over the cornmeal mixture. Pour in the milk mixture and stir until just combined. Add the corn and stir. Pour into the skillet.

Bake 20 to 25 minutes or until a cake tester comes out clean.

BOURBON APPLE FRITTERS WITH BOURBON CARAMEL SAUCE
RPC142

2 large sweet apples, such as Fuji
1 cup flour
2 tablespoons sugar
1 1/2 teaspoons baking powder
1/2 teaspoon ground cinnamon
1/2 teaspoon salt
2 tablespoons bourbon
1 egg
1/2 cup milk
Corn oil for frying (40 ounce bottle)
Powdered sugar

Peel and core the apples. Cut into slices about 1/4 inch thick. In a large bowl, mix the flour, sugar, baking powder, cinnamon, and salt. In a separate bowl, mix the egg with the milk and bourbon. Whisk the milk mixture into the flour mixture. Pour the corn oil about three inches deep in a pot and heat until a drop of water sizzles in it. Dip the apple strips into the batter and gently lower them into the oil. Do not crowd them. Fry until golden. Remove to a paper towel to absorb any excess oil. Sprinkle with powdered sugar and serve with

Bourbon Caramel Sauce. Note: these are best the day they are made.

BOURBON CARAMEL SAUCE
BAF7168

1/2 cup packed dark brown sugar
1/2 cup butter
1/2 cup heavy cream
Pinch of pink salt
2 tablespoons bourbon
1 tablespoon powdered sugar

Add the dark brown sugar, butter, cream, and salt to a small pot and bring to a boil while stirring. Continue to cook at a simmer for one minute while stirring. Remove from heat and stir in the bourbon and powdered sugar.

HOMEMADE PUMPKIN SPICE LATTES
CPS3811

2 cups 2% milk
1/2 cup canned pumpkin
1/4 cup packed brown sugar
1/2 teaspoon cinnamon
1/8 teaspoon nutmeg
Pinch of cloves
1 teaspoon vanilla

Place milk, pumpkin, brown sugar, cinnamon, nutmeg, and cloves in a large pot and whisk together. Heat until the brown sugar is melted and everything is combined. Stir in the vanilla. Pour into individual mugs and spoon sweetened cream on top. Sprinkle with just a hint of nutmeg.

Sweetened Cream
1 cup heavy cream
1/3 cup powdered sugar
1 teaspoon vanilla

Beat the heavy cream until it begins to take shape. Add the powdered sugar and vanilla and continue to beat until the cream holds a firm shape.

BRANDIED APPLE CIDER
GMP434

4 cups apple cider
1 cinnamon stick
1/2 teaspoon nutmeg
Pinch of cloves
1 cup apple brandy

Place all ingredients in a pot and simmer for 20 minutes. Pour into mugs and garnish by adding a cinnamon stick to each mug.

CREAMY MACARONI AND CHEESE
BCS417

1 8 × 8 baking pan

8 ounces dried macaroni
4 tablespoons butter
4 tablespoons flour
2 cups milk
1 teaspoon paprika
1 tablespoon yellow mustard
1 teaspoon garlic powder
1 teaspoon salt
4 ounces sharp cheddar cheese, such as
  Kerrygold, shredded
4 ounces Colby cheese (not Colby-Jack),
  shredded
1/2 cup panko
1/2 cup freshly grated Parmesano Reggiano

Cook the macaroni according to its instructions, then drain and set aside. Preheat the oven to 400°F.

Melt the butter in a large pot over medium-low heat. Whisk the flour into the butter. Stir while cooking until it begins to smell a little bit nutty.

Stir in the milk, paprika, yellow mustard, garlic powder, and salt, and whisk well to combine. When the milk mixture is very hot but not boiling, add the cheddar cheese, the Colby cheese, and the cream cheese and stir to melt. Pour into an 8 × 8 baking pan. In a small bowl, mix the panko and the Parmesano Reggiano. Sprinkle over the mac and cheese. Bake 20 to 30 minutes. The top should be golden, and the sides should be bubbling.

CARROT PUMPKIN SOUP
CCT1085

2 tablespoons butter
2 medium onions
3/4 teaspoon rubbed sage
Pinch of thyme
2 ribs of celery
5 large carrots
4 cups chicken broth (vegetable broth
   would work fine)
1 pear
1 cup pumpkin puree
1 cup half-and-half
Salt to taste
Toast or croutons

Melt the butter in a large soup pot at medium to medium-low heat. Dice the onions and add to the pot. Give them an occasional stir while they cook. Add the sage and thyme. Slice the celery and add to the pot.

Peel and slice the carrots while the onions cook to the point where they just begin to tinge a little bit brown. Add the carrots to the pot. Peel and core the pear and throw it into the pot.

Add the chicken broth and place a lid on the pot. Bring to a boil, then reduce the heat and simmer for about 45 minutes. The carrots should be soft. Use an immersion hand blender to puree in the pot. It's up to you to decide how smooth you want the soup to be.

Add 1 cup of pumpkin and 1 cup of half-and-half. Mix well and bring back to a boil briefly before serving.

Garnish with toast or croutons, or serve with rustic bread and butter or cheese.

WESLEY'S FAVORITE MEATLOAF
CMC3610

1 green or red bell pepper
1 large onion
1 extra-large egg
1/2 cup oatmeal
2 tablespoons yellow mustard
2 tablespoons Worcestershire sauce
Dash of salt
Dash of black pepper
2 pounds ground beef
Barbecue sauce (or 1 cup ketchup)

Preheat oven to 350°F. Grease a loaf pan.

Finely chop the green or red pepper. Chop the onion. Whisk the egg in a large bowl. Add the oatmeal, mustard, green pepper, onion, Worcestershire sauce, salt, pepper, and beef to the bowl. Mix well and place in the loaf pan. Bake for 30 minutes.

Spread barbecue sauce on the top and bake another 30 minutes.

BONUS RECIPE!

FRANKENSTEIN MARSHMALLOWS

These are easy to make at home and will thrill children.

Green candy melts
Large marshmallows
Straws
Chocolate sprinkles
Candy eyes
Chocolate chips

Melt the green candy melts. Dip the marshmallows in the green candy so they are covered completely. Insert the straws into one marshmallow side to create the stick to hold on the bottom. Dip the marsh-mallow tops into the chocolate sprinkles. Place two candy eyes on one side to make the face. Stand them up in a glass to dry. To speed up the process, you can place them in the fridge.

When the green candy has set, melt some chocolate chips and use a toothpick to draw a hatchmark "scar" on each marshmallow face. A straightish line with three smaller lines crossing it will work fine. Next, use the toothpick to draw a jagged mouth. Then dip the pointed ends of two chocolate chips into the melted chocolate and push a chip on each marshmallow side as ears.

Store in an airtight container in the refrigerator.

Guide to Recipe Code

Letters are the names of the recipes.

First number: line of recipe.

Second/Third numbers: the corresponding letter of Peyton Poulon's name (count spaces, too).

Last number(s): order in which they belong.

GPP251	P	Grandma Peggy's Pumpkin
RPC142	E	Roasted Parmesan Chicken
MGB4143	Y	Maple-Glazed Brussels
GMP434	T	Garlic Mashed Potatoes
CCT1085	O	Cornbread Corny Twist
HPS5106	N	Homemade Pumpkin Spice
BCS417	P	Bourbon Caramel Sauce
BAF7168	O	Bourbon Apple Fritters
BAC149	U	Brandied Apple Cider
CMC3610	L	Creamy Macaroni and Cheese
CPS3811	O	Carrot Pumpkin Soup
WFM2912	N	Wesley's Favorite Meatloaf

ABOUT THE AUTHOR

Krista Davis is the *New York Times* best-selling and four-time Agatha Award-nominated author of the Domestic Diva Mysteries, the Pen & Ink Mysteries, and the Paws & Claws Mysteries. She lives in the Blue Ridge Mountains of Virginia with two cats and a brood of dogs. Her friends and family complain about being guinea pigs for her recipes, but she notices they keep coming back for more. Please visit her at KristaDavis.com.

The employees of Thorndike Press hope you have enjoyed this Large Print book. All our Thorndike, Wheeler, and Kennebec Large Print titles are designed for easy reading, and all our books are made to last. Other Thorndike Press Large Print books are available at your library, through selected bookstores, or directly from us.

For information about titles, please call:
  (800) 223-1244

or visit our website at:
  gale.com/thorndike

To share your comments, please write:
  Publisher
  Thorndike Press
  10 Water St., Suite 310
  Waterville, ME 04901

DISCARD